Intimate Strangers

by

Anna M. Figueroa

Title: Intimate Strangers
Author: Anna M. Figueroa

Published by Pine Tree Press

www.pinetreepress.com
Printed in USA

DEDICATION

This book is dedicated to my mom. We both enjoyed an exciting novel and often exchanged books until the day I lost her. I miss her every day.

ACKNOWLEDGMENTS

I would like to thank my dear friend, Maria Rivero, who was the first person to ever read this. As always, she encouraged me to fulfill my dreams and stop waiting. To the very best of friends.

CONTENTS

INTIMATE STRANGERS

Chapter One

The room was dark; only a crack of light beneath the door relieved the ink-black darkness. Instinctively, she knew the door was locked. There was no way out. The stench was overpowering, the air thick with sweat, human waste, and fear. She could hear him groaning… "Help me, please…"

Laurie fell over her desk, the pain washing through her in waves. Who was he? Christ! This had to stop! The flash of pain was so sharp it doubled her over. Laurie gripped the arms of her chair and tried to breathe, to calm her twisting stomach muscles. She squeezed her eyes shut, willing the stabbing agony to stop. Tears streamed down her face, and she was dimly aware of their damp coolness on her silk-clad knee.

Slowly, the pain abated. She remained doubled over, afraid to move in case it returned. After a few moments, she forced herself to release her fierce grip on the smooth arms of the chair and take deep breaths. She risked straightening and was grateful when no new wave hit her. With trembling hands, she lifted the mug of herbal tea she had prepared just minutes before the attack and sipped slowly. Little by little, her breathing steadied and her pulse eased.

Just as her muscles began to relax, the door banged open, making her jump and spill the tea. Dorothy, her assistant, marched in with her usual sunny expression, one that quickly shifted to concern.

"Laurie! You're as white as a sheet!"

Laurie almost managed a smile at how quickly Dorothy bustled around the desk. It always amazed her how agile the woman was, considering her magnificent proportions. At her last weigh-in, Dorothy was a glorious two hundred and fifty pounds, a full, voluptuous figure wrapped in the most flamboyant outfits Laurie had ever had the fortune – or misfortune – to see. Today's ensemble was a brilliant orange caftan-like dress with long orange and yellow ruffles along the rather indiscreet neckline. Matching yellow and orange high-heeled sandals completed the outfit, and plastic bangles in coordinating shades adorned each chubby wrist.

One of those wrists now hovered directly in Laurie's line of vision. Without waiting for an answer, Dorothy pressed her palm to Laurie's still-clammy forehead.

"Dorothy, I'm fine, really," Laurie said in a shaky voice that betrayed her. Even so, she firmly removed the older woman's hand.

"You don't look fine to me!" Dorothy accused. "You've had another one of those... those fits, haven't you? Why haven't you gone to the doctor?"

"I don't need a doctor, Dorothy. It's just stress... nothing some rest won't cure." She clenched her teeth and tried to force the most reassuring smile she could manage.

"Nonsense!" snapped Dorothy, her face settling into maternal concern. Her bright orange brows – color-coordinated with this month's hair – lowered over worried blue eyes.

"Don't start, Dorothy." Laurie's tone sharpened, losing its usual mildness. She turned and looked out the window, pushing a strand of thick brown hair behind her ear. She stared, unseeing, at the people dotting the bustling street below.

Dorothy believed she was working too hard, but people's dreams depended on her work. Laurie was an immigration lawyer. When she lost a case, someone's dream died – the American dream held so dearly by immigrants around the world. The weight of letting people down never sat lightly with her. Thankfully, it didn't happen often.

Focusing once again on the colorful flow of humanity below, Laurie noticed an elderly couple attempting to cross the busy street, their hands tightly clasped. The sight reminded her of her parents. She sighed and leaned her forehead against the cool glass. Dragging her hand through her hair, she sighed again, the sound pulled from deep within her.

The tap of Dorothy's heels pulled her back to the moment. The painful attacks had begun three days ago.

Until yesterday, no one else knew. Dorothy, in her usual unprofessional manner, had burst in during a mind-searing spasm. Laurie had made her swear not to tell her parents or her brothers, though she knew that promise wouldn't last long.

She brushed her hand across her eyes as if she could wipe away the memory of the pain. She was still weak and in no mood for Dorothy's lecturing. Knowing Dorothy was still hovering across her desk, she turned. "Please don't worry," she said softly. "I promise, I'm fine."

Dorothy threw her hands up in defeat and scowled as she strode to the door. Without looking back, she warned, "Don't think for one minute I'm going to keep quiet for long. You go see your doctor right now, whether it fits your schedule or not! Otherwise, I'll drag you there myself!"

As the door slammed shut behind Dorothy's broad back, Laurie sighed and took another sip of lukewarm tea. Her mind drifted to what had happened three days ago – the moment she knew had triggered the attacks...

She had left the courthouse around midday, euphoric after winning a case for Emilio Lopez. With almost no money and even less hope, he had entered her office with his wife, Esperanza. It was Esperanza who convinced him to try Laurie after a friend at the factory insisted she could be trusted.

The judge granted the Guatemalan couple political asylum after reviewing documentation of their torture and the disappearance of their oldest son. The grisly photos and signed affidavits from the priest in Emilio's village were more than enough to prove their case. Laurie shivered on the sunlit courthouse steps as she recalled those images.

Shaking off the morbid thoughts, she decided not to return to the office. The day was gorgeous, and she was minutes from the beach. She climbed into her car, called Dorothy, and told her to take the rest of the day off. Dorothy's loud, "Well, I'll be damned!" had topped off Laurie's good mood.

She drove to her favorite deserted stretch of Miami Beach beside the old Coral Reef Hotel, condemned after Hurricane Irma. The ongoing litigation between the owners, the City of Miami Beach, and the contractor had dragged on endlessly – which suited Laurie perfectly. It left her one of the prettiest spots in the city all to herself.

After changing into the bathing suit she kept tucked in her trunk, she spent the afternoon sunning and taking quick swims. As the sun lowered, she began nodding off.

Before her eyes fully closed, the hair on the back of her neck rose and her heart began to race. She sat up quickly, dizzy as the blood rushed to her head. She didn't know what caused the sudden fear, but she didn't hesitate. Once the dizziness passed, she yanked her shirt over her swimsuit and gathered her things in a rush. Without stopping to question the irrational feeling, she sprinted toward the parking lot.

As her bare feet hit the concrete sidewalk, she saw three men walking toward the old hotel. Goosebumps ran along her arms. They weren't dressed for the beach. Two wore dark suits, and the third – much taller than the others – wore slacks and dress shoes. Instinct told her not to make eye contact and to get off the beach, but something kept pulling her gaze toward the tall man.

From where she stood, nothing indicated he was there unwillingly. He walked between the men at a steady pace, not hurried. But she was certain he wasn't there by choice. She shook her head at herself. How the hell could she know that? She must have been in the sun too long.

She picked up speed again, reaching her car in seconds. As she slid the key into the door, some force made her look up.

He was staring at her.

The tall stranger's gaze locked onto hers. She couldn't make out his features, but she could see he was powerfully built, radiating a tense energy she could feel from across the lot. A chill swept through her.

She had never reacted to anyone like that. It wasn't logical – it was still daylight, and the men were walking away, not toward her. But the sense of danger felt real enough to shake her.

The man turned as one of the others said something to him. Snapping out of her strange reverie, she jumped into her car and slammed her foot onto the accelerator, fear pulsing through her.

But another emotion hit her as she sped blindly through the streets.

Anguish.

The word tore from her throat with a rawness that startled her. She felt anguish because she had left the stranger behind.

She bit her lip, refusing to let that thought settle.

The dreams began that night.

Shaking off the memory, Laurie decided to head home. Her nerves were shot.

Once in her car, she switched on the old radio and turned the dial to the local jazz station. The car was one of her favorite possessions—a 1964 Chevy Corvette painted a shiny metallic blue. She loved the feel and sound of the engine when she hit the highway. She admitted to herself that the way she had purchased the car had something to do with the pleasure she took in owning it.

She had outbid her brother Tom for it a few years back. His next-door neighbor had gleefully accepted the extra thousand dollars Laurie offered, telling Tom that his little sister would look better in it anyway. Laurie doubted Tom would ever truly get over the defeat. He still looked near tears every time he saw the car. He even refused to drive it, accusing her of being a sadist for even suggesting it.

She shifted gears, trying to shake the guilt she felt about leaving the office early. She knew better than to take a threat from Dorothy lightly. Although the woman was fiercely loyal, she was also intensely protective. Dorothy might not be able to drag her to the doctor, but she could certainly get Laurie's family involved.

The last thing Laurie needed was her family worried and fussing over her. Her mother would insist on staying with her, hovering and tending to her every move. Laurie grimaced at the thought. She loved her mother dearly but had no desire to be cooed and clucked over. Worse, she didn't want to frighten her. Her mouth tightened grimly at the thought of how the attacks would terrify her gentle mother.

Traffic was light, and in less than fifteen minutes, Laurie was turning into her driveway. The old Spanish-style house sat conveniently close to her office. She loved the quaint place with its oddly shaped windows and spacious kitchen. Many restless nights were spent on the back porch, sitting in her grandmother's old rocker, sipping wine and staring at the moon.

On those nights, she allowed herself to admit that she was lonely. She was surrounded by people constantly—people she knew cared about her. It should have been enough. But it wasn't.

Locking the car door, she walked around to the back entrance and stepped into her sunny kitchen. The phone was ringing shrilly. Dropping her purse and briefcase, she snatched up the receiver.

"Hello?"

"Laurie! How are you? Why haven't you come for dinner like you promised? What is going on?" Maria James rushed on without pausing for breath or an answer, as was her way.

Smiling despite herself, Laurie replied, "Mom, hold on. I'm fine. I promise I'll come sometime this weekend–honest. Listen, I have to go. I love you."

"Are you sure? Why don't you come tonight? Your father is having some friends over, and I know they would love to meet you." Her mother's melodic voice brimmed with hope.

Groaning silently, Laurie forced herself to sound cheerful. "I'm sorry, Mom. Tonight is impossible. I'll call you tomorrow... bye." She hung up before her mother could wear her down. She was in no shape to make polite conversation with stuffy bankers. And she didn't dare risk another attack in full view of her overprotective parents.

She moved down the long hallway that connected the kitchen to the two rooms on the east side of the house and stepped into the coolness of her bedroom. She began to undress. Stripping down to her bra and panties, Laurie slipped quietly into the bathroom and bent over the antique tub. A warm bath was exactly what she needed to unwind after the last few days.

As the tub filled, Laurie stared at herself in the slightly steamed mirror. She made a conscious effort to relax the tightness around her mouth and across her brow. Running her hands over her face, she tried to think of something pleasant.

Failing miserably, she stared at her reflection. Tense emerald eyes stared back at her. As the mirror fogged further, dizziness washed over her, and she lost sight of herself. Her face faded as darkness and fear closed in once again. Desperate, she cried out, "No! I'm awake, damn it! No!"

The darkness dragged her down.

"Help me, please..."

Laurie gripped the edges of the sink, fighting the rising pain and terror. His voice was there–begging her. She must be losing her mind.

Her heart fractured inside her. She was losing him. He wouldn't last much longer. As the blackness closed in, Laurie grieved for the stranger. When the physical pain fused with the grief, her knees buckled and she slid to the cold tile floor.

Jake North lay slumped in the corner of the hellhole he had called home for the past three days. He was barely conscious. The darkness pressed in on him, heavy and suffocating. He almost welcomed it.

Idly, he wondered if there was some threshold in the human body—a point beyond which pain simply ceased.

Sure, it was called death, he thought grimly.

He had taken to answering his own thoughts over the last few hours. He figured he was hallucinating anyway, so why not?

Shaking his head, Jake fought to stay awake. No. He wouldn't die yet. There were too many unanswered questions.

His cover had been solid—the best. He'd come personally recommended to Lacayo by Jimmy Fanucci, the infamous henchman for the Ponti family in New York. Fanucci had conveniently "died" of a heart attack one week later. Only Jake, along with select members of the NYPD and FBI, knew that Fanucci was actually thousands of miles away, enjoying a new life courtesy of the U.S. government.

Yes, his cover had been airtight. He'd gone in deep—so deep that Lacayo had chosen him for the next shipment. It had taken nearly six months to fully infiltrate the drug dealer's operation and gain his trust.

Six months of work destroyed in less than twenty-four hours.

In the hours after he woke up alone—before Lacayo took personal pleasure in his interrogation—Jake replayed the last few days over and over in his mind. He couldn't figure out where things had gone wrong.

Less than four days ago, Lacayo had believed him completely. Then, without warning, Diaz and Gruber had shown up at Jake's apartment, explaining that Lacayo wanted to see him at the penthouse on Miami Beach. When Jake asked what was going on, Diaz reassured him that the boss always reviewed every detail of an operation multiple times before execution.

Gruber had smirked at the word.

Jake realized now that the smirk should have warned him. Gruber never showed emotion—certainly not humor.

The two goons brought him here. They'd knocked him unconscious but hadn't been overly vicious. They knew better than to deprive their boss of the pleasure of inflicting pain himself. The sadistic bastard had actually giggled as Jake screamed and writhed.

Who had tipped him off?

It had to be someone on the inside. The realization struck hard, making him nearly as sick as the beatings and the hunger gnawing at his gut. They hadn't fed him in three days. Lacayo had ordered water only—just enough to keep him alive.

Long enough to stretch out the enjoyment.

Each time Lacayo worked him over, Jake was certain he wouldn't survive. Each time, as the blackness crept in, he felt... not alone.

It was crazy—but why the hell not believe it? Believing had kept him alive so far. He felt her—imaginary or not. He felt her fear. Fear for him, and fear for herself.

He could have sworn he'd heard her voice more than once. Strangely familiar.

He found himself calling out to her, straining for a reply. Maybe she was an angel, come to escort him to whatever waited next.

He laughed weakly, the sound emerging as a rasp from cracked, bleeding lips.

Angel. Hell, the odds of that were slim to none.

No—he was hallucinating.

His thoughts drifted to the curvy brunette on the beach three days ago. He'd felt an inexplicable pull toward her. Even as he walked toward what he knew might be his death, the sight of her had shattered his concentration.

Closing his eyes, he thought that if he had to lose his mind, at least the madness had taken on a sweet shape.

Laurie moaned as warmth lapped around her body.

God, her head hurt.

Groaning, she opened her eyes and focused on the steady stream of water spilling over the edge of her porcelain tub and onto the tile floor. Slowly, she pulled herself upright and shut off the tap.

Dropping back into the pooled water, she wrapped her arms around herself and shivered.

What was she going to do?

The pain had eased, but its intensity had left her weak and shaken. The nightmare had bled into her waking hours, striking without warning. It had felt so real.

What if it *was* real?

"Oh God... what am I going to do?" she whispered, fear threatening to swallow her whole.

Urgency surged inside her. The man was in danger. He had to be. She wasn't insane–she knew it. The certainty lived deep in her gut, impossible to ignore.

Laurie had never experienced telepathic abilities. She'd studied the subject briefly in college and later researched the paranormal after her cousin confessed to visiting a Tarot reader. At the time, Laurie's goal had been to prove her wrong–to show how easily "seers" pulled information from unsuspecting clients.

Instead, she'd found study after study suggesting that telepathy and precognitive visions might, inexplicably, exist.

Amanda had remained a believer. Laurie had backed off.

Now, it didn't matter.

She had to save him–whoever he was.

Dripping wet, Laurie staggered back to her bedroom and sat on the edge of the bed. Grimacing at the spreading wet stain beneath her, she reached for the phone.

After three rings, a loud nasal voice answered, "Amanda's Beauty Salon, may I help you?"

Forcing calm into her voice, Laurie said, "Hi, Martha. It's Laurie. May I speak to Amanda, please?"

"Laurie! It's so good to hear from you! Do you have a man yet?"

"No, Martha. No man yet. Amanda, please."

"Well, you better hurry. People are going to start thinking you're an old maid!"

The sting was softened by Martha's booming laugh.

"Thanks for the advice," Laurie replied tightly. "I'll keep it in mind."

She tried to relax as Martha yelled for Amanda over the roar of dryers and music. If she sounded tense, Amanda would pounce in seconds.

Laurie had never been good at keeping secrets from her cousin. No one was—especially Amanda's customers. Somewhere between the shampoo and blow-dry, people spilled their deepest confessions. Amanda listened, nodding sympathetically, her scissors snipping in rhythm.

"Laurie! It's so nice of you to call! Where have you been hiding?" Amanda's cheerful voice warmed Laurie despite her shivers. "Never mind—I know. That stuffy old office of yours."

Trying for their usual banter, Laurie replied, "What do you mean, stuffy?"

"Stuffy. You know–staid, formal, boring." Amanda paused. "What's up, cuz?"

Feigning nonchalance, Laurie said, "Nothing really. I was just wondering if you still had the number–or address–of that woman you saw before marrying Max."

"Are you home?"

"Yes."

"Don't move. I'll be there in ten minutes."

"Amanda–"

"I said don't move!"

The line went dead.

Laurie groaned. "Shit."

Amanda was pounding on Laurie's door exactly seventeen minutes later.

"Hold on! I'm coming!" Laurie yelled, swinging it open. "For Pete's sake, Amanda–you didn't have to drive like a maniac!"

Amanda–all five feet three inches of her–stood on the porch with narrowed brown eyes. Except for her size and lack of a weapon, she could have passed for an Amazon. Curvy, fierce, and dressed in a tight red blouse and snug jeans, her long black hair framed her heart-shaped face. The extra three inches came from her sky-high heels.

Her gaze swept Laurie–from her loose hair to her wet underwear.

"Nothing's wrong, huh?" Amanda snorted. "When was the last time you were home this early—much less dressed like *that*?"

She marched inside without waiting.

Laurie followed, closing the door and glancing down at the robe still clutched in her hand. She'd been headed for the closet when the pounding started.

Slipping into the silk wrap, Laurie opened her mouth to deliver her rehearsed lie.

Too late.

"Don't tell me it's for someone else," Amanda said evenly. "You'd never recommend this kind of 'counseling.' You'd deport them first."

"Okay, okay," Laurie muttered. "I'll tell you. Someone needs to tell me if I'm losing my mind—and it might as well be you."

She sank onto a kitchen stool.

Amanda perched opposite her, one eyebrow arching.

Laurie twisted the belt of her robe and stared at the yellow-and-white counter. She felt ridiculous. Maybe she *was* wrong.

The eyebrow rose higher.

"Fine," Laurie said. "Here goes. I've been having these terrible dreams. Nightmares. Except... now they don't wait for night."

Her voice dropped to a whisper as she met Amanda's eyes.

"They're not dreams. He's out there. In that filthy room. And I have to save him."

Chapter Two

Laurie checked the number on the door: C-15. This was it. She looked dubiously at the knocker. What was she doing here?

"Amanda, this is crazy. Let's just go to the Coral Reef and check if he's really there," she pleaded.

"Crazy? You're crazy! If this is real—which it probably is—that means this guy is with some very bad people, Laurie." Sarcasm dripped from Amanda's voice. "What are we going to do, waltz in and say, *I'm sorry, please excuse us, but could we possibly take poor what-his-name in the corner there home with us? My cousin really needs a good night's sleep!*"

Scoffing, Amanda knocked with more force than was necessary.

Suddenly panicking, Laurie began to back away. The door opened, revealing a pretty, petite redhead dressed in a plain white T-shirt and jeans. The woman broke into a warm smile that transformed her from merely pretty into beautiful as she extended her hands toward Amanda.

"Hi there!" She stepped back and motioned for them to enter. "You must be Laurie. Won't you please come in?"

The woman's voice was low and melodious. Her gray-blue eyes were bright and filled with humor. Laurie had expected something more sinister, for reasons she couldn't quite explain. As she followed her cousin inside, she felt obliged to confess, "I'm not sure about this."

"I know. Amanda warned me." The musical voice was filled with warmth. "I'm Claire, by the way—Claire Murphy."

Claire held out her hand. As Laurie shook it, her uneasiness was temporarily checked. There was strength in the hand that held hers.

The room was dim; no sunlight was allowed in through the tightly shut wooden blinds. The living space was spare and uncluttered. The walls were adorned with a combination of black-and-white photographs, obviously taken somewhere in the Southwest. At the back of the room, another door stood slightly ajar. From what Laurie could see through the crack, it appeared to lead to a bedroom.

To the right was a small kitchen, from which came a curious scent that reminded Laurie of a flower she could not name. The refrigerator was covered with photographs of small children and a mixed group of adults, many as red-haired as her host, all smiling warmly. She took what comfort she could from their seemingly benign faces.

Claire beckoned them to a small table in the corner of the room. It was a beautifully carved wooden table with two matching wooden chairs set facing each other across it. On the table sat a large glass filled with what appeared to be water and an antique lamp. Beside the glass lay a deck of cards—Tarot cards. Laurie recognized them from her less-than-successful research, and she felt her uneasiness return.

She jumped at the sound of Claire's soft voice behind her.

"Laurie, relax. I'm not going to pull out a crystal ball—at least not yet." Claire wiggled her eyebrows comically, then sat in one of the chairs and motioned for Laurie to take the other. Seeing Laurie's look of horror, she hurried to add, "I'm kidding. I'm kidding."

Amanda settled onto the arm of the deep, comfortable-looking sofa against the opposite wall.

"Listen, Laurie, if it'll make you feel any better, the cards are just a tool—just a way for us to get started." Claire began shuffling them methodically.

Laurie sat stiffly, wondering how on earth she had fallen down the rabbit hole.

"Okay, Laurie, shuffle and split the deck in three." Claire held the cards out to her.

Laurie did as she was told. Curiosity began to get the better of her, and she leaned forward as Claire neatly separated the three stacks of cards.

"Amanda said you've been troubled by bad dreams. Let's see if we can figure out what's going on." Claire's voice had become low and serious. She looked directly into Laurie's eyes, waiting for a sign that she was ready to begin.

Laurie returned the stare, observing Claire the way she observed a client the first time he or she walked into her office. Laurie could always tell if someone was lying or hiding something by their body language and the way their eyes wandered around the room instead of staying on hers. Claire's body was relaxed, her eyes steady on Laurie's.

Laurie nodded and took a deep breath. "What the hell? I'm already pretty sure I'm crazy. Let's do it."

Claire began taking cards from the top of one stack. With great precision, she laid them side by side in the order they were drawn. Then she stopped suddenly and looked up at Laurie. Carefully gathering the cards, she offered the deck to Laurie again to shuffle and divide once more.

Again, she laid the cards out side by side.

Again, she stared at Laurie.

Her gaze was penetrating, and Laurie felt a sudden slash of fear.

"Well?" Amanda asked anxiously, leaning so far forward that she nearly fell off the arm of the sofa.

Claire looked only at Laurie. "These dreams you've been having–they're vivid, aren't they? So much so that they seem real… frighteningly real. You feel his pain, don't you?"

As Claire asked each question, she never really gave Laurie time to respond. Instead, she seemed to be searching for the answers in Laurie's eyes.

Laurie gasped. "How did you know it was a man?"

"How long have you been together?"

"I don't even know him."

"What?" Claire's tone was incredulous. "Laurie, the cards show that this man is very close to you. His card repeatedly follows yours... he's tied to you. The bond is very strong."

Amanda wriggled excitedly and stared at Laurie, who squirmed nervously in her chair.

Laurie shook her head at Claire. "It can't be. I don't even know him. I just became fixated on some guy I saw for two minutes on the beach. Christ! What I need is a psychiatrist. I think I hear his cries; I think I feel his pain. I must be losing my mind!"

Excited, Claire leaned forward. "You can hear him? What do you mean? You've had communication with him?"

"No!"

"Laurie! What do you call these weird dreams if not communication?" Amanda had jumped up from the sofa and now turned to Claire. Exasperated, she continued, "She dreams that he's being held in some filthy room. He's tied up. Every afternoon some creep comes in and tries a different kind of torture on him. Just listening to her describe it made my stomach turn."

Claire drummed her fingers furiously on the polished wooden surface of the old table. "He needs you. The strength of your bond may have developed into a sort of mental link." She seemed to be speaking more to herself than to Laurie.

"Are you crazy?" Laurie jumped out of her chair, nearly knocking it over. She backed away from the menacing cards spread across the lustrous wood. When she felt she was at a safer distance, she began pacing back and forth frantically.

It couldn't be real. It couldn't. If it was, that meant he was dying. She had felt how close he was to giving in to despair and pain during her last, most terrible vision.

Oh God. He couldn't die.

The thought tormented her even more than the visions themselves.

Claire sat still, watching her. "Yes, Laurie. He's close to dying. The card of death continues to follow his card."

Suddenly, Laurie felt a violent surge of rage. "No! He can't die–do you hear me?" she yelled. "I won't let him die!"

Shocked by the vehemence of her own outburst, she whispered, "How did you know I thought he was dying? Never mind–I don't want to know." She closed her eyes. "What am I going to do?" she whispered.

Claire stood and came over to Laurie. Placing an arm around Laurie's shoulders, she looked first at Amanda and then back at Laurie. "Whatever the reason, he's been able to connect with you, Laurie. It's obvious he needs your help. I'd like to know whether you'd be willing to try something–something that might help you reach him and help him."

Laurie's head came up; fear and doubt reflected in her emerald eyes. "What do you mean?"

"I want to try hypnotizing you."

"What?"

Amanda looked at Claire searchingly. "Are you sure?"

"If this is some kind of telepathic connection, it means he could communicate his whereabouts to her. On the other hand, she could verify whether this is actually happening or whether it's a memory or a dream. Hypnosis could help her know for sure. It could also help her explore the source of their connection."

Determined, Amanda moved closer and grabbed Laurie's arms firmly. "Besides her psychic abilities, Claire is a hypnotherapist. I did it once myself, Laurie. It was very helpful–and perfectly safe."

Laurie looked at Amanda helplessly. "Amanda… this whole thing is too weird. I don't think I could be hypnotized even if I wanted to be. God, I'm pulled as tight as a rubber band." Turning toward Claire, she tried to convince them both. "The whole thing is probably the result of too much stress and an overactive imagination. Besides, the pain is getting worse each time. I don't think I can handle it anymore."

Sensing an opening, Claire pressed her advantage. "You'd be able to control it. You might be able to reach him and find a way to help him survive."

Help him survive.

Laurie sank down onto the nearby sofa. In her heart, she knew this was no figment of her imagination. She knew it wasn't even a memory; the pain was too real. She had no choice. She could not let him die–not with this bond between them. She didn't know who he was, but it didn't matter anymore. She knew how he felt. She had shared his fear and his despair.

She had no choice.

◐○◑

Jake felt himself floating through a dark tunnel. At the end of it, he could see a bright light. He made no movement, yet felt himself pulled toward it by a force stronger than anything he had ever known. Closer and closer it came. He could hear voices–soothing voices–calling to him from the light.

"No!"

Jake felt a tug behind him. That voice did not belong here; he knew it instinctively. He tried to shake it off.

"Please! Don't die–don't do it! Help me find you, please! I'll help you, I promise!"

It was the angel. Why was she calling him back? If she was an angel, she should be here with him. The light seemed to dim.

No.

He didn't want to go back. He couldn't take any more. He tried to propel himself toward the light.

"Please!" He could hear the terror in her voice, and for a moment he marveled again at the strange familiarity of it. "Please, don't leave me. It's not fair! I've only known your pain. You come back, damn you!"

The voice shifted from pleading to demanding.

He wondered idly if she would get in trouble for swearing in the tunnel. Hell, she was right—he owed her. She'd kept him alive until now. He knew now, deep inside the tunnel, that she was the brunette who had stared at him on the beach. Maybe she was some kind of guardian angel, and that was why she had shown herself to him that day. To warn him.

He wasn't sure what the explanation was, but he found her pull stronger than that of the voices at the end of the tunnel.

With a deep sigh, he turned away from the ever-dimming light and back toward the darkness—toward her voice.

"Where are you?" the voice demanded again.

"Who are you?"

"Forget that. It doesn't matter. Just tell me where you are so I can help you!"

"No way. I'll probably be dead by the time you get here. I want to know your name before I die."

"Laurie. Laurie James. Now where the hell are you?"

"Nice to meet you, Laurie James. I'm Jake North."

"Are you still at the beach? Tell me!"

"I guess it can't hurt. At least someone will give me a decent burial."

"Stop that, damn you!"

"Coral Reef Hotel. Abandoned cabanas near the pier."

"Jake, help is on the way. Jake? Jake!"

"Yes, Laurie?"

"If you die, I'll kill you! Jake? Jake! Oh God, not again!"

Laurie rode with Claire in the back seat of a City of Miami Police squad car. Sirens wailed as they sped toward the Coral Reef Hotel in Miami Beach. Somewhere in the rubble of the crumbling hotel, a man named Jake was dying—beaten to a pulp and abandoned. A man she could not possibly know, and yet she did… intimately. She knew, though she didn't know how, that he had been alone since yesterday afternoon. Apparently, his tormentor had grown bored or too busy and had left him there to die.

Not again.

The words echoed through her mind. She could not deny what she had experienced during her terrifying session under hypnosis. Tears streamed down Laurie's face as the sharp stab of loss tore through her.

Beside her, Claire sat handcuffed and nervous. She still couldn't believe the events that had landed her here. How could she not have seen this coming?

After the session, Claire had been deeply disturbed. At Laurie's request, Amanda had gone home. Max, Amanda's husband, had called her twice. The first time, Amanda hadn't returned the call. The second time, she had answered and given him a lame excuse about buying dog food as the reason she wasn't home yet. Realizing that Max was not a happy camper, Laurie had insisted Amanda go home, promising to call her and let her know what had happened during the session.

Laurie had gone under after almost an hour of fighting it. Finally, she had been able to reach Jake without feeling the pain—not because she could control it, but because he was past it.

Claire felt a shiver of fear run through her body.

Laurie had called him back.

She had made him come back.

With her help, Laurie had interfered with a man's death.

Laurie had been exhausted when she came out of the hypnosis. Claire had tried to get her to rest, but like a trapped animal, Laurie had snarled a demand that she contact the police. Shaken, Claire had obediently dialed.

After hearing Jake North's name during Claire's jumbled explanation, the dispatcher had gone silent for a moment and then put her on hold. Seconds later, a man identifying himself as Chief Sam Hollinger listened silently as Claire repeated herself. When she finished, he asked to speak to Laurie directly.

The man began barking at Laurie, firing questions at her a mile a minute. Barely coherent, she launched into a frantic rant about Jake and the Coral Reef Hotel. "You've got to go get him. Please! He's so weak!" Chief Hollinger promised to dispatch a patrol car immediately and then requested to speak to Claire again.

With infinite patience, he asked Claire the same questions he had asked Laurie. He didn't know how the hell these women knew where Detective Jake North was when the entire City of Miami Police Department and the NYPD couldn't find him, but he was sure as hell going to find out.

Furious at the continued discussion while Jake lay dying, Laurie tore the phone from Claire's grasp. Yelling at the top of her lungs, she demanded that Hollinger come get her. "I'm the only one who can take you to him! I'm the only one who can keep him alive–do you hear me?" At the time, she hadn't realized how threatening she sounded.

Hollinger asked for the address and tersely instructed her not to move until he got there. He arrived at Claire's apartment within minutes, sirens wailing and lights flashing. He didn't bother with introductions. He simply ordered the officer with him to recite their rights as he handcuffed them both.

Laurie was so relieved by his swift arrival that she didn't even object. Though she felt a tremor of doubt at the barely controlled violence in Chief Hollinger's handsome ebony face, she told herself it would all be sorted out later. At least, she hoped so. Claire yelled and argued until she was hoarse, but it made no difference.

Now she sat awkwardly, handcuffed, praying with every ounce of strength she had left that Jake—whoever he was—was still alive... for his sake as well as theirs.

◐◯◑

The officer driving Chief Hollinger slammed on the brakes, stopping a block away from the abandoned hotel. Hollinger jumped out immediately. Approximately eight patrol cars and three unmarked vehicles were already there, along with an ambulance standing by. He nodded to the men waiting for instructions.

Then he turned, opened the back door of the squad car, and fixed Laurie with a hard stare. "This better be for real, lady, because if it's not, you're going to be in some deep shit. Now where the hell is he?"

Laurie returned his gaze. She had to see Jake. She had to be the first to talk to him. Instinct told her it was her voice he needed to hear—if she wasn't already too late. She lifted her chin and said in her best courtroom voice, "I don't have to tell you a damned thing. Follow me, and I'll take you to him."

She had tried to reach him again, not caring if she felt the pain, but it was as though the link between them had collapsed. Her throat constricted at the thought. This time, the searing pain in her chest was her own.

Roughly, Hollinger reached in and, with one powerful hand, dragged her out of the car by the front of her blouse. Claire yelled at him to stop. He ignored her.

"Alright, Ms. James, where is he?" He seemed to spit each word out in a growl.

Shaking free with surprising strength, Laurie broke into an awkward run toward the beach. "Come on–hurry!" The entire time, she kept chanting over and over in her mind, *don't you do it. Don't you die, damn it!*

Finally, she caught sight of the abandoned cabanas. Sprinting, breathing harshly, she tried to yell at the top of her lungs, "Jake! Jake! Where are you?"

Hollinger was right behind her. "Shut the hell up, lady! What are you trying to do–warn somebody we're coming?"

The fury in his voice silenced her. It hadn't occurred to her that the men holding Jake might still be guarding him. She had been certain they'd left him to die.

She stopped in front of the cabanas. They stretched along the sand like decaying teeth. As she struggled to catch her breath, the unpleasant odor of humidity and rotting wood hit her. A terrible silence filled the air.

Suddenly, she heard a muffled thump from the cabana to her left.

Like a madwoman, she ran and threw herself at the rotting door. It wouldn't budge. Tears streamed down her face as she slammed her shoulder against it again.

Strong hands grabbed her from behind and hurled her down into the sand. Pulling his gun from its holster, Hollinger shouted, "Police!" as he stepped aside from the door. He waited for the second officer to get into position, then raised his hand and motioned when he was ready.

The officer moved quickly and, on a count of three, kicked in the door, keeping his pistol raised and ready. After only a few seconds, he called out, "All clear, Chief!"

Hollinger barreled through the doorway. Swinging his head wildly, he searched the dark space for his friend. A large, dark mass twitched in the corner.

"Jesus Christ! Jake, is that you?"

Hearing the shock in the man's voice—then what sounded like retching—Laurie struggled to get up, ignoring the pain in her shoulder and wrists. She rushed into the cabana, only to reel back at the sight that greeted her.

In the corner, tied like an abused animal, lay the man named Jake, still as death. Hollinger stood just inside the doorway, seemingly paralyzed, as the younger officer who had entered first dropped to his knees and vomited.

A cry of anguish tore from Laurie's throat. She rushed to the prone figure, falling to her knees beside him. He was covered in blood. The stench was overwhelming.

How long had he been here?

No—she knew the answer.

Three days.

Unable to touch him or lift his head because of the handcuffs, she nuzzled him clumsily with her face, ignoring the blood and filth that smeared her skin. Her tears splashed onto his bruised, grimy cheek as she knelt over him, sobbing.

"Please don't be dead. Please."

She felt the slightest movement of his head and heard the barest rasp of a voice. "Angel?"

"Yes!" she sobbed, then turned toward the doorway, where Claire stood behind Chief Hollinger, horror etched across her face.

"He's alive—he's alive!" Laurie shouted frantically.

Bending back down to him, she murmured over and over that it was over, that he was going to be all right. She could hear Hollinger radioing desperately for the ambulance, his breath coming in violent rasps.

Her tears flowed over the intimate stranger who was Jake North.

Six hours later, Jake North woke up—sort of. Heavily drugged, with all sorts of tubes running in and out of him, he could barely make out the shadowy figures of doctors and nurses. He tried to remember how he had gotten to the hospital, but all he could recall was the angel's voice.

A wave of overwhelming grief washed over him at the realization that she was gone. He hadn't even been able to thank her. He hadn't been able to ask her all the questions he had. Now he would never know the answers. He would never hear that sweet voice again.

Why hadn't she just let him die?

A sharp ache bloomed in his chest. His breathing grew agitated. Wildly, he tried to pull the tubes from his throat and arms. Monitors began beeping frantically. He heard people shouting, though he couldn't make out the words.

He had to go. He had to find her again.

What was her name?

Christ, his head hurt.

Her name... her name was–

"Laurie!"

Her name rang out like a gunshot.

Laurie sat across a scratched metal table from Claire in what she imagined was an interrogation room. Still numb from the shock of the last few hours, she was having trouble concentrating on what Claire was saying.

"Laurie? Laurie, are you listening to me? They say we're not under arrest, but they're holding us for questioning. Laurie?"

Claire's eyes had turned slate gray, clouded with genuine fear and concern for the young woman across from her. Laurie had bordered on catatonic since the paramedics had pulled her away from Jake in that horrible cabana. Claire shuddered at the memory of the bloody scene. Only a monster could beat and torture someone so viciously and then leave him to die alone in his own filth.

She squeezed her eyes shut against the image—against memories of other such monsters. Shaking her head to clear her thoughts, she stared down at the scarred surface of the table.

Claire had tried to reason with Hollinger about letting Laurie stay with Jake, but he was still convinced that Laurie had something to do with the crime. Laurie hadn't said a word, but Claire knew it had torn her apart when they'd driven her away from him. She had somehow convinced herself that only she could keep him alive. Remembering their session in her apartment, Claire suspected there might be some truth to that.

She knew about soul mates—people bound to each other by emotions so deep they followed one another into the next life. Laurie hadn't regressed to a past life, but during her communication with the man, she had cried out in fear that he was dead *again*. Claire doubted Laurie remembered that particular word or feeling, at least not on a conscious level. But then again, maybe she did. That might explain her reaction to having him taken from her.

Hollinger had handed them over to a uniformed officer, instructing the man to take them to the station until they could be properly questioned. Claire was grateful she'd been allowed to stay with Laurie, even if it meant remaining in handcuffs. She was afraid to leave her.

Laurie had hardly spoken in the past hour. She sat perfectly still, eyes unfocused, her body held like a tightly coiled spring. In a way, Claire felt responsible for the trauma Laurie was enduring. She had pushed her into the hypnosis. It had saved the man's life—but Claire wasn't sure what permanent effect it might have on Laurie.

Patiently, she tried again to reach her. "Laurie, please look at me. Is there someone I should call? Your lawyer? Should I call Amanda?"

At the mention of her cousin's name, Laurie snapped to attention. "No! Don't call anyone!"

Claire flinched at the harshness of her voice. "I'm sorry, Laurie. I'm so sorry. This is all my fault. I shouldn't have pushed you the way I did earlier. I didn't see this coming."

Claire's normally even voice was pitched high with emotion.

Hearing the anguish in Claire's voice, Laurie made an effort to focus. Clearing her throat, she forced the words out. "Claire, it's okay. Don't be sorry. Without you, we wouldn't have found him in time—if at all. You saved him."

"No, Laurie. You saved him. You took a chance, and you reached him. He owes you his life."

Laurie stared past Claire. She would have done more than go under hypnosis for this man. She wanted to kill whoever had done this to him. She had never felt such raw hatred in her life. Suddenly, the emotions she had been struggling to control surged over her. She began to shake violently.

Frightened, Claire jumped up and moved closer. "It's okay, Laurie. It's okay. Come on, just let it all out. That's it." She leaned her shoulder against Laurie's, trying to comfort her.

Coming apart, Laurie keened desperately. "Oh God! What kind of animal could hurt him like that? Did you see him? He was barely alive! Christ, what if he doesn't make it? I couldn't bear it." She ground out the words as if they were choking her. "If he dies, I'll kill whoever is responsible–I swear it, Claire!"

Alarmed, Claire leaned closer. "Come on, Laurie. You'll cause a commotion, and believe me–you don't want to do that twice in one day to the City of Miami's finest." She tried to smile, though the tremor in her voice betrayed her anxiety.

Fighting to regain control, Laurie took several deep breaths. She slowly straightened her shoulders and gave Claire a watery smile in return. "We sure have kept the poor Chief entertained, haven't we?"

Laughing shakily in relief, Claire replied, "We're probably the most exciting thing that's happened to him since he lost his–"

At that precise moment, the man in question burst through the door. If possible, his face was even grimmer than it had been when he shoved Laurie toward the officer who had escorted her downtown.

"Alright, Ms. James, let's go," he said roughly as he reached for her arm.

Claire had had just about enough of the tough-cop routine. "You listen to me, you dumb ox! This woman has nothing to do with what happened to that man–nothing! She found him when you couldn't! If you would just listen–"

Hollinger didn't give her a chance to finish. Looking only at Laurie, he growled, "He's going nuts, tearing all the tubes out of himself. He's screaming for the angel." He paused, then added, "An angel he calls Laurie."

Laurie seemed to come back to life. "Oh my God! Please–you have to take me to him!"

Hollinger stared at her, hard, then nodded curtly. "Let's go."

Laurie realized she was still handcuffed as they pushed through the doors of the intensive care unit. Her arms were growing numb. Chief Hollinger hadn't even noticed–or perhaps he still believed she was dangerous. It didn't matter. She had to get to Jake before he hurt himself further.

The police officer standing at the door of Jake's room looked surprised but stepped respectfully aside as Hollinger hurried Laurie past him into the small hospital room.

Laurie felt faint at the sight of the man in the bed. His face was partially swollen and bruised. His torso was heavily bandaged from beneath his arms to somewhere under the sheet covering his waist. Tubes ran into his nose and his forearm. His eyes were closed, his breathing irregular. His arms were strapped down.

Slowly, she approached the bed. "Can you hear me?" There was no response.

Hollinger positioned himself inside the curtain that curved around the hospital bed, saying nothing. Laurie turned awkwardly and sat on the edge of the metal-framed bed.

Bending close to his ear, she murmured, "It's okay. I'm here now. I won't go anywhere–I promise. But you have to promise me," she whispered in a hushed, soothing voice meant only for him, "you have to promise you'll let the doctors help you. You can't fight them anymore, okay?"

Jake moaned, but his eyes remained closed. So softly she almost didn't hear him, he rasped, "Don't go..."

Leaning closer, she whispered, "I won't leave you. I promise. Rest now, okay? I'll be here when you wake up."

Laurie straightened, relief coursing through her. She stared at him, wanting to touch him. The restraints on her hands made that impossible. She turned and fixed Chief Hollinger with a pointed look.

"Chief, I understand your doubts about me, but you and I both know there's no reason to keep me handcuffed. Please remove these damned things from my wrists."

Hollinger stared at her arms behind her back as if seeing them for the first time. He said nothing, but reached for his keys and released her. He looked away as she rubbed her wrists, trying to ease the pain and restore circulation.

"I still have to question you," he stated, almost defiantly.

"Fine. You can question me here." She raised a tingling hand as he started to protest. "Here. You care about him–you know that. And you know he wants me here. Neither of us wants him to lose it. If you have to stay with me or assign someone to watch me, do it. I couldn't care less." She paused, then added, "I'd like to have someone pick up some clothes and personal things from my home, if that's alright with you. I have a feeling I'm going to be here for a while." She sighed tiredly. "There's no need to shock the hospital staff–or him, once he's conscious–with my appearance."

Sam Hollinger didn't often find himself at a loss. His world was usually black-and-white. The Murphy woman had tried to convince him that this young woman shared some kind of mental telepathy with Jake–that that was how she'd known where he was.

Gray. Very gray.

He hated gray.

For the first time, he looked at Laurie James without emotion. She wasn't acting guilty or afraid. In fact, she was looking at him as though he were a slow child, patiently waiting for him to grasp the obvious. Jake's blood was still smeared across her clothes. One of his officers had wiped her face with a paper towel from the station restroom.

He decided it didn't really matter what he thought or believed.

What mattered was that Jake wanted her here—apparently needed her here. If this was what Jake required to maintain his fragile hold on life, then this was what he would have. Sam would make sure that Jake's "angel" was there when he woke up.

He owed Jake. Big time.

He would do whatever it took to keep him alive.

Turning toward the door, he called out, "Brown! Get in here!"

The young officer hurried into the room and snapped into an almost military stance. "Yes, sir?"

"Call the station. Have Darlene get Claire Murphy—she's being held for questioning. Get her on the radio for me."

"Yes, sir."

Laurie could hear the crackle of static from the police radio as the young man dutifully followed instructions. Sighing, she sat down on the edge of the bed and contemplated the mess that was Jake North. She rolled his name around in her mind. It was a nice name—strong and simple.

Slowly, she took a physical inventory of the man lying helplessly before her.

He had black hair that fell limply to his shoulders. She imagined it would shine almost blue if it were washed. He was big… really big, she noted with mild surprise. She hadn't been sure whether the brief moments she'd seen him on the beach had made him seem larger in her mind. She was grateful for his size. A weaker man would never have survived the kind of torture he had endured.

Idly, she reached out and placed her hand over his, wincing as her arm protested the movement with sharp pain. His hand was warm and rough, mapped with old scars and bloodied new nicks. She liked the way her hand looked resting on his.

Her gaze returned to his face. She realized she didn't know what color his eyes were. She found that she wanted to know more than she had wanted anything in a long time.

Sam Hollinger was dead tired. The day had been an emotional roller coaster, taking him from fury to relief in the space of a few hours. The acidic taste of bile still rose in his throat at the memory of how they had found Jake.

He looked uneasily at the woman bent over his friend. She had fallen asleep in the hard-backed chair beside the hospital bed, her head resting on her arm, her fingers entwined with Jake's.

He had received the results of her background check an hour earlier. She was a lawyer. God, he hated lawyers. But apparently, Miss James was not your average, run-of-the-mill predator. From what he had read, she seemed not only to be an excellent attorney but also to possess a conscience.

What the hell was this woman doing in the middle of this mess?

The Murphy woman was another puzzle entirely. She was a professor of Celtic mythology at the local university, originally from out west, and apparently a part-time psychic on the side.

Shit.

Restless, he shifted in the vinyl armchair. Once again, he reviewed the few facts he possessed. Jake North was a loner and always had been. They had met during their stint together in the Marines. Hollinger didn't know a hell of a lot about Jake's past, but he was certain it hadn't been anything resembling a *Leave It to Beaver* episode. Still, Jake had been one hell of a good soldier—and a good friend.

Hollinger had never understood why Jake had befriended him. Maybe it was simply because he never asked questions. Hollinger had been one of only two African Americans in the small, specially trained unit. He had taken great pride in serving in one of the most elite units of the United States Marine Corps.

While in training, one of the other cadets had a problem containing his racism. He constantly muttered to himself, complaining to no one in particular that the Marines were going to hell now that they were lowering their standards to appease the "liberals" running the government. For the most part, everyone ignored the ignorant son of a bitch. They all figured they'd be rid of him soon enough, since he was the sloppiest and poorest performer of the lot.

They were right.

He was disqualified almost immediately. He openly accused his superiors of getting rid of him just to maintain a "quota." Then he spat in Hollinger's face.

Before either Hollinger or the sergeant could react, Jake smashed the man's nose and knocked him flat. A second later, Jake calmly looked down at him and said, in the flattest voice Hollinger had ever heard, "You're nothing but white trash. You're lazy and sloppy, and that makes you dangerous to anyone around you. Both these men are four times the man you'll ever be–and they had to work twice as hard to prove it."

Hollinger remembered the chill that had run up his spine at the danger in Jake's voice.

Jake served his punishment for breaking the man's nose. He had acted without allowing his superior to intervene, and he had been out of line. Hollinger never forgot it. On more than one occasion afterward, the two men had saved each other's asses. With each mission, their friendship grew stronger, though neither of them ever spoke about their personal lives beyond the superficial.

None of the former members of the unit ever spoke about the nature of their assignments during their time on active duty. They never received recognition for their valor or sacrifice beyond that of their commanding officer. Still, it had been enough to know that they had served their country–and each other–well.

When he finished his commitment with the Marines, Hollinger went on to a career in law enforcement and returned to Miami, his hometown. Years passed before he heard from Jake again. Jake had reenlisted twice and was eventually promoted to commander of his unit.

A couple of years ago, Jake called and invited him to lunch. They met at a tiny seafood restaurant along the Miami River. Jake had just joined the NYPD. He offered no explanation, saying only that he was finished with the Marines for good.

Once again, Hollinger asked no questions.

Jake had never been the life of the party, but there was a strange distance about him now that hadn't been there before. Hollinger congratulated him, bought him a beer, and showed him pictures of his wife and kids. As he relaxed, Jake teased him about his domesticated life.

It was only afterward that Hollinger learned about the friendly-fire death of one of the young men under Jake's command.

They had been in South America on a highly classified operation. After completing the mission, Jake's unit radioed for airlift extraction. His troops were mistaken for members of the cartel they had been sent to dismantle. By the time the pilots realized their mistake, one of Jake's men was dead.

According to Hollinger's source, Jake quit after learning that the soldier's family had been told he died due to his own carelessness during training exercises.

Hollinger didn't hear from Jake again until a month ago. Jake called him at home from a pay phone. He said he was working undercover in Miami and would contact Sam when it was safe to do so. He asked him not to say a word to anyone, then hung up abruptly.

Three days ago, Chief Robert Morris of the NYPD contacted Hollinger in an official capacity to inform him that one of his detectives, Jake North, was missing and that his last known location was South Beach in Miami. It was clear that Chief Morris had no idea of the personal relationship between Hollinger and Jake.

For his own reasons, Hollinger chose to keep it that way.

Morris asked for assistance in locating Jake but specified that Jake's status as a police officer should not be revealed.

For three days, Sam's men had searched for Jake. Although they had found people on South Beach who had seen him recently, he seemed to have vanished off the face of the earth. Sam had instructed his force—as well as all dispatchers and desk personnel—that any information regarding the "suspect," or Jake North, was to be routed directly to him. That was why the call from the Murphy woman had been put straight through to his office.

He glanced over again at the woman and his friend. Thankfully, she had bathed and changed once her cousin—Amanda something-or-other—had brought her clothes. He grinned to himself as he remembered the scene the cousin had staged outside Jake's hospital room.

She was a tiny thing, no more than five feet tall. She had Officer Brown stammering as she railed at him and the "fascist police force" that had dared to hold her sweet, innocent cousin in jail. Before Brown could clarify that Ms. James had not, in fact, been in jail, the woman launched into accusations of both incompetence and ingratitude. Apparently, they were all supposed to be grateful to Ms. James for helping them find Jake. The Murphy woman had yelled much the same thing at him only a few hours earlier.

Ms. James had finally stepped in and calmed her cousin down. Once Amanda had caught her breath, she stared hard at Jake. "That's him, Laurie? That's the guy? Gosh, he looks like he's been hurt pretty bad. Could be cute, though—nice chest, big hands... you know what they say about big hands and feet..."

"Amanda!" Ms. James had turned an attractive shade of pink. To their credit, both he and Brown managed to keep straight faces.

Once it was just the two of them with Jake again, they hadn't said much. Sam still hadn't questioned her. He hesitated to distract her from Jake; she seemed entirely focused on the man lying unconscious in the hospital bed. It also allowed him to observe her more closely.

She was a pretty woman, though not his type. Her most striking feature was her eyes—not so much their color, lovely as it was, but the depth within them. She looked a man straight in the eye.

What the hell was she doing here? How did she know Jake? Sam found it difficult to believe she had never met him before. The room was charged with the emotion radiating from her.

Frustrated, he shifted in his chair and dragged a hand across his beard-roughened face. He should call his wife. Trish would be worrying by now, even if she pretended not to be. He stood and, as quietly as possible, stepped outside to use the phone in the intensive care waiting room.

Claire slowly turned the key and leaned back against her apartment door. Her purse slipped from her fingers as tears welled in her eyes. She knew the shakes wouldn't be far behind. Letting her knees buckle, she slid silently to the floor. Wrapping her arms around her knees, she held on as the tremors overtook her small body.

It had been a long time since she'd experienced this level of emotional and spiritual exhaustion. Six years had passed since the murder of Betsy Williams. It had taken Claire months to recover from the horror of her session with Betsy's mother and father.

She had worked frequently with the police department in the small town of Cardozo, New Mexico. The sheriff was a second cousin who knew she had inherited the special gift shared by many of the women in the family. It was routine for him to ask her to visit a child's home, posing as a regular police officer, when a little girl was reported missing.

What was not routine were the violent visions that struck her almost as soon as she entered the Williams home. The evil that had occurred there was so strong that she knew immediately the little girl was dead–and that the parents were responsible. She could not, however, say so. She had to find proof. She had to sit in the impeccably clean-living room with Mr. and Mrs. Williams and speak to them as though she knew nothing. She had to look into their frighteningly normal faces–benign faces she knew masked monsters beneath.

She drank coffee with them as they spoke of how desperate with worry, they were over the disappearance of their beautiful little daughter, while images of brutal beatings flashed wildly through her mind. She stayed until she could see what they had done with the child's body.

Finally, she sensed that the girl had been buried in a damp place that smelled of gasoline and was crowded with cold metal objects. As soon as the image clarified in her mind, she practically fled the house. With a vague excuse about being needed at the police station, she stumbled down the porch steps and sped away in the patrol car. Two blocks later, she was forced to pull over and vomit violently at the side of the road.

That same afternoon, the sheriff obtained a warrant to search the Williams property. They found the small, broken body buried in the shed Carl Williams used to tinker with his old, beat-up cars. Both parents were arrested immediately. Later, they testified against each other in court, each hoping to save themselves by sacrificing the other. Claire knew that no matter who had struck the final blow, they were both murderers.

She hadn't slept for months afterward. Nightmares of Betsy haunted her. When she learned that Maude Williams would be released a year and a half later, Claire decided to leave Cardozo. She knew she couldn't live in the same town as that woman and survive. Every encounter would force her to relive the horrors of what Maude had done.

So she moved to Miami—a place so different from Cardozo that it helped her forget. She never married and had no children of her own. She likely never would. Her gift and her lifestyle were not what most men looked for in a wife. She had occasional lovers but avoided true intimacy. The emotions ran too deep, and the men she might have loved were usually frightened off anyway.

And here she was again, sitting on the floor in the fetal position—a position she knew well six years earlier. Only this time, she hadn't been the one having the visions. This time, she had helped save a life, not uncover a stiff, broken body.

She took a deep breath and ran her fingers through her curly auburn hair. She should take a shower. Though she hadn't touched anything in that filthy cabana, she had pressed close to Laurie more than once. She knew without looking that some of the man's blood stained her clothing. The scene had been horribly similar to the visions she'd had of poor Betsy Williams. It took an exceptionally sick, evil person to inflict that kind of torture. She knew—she had been inside that kind of mind before.

She also knew that both Laurie and Detective North were still in grave danger.

She had felt it the moment Chief Hollinger took her from the interrogation room.

Claire didn't want to be involved any further. She had realized too late how much evil surrounded the young woman and the man in her visions. She had allowed her excitement over the telepathic connection Laurie and Detective North shared to override her carefully constructed defenses.

Interrupting her dark reverie, Moses—her adopted alley cat—appeared out of nowhere and began rubbing his rough head insistently against her bent legs. He weaved in and out between them.

"Sorry, old fella," she murmured. "I guess I forgot about you today."

She pushed herself up off the floor. She felt steadier now. Moses stayed close at her heels as she went into the small kitchen. Reaching up, she grabbed a can of cat food from the stack perched on top of the refrigerator and opened it for the hungry tomcat.

While he ate with the intense concentration particular to former strays, she reached into a cabinet and pulled out a half-empty bottle of Jack Daniel's. She poured herself a double, straight up, and stared at the ceiling. Tossing back enough whiskey to make her shiver, she wondered what the hell she was going to do about Laurie James and her mysterious soul mate.

Amanda Tavares couldn't sleep.

She had lied to her husband, who was now angry with her. Laurie hadn't called—she was at the hospital keeping watch over a total stranger and hadn't even had the decency to give Amanda the lowdown. But what was really keeping her awake was the fact that she couldn't tell the juiciest story she'd ever heard to anyone.

Laurie had made her swear to secrecy.

Secrecy was a difficult concept for Amanda. She had very little practice keeping things to herself. Not telling Max had been especially hard. He was the jealous type. His first wife had cheated on him, and although he swore up and down that he trusted Amanda, she knew her excuse for being late had been weak at best. She had always been a terrible liar.

She'd learned early in life to stay out of trouble–not because of a superior moral code, but because of a strong sense of self-preservation.

She always got caught.

Turning over, she faced Max's broad back. With a sigh, she realized this was the first time since their marriage that he had gone to sleep turned away from her.

She tossed and turned for a few more minutes. What she needed was to burn off all this pent-up energy. She also needed to make things right with her stubborn, adorable husband.

Slowly, she inched across the bed until she was pressed against his back. Reaching around his waist, she began rubbing his stomach in gentle, circular motions. Each movement carried her small hand a little lower along his abdomen. With her usual enthusiasm, she began warming to the task.

She startled when a very awake Max murmured, "Babe, are you trying to distract me with sex?"

Laughing delightedly, she scrambled over him, forcing him flat onto his back. "You better believe it, you gorgeous stud. How am I doing?"

"Well, I think you might be slightly more successful if you tried a more direct approach."

Giggling, Amanda slipped her hand under the waistband of his boxers at precisely the same moment he slid his tongue into her eager mouth. Closing her eyes, all thoughts of Laurie and her beaten, nightmare man faded away.

Unblinking and cold, dark reptilian eyes stared out at the black ocean in the distance. He had chosen the penthouse of the exclusive condominium for the privacy the building offered, as well as for the pleasure he took in the view. When storms rolled in, he could watch lightning bolts strike the sea. He thrilled at the unleashed power of the deadly light show.

Tonight, the ocean was still. A thin slice of moon did little to relieve the inky blackness of sky and water. It was impossible to tell where one ended and the other began.

He studied his reflection in the glass door for a moment. He was not a tall man. At five feet four inches, most women towered over him. His height was the one thing he had never been able to change. Still, the elegantly groomed man staring back at him bore no trace of the dirt-poor boy who had hustled the streets of Managua so many years ago.

Turning, he faced the two men standing behind him, their tension radiating across the room.

The shorter of the two was built like a bulldog–wide, muscular, and ugly as sin. His dark hair was slicked back on his skull and bound at the nape of his neck with a leather band. Dressed in an expensive Italian suit, he looked exactly like what he was: a thug in fine clothes.

The taller man was the polar opposite of his companion. Lean and elegant, he exuded breeding and class. So blond and fair he was nearly albino, his appearance was his one liability. People remembered Gruber. Diaz, on the other hand, looked like every other arrogant punk on the street.

Clearing his throat, Lacayo lifted his glass and sipped the expensive brandy. He regarded the two men in silence. Gruber stood motionless, eyes fixed straight ahead. Diaz began to fidget nervously.

Only when beads of sweat glistened on the brute's upper lip did Lacayo finally speak.

"What do you mean–he's gone?"

Diaz began speaking rapidly. "The body–it's gone, boss. We went back to dispose of it, when–"

"You went back?" The words were almost a whisper. "Where the hell did you go?"

Diaz began to stutter.

Realizing that his grip on the glass had become dangerous, Lacayo gently set it down on the glass table beside the white leather sofa. "Shut up." Shifting his gaze, he asked, "Gruber?"

The man nodded. "Sir."

"What were your instructions?"

To Gruber's credit, not a muscle twitched. "We were to stay at the beach until you instructed us otherwise."

"Why did you disobey me?" The snake eyes narrowed dangerously, and once again, the voice was soft and low.

Gruber swallowed hard. "The man was as good as dead. The stench was awful. We figured it would be inconvenient if someone passing by reported the smell and we were caught at the scene." Only the telltale movement of his Adam's apple betrayed any nervousness. Both he and Diaz had seen how this man exacted vengeance, and neither wanted to be on the receiving end of it.

It wasn't that Gruber felt any sympathy for the traitor. He despised him. If they hadn't been tipped off, Gruber would be sitting before federal agents in a grungy, cement-gray cell instead of standing in the elegant, all-white living room of his boss's penthouse. He had been imprisoned before, and he would die before going back.

He just didn't want to die Lacayo's way.

Gruber couldn't comprehend the pleasure Lacayo took in causing pain. It was that twisted pleasure that had prolonged the cop's death and placed them all in this precarious position. Gruber didn't mind killing—he'd done it so many times he no longer kept count. It was business. He neither enjoyed it nor hated it. It was simply part of the job.

He approached killing the way he approached everything else: with mathematical practicality. The surest, quickest route from point A to point B. Efficiency he understood. Lacayo's bloodlust was wasted energy. He didn't understand it—but he feared it.

And he could feel that fear clawing at his insides now.

He could smell the fear rolling off Diaz in fat beads of sweat. Gruber felt an urge to smash the idiot's face in. He had always hated working with anyone else. He worked best alone. No matter how much he'd tried to polish Diaz, the man remained the same dumb punk Lacayo had brought on board.

Gruber watched as Lacayo stared at them without blinking, the way a rattlesnake watches its prey. Manicured hands stroked the alabaster statue that adorned the table where Lacayo had set his drink. The sculpture depicted two men locked in an explicit sexual pose. It had cost a bloody fortune.

Lacayo loved it, calling it a sound investment.

Gruber thought it was tacky.

Diaz hated it. It made him deeply uncomfortable.

Sadistically, Gruber always made a point of positioning Diaz so that he faced the sculpture whenever they gathered to discuss business in the penthouse.

The hand stilled.

The black eyes narrowed.

And the command came softly.

"Go back and find out what happened to him."

Chapter Three

Laurie was deep inside another dream, but this one was different. She rode in a wagon, her backside aching while her spirits remained high. The surrounding countryside was beautiful. She surveyed the valley below with a quiet, possessive pride. The sound of the small river, running from the mountain where they had stopped and winding down into the valley, was musical and full of promise. In the distance, she could make out the small log cabin her husband had built the summer before, knowing he would come for her and their children this spring, when the crossing was more favorable.

At the sound of approaching hooves, she turned. Once again, pride filled her heart. Her husband was the most handsome man she had ever laid eyes on. Most women she knew would argue that. He had the look of a predator, a hardness that frightened the swooning, tittering women of her hometown back east. He was a hard man, and he had reason to be. But he was also a loving one. Memories of their reunion made heat rise to her cheeks.

"You keep looking at me like that, and I'm going to have to drag you off that wagon and embarrass the both of us in front of the children!"

His laugh washed over her like a warm, sweet wave. How she had missed him.

"Well, seeing as how the children are all asleep," she said, smiling, "I think it's safe to say we wouldn't be in danger of embarrassing anyone but ourselves by being too rusty to remember how."

Laughing harder, the tall man swung down from the big bay horse and headed toward her. Without a hint of shame, she jumped from the hard buckboard seat. He caught her as she fell, pulling her tight against his chest before looking down into her eyes. Heat mixed with laughter in the intriguing silver-gray gaze fixed on her. Her heart tightened as the laughter faded, leaving only that wondrous warmth. The silver gleam disappeared as he closed his eyes and pulled her up to meet his kiss.

She was finally home.

Jake awoke to a dim room and unbearable pain. Where was he? He tried to move, only to discover that his arms were tied down.

Shit.

He was still in the piss-hole Lacayo had left him in.

Despair flooded him as he tried to retreat back into the dream he had been enjoying before waking. He had been a cowboy, or something like one. He'd had a wife and children.

He'd had hope and happiness. Squeezing his eyes shut, he willed the image of the beautiful woman he'd been holding in his arms to return. He had been drowning in those deep green eyes...

Suddenly, he felt movement on his arm.

He was instantly wide awake and intensely afraid. He could bear no more. He would not survive another game with Lacayo. His body went rigid with fear.

"Jake? Jake, are you awake?"

It was the angel's voice.

Joy flooded through him at the sound of it. She was back. Turning his head sent spears of pain ripping through him, and he gasped before forcing himself to breathe deeply and bring his eyes into focus. She was close, closer than he'd realized. Only then did he notice she was holding his hand.

He gripped her hard, trying to pull her closer, but the restraints on his arms stopped him.

"Get these off." He barely recognized his own voice. It sounded like sandpaper dragged across rough wood.

She leaned closer. He found himself staring into beautiful green eyes, deep as the sea. The kind of eyes a man could drown in.

Shit.

She had started to speak but stopped, a sharp, shocked gasp replacing the words she'd begun to murmur. "Your eyes," she said. "You have silver eyes." The words sounded almost like an accusation.

He didn't know this woman.

But he did.

She was the angel. She was his dream wife. Despite his confusion, he forced himself back to the immediate problem. "Untie me," he said gruffly, his softer "please" sounding like an afterthought.

She blinked twice, still staring at him. Just when he was certain she hadn't heard him, he saw determination settle into her gaze. "First, you have to promise to stay still and not try to pull out the tubes."

It dawned on him then that he was in a hospital. He still wasn't entirely sure whether she was real or not.

"Are you an angel?"

The moment the words slipped out, embarrassment followed. He couldn't believe he'd said them aloud.

As her smile slowly reached her eyes, he felt a different kind of pain. It was a dull ache that began in his chest and sank into the pit of his stomach. He swallowed hard, stunned to realize he was holding back tears. He hadn't cried since he was four years old.

The smile faded, replaced by a worried frown. "Are you alright?" she asked gently. "Would you like me to call the nurse?"

She wasn't beautiful in the way movie stars or models were. She was more. Her smile filled him with longing, and the anxiety in her eyes filled him with regret.

"No, don't... I wanna talk..."

The words were as raw as his thoughts.

She searched his eyes for a few seconds, unconsciously laying her palm against his cheek. He almost cried out when she pulled her hand away but bit the sound back. She must have convinced herself that he was alright, because she smiled again, tentatively, and said, "I'm no angel, believe me. You can ask anyone I know. They'll relieve you of that misconception quickly enough."

Relief coursed through him. If she was real, that meant she wasn't going to disappear just yet. "Untie me... won't move."

He was rewarded with her smile again. He realized he wanted to see it once more and frowned at the thought as memory crept back in, bringing with it where he had been and why.

She was calling the nurse now. Within seconds, an efficient-looking woman with tight salt-and-pepper curls bustled into the room. Laurie explained that he wanted to be untied. The nurse looked at him disapprovingly.

"I don't think that's a good idea. You almost hurt yourself, young man. I won't be responsible if you cause another scene like the last one."

Silver eyes glittered dangerously. Laurie looked as though she was about to speak, but he cut her off in a hoarse voice. "I won't be any trouble at all. Please." The words grated out of him.

The nurse stared at him in a way that reminded him of the librarian at his first elementary school. Then she looked at Laurie, sitting at the edge of the bed. "You'll have to be responsible for him," she said, her voice almost petulant.

Laurie and Jake looked at each other. Laurie smiled, and Jake's bruised face seemed to relax. Laurie turned back and replied, "I have been for three days."

The nurse wasn't sure, but she thought she heard something that might have been laughter coming from the bed. She unbuckled the straps and bustled back out of the room.

◐◯◑

"You're the one. You're her, aren't you?"

Laurie's smile faded as she looked at Jake. She wasn't sure whether he had experienced things the way she had. She wasn't even sure he would remember any of it. "Am I who?" she asked.

"The one on the beach that day."

Deep disappointment washed through her, but she answered in a neutral voice. "Yes, I was the one on the beach."

"You're the one in the tunnel," he whispered. "You brought me back."

Unexplainable relief replaced her disappointment. She hadn't imagined it all. She hadn't been alone in that strange dream. "Yes."

"I'm glad."

"So am I."

An awkward silence settled between them. They were strangers, yet they were closer than most people ever became in a lifetime.

Jake was the first to break the impasse. "I was dreaming of you before I woke up…"

Her eyebrows lifted, and she asked cautiously, "What were you dreaming?"

"We were married. I was about to kiss you."

For a moment, they simply stared at each other. Laurie's heart pounded. He had been dreaming that they were married. She had dreamt the same thing. It seemed outlandish, but after everything they had been through, why shouldn't it be true? "How did you know it was me?"

"I didn't," he said. "I realized it when I woke up and saw your eyes."

"My eyes?"

"Yeah. You were dressed differently. You had a bonnet on that kind of shielded your face. But your eyes… I couldn't confuse them if I wanted to." He spoke slowly, carefully easing the words out.

Her heart raced. She clenched her fists into the hospital sheets and repeated dumbly, "I had a bonnet on?"

"Yeah. It was a little weird. I was riding this big horse, and we were—"

"We were on a mountainside, looking down at the valley where you had built our cabin the summer before." Laurie went pale.

Jake stared at her. They had both had the same dream. A chill moved through him. Until the tunnel, despite the efforts of countless foster parents, he had never believed in God. If there was a God, he had certainly never met Him. And yet here was this beautiful woman who had somehow saved him.

At that precise moment, the door opened, and Sam Hollinger strode in. Almost grateful for the interruption, Jake shoved the thoughts and emotions churning inside him into that dark place he reserved for things he couldn't—or wouldn't—deal with.

"Jake! You're awake! Jesus H. Christ, Jake, what the hell happened?"

What the hell happened?

He'd had three long days, in between torture sessions, to think about it. He knew he could trust the two people in this room. He could trust Laurie because she had nothing to do with it. He knew that in a way no one else could understand. He could trust Sam because he hadn't been involved in the investigation.

A brief flicker of shame passed through him at the realization that he would have distrusted his old friend otherwise. He brushed it aside just as quickly. He had learned not to trust, and that lesson had kept him alive. He liked Sam and respected him. They had saved each other's lives more than once. But he had also seen men he liked and respected just as much give in to the lure of money and power.

And someone he had trusted had betrayed him three days ago.

"Sam. Good… to see you."

He watched his friend's face soften. Sam had always been easy to read.

"Jake, you don't know how good it is to know you're okay. I thought you were dead when we found you."

Hollinger's expression shifted as he gestured toward Laurie. He looked back and forth between her and Jake, then straightened.

"Do you know this woman?" His voice was threaded with suspicion.

Jake glanced from his old friend to Laurie. He could see the tension in Sam's massive, crossed arms. It suddenly dawned on him that she had led the police to his rescue. She would have no plausible explanation for knowing where he was, none that the department would believe, anyway.

Both of them were watching him now. The look on Laurie's face startled him. She was smiling serenely, her expression open and unguarded. The trust there scared the hell out of him. It was clear she expected him to tell Hollinger the whole improbable, impossible truth.

He had to be careful. Very careful. Leaving himself room to maneuver was not going to be easy.

"Yes," he said finally. "We know each other."

He offered nothing more.

"How does she figure into what happened to you?" Hollinger asked. His voice had taken on a faintly threatening edge as he stared at Laurie.

"She doesn't."

Hollinger's head snapped back toward him. He stared at Jake for a full thirty seconds without saying a word. Then he could contain himself no longer. Almost spitting out the words, he demanded, "You're telling me you believe in this psychic bull?"

"She told you?" Jake asked.

"Of course I told him! So did Claire. Or at least we tried to." Laurie snapped. "Both of you stop talking as though I weren't in the room!"

Her irritation darkened her eyes to a deeper green, and a pink flush crept into her cheeks. She crossed her arms and took a steadying breath, forcing herself to calm down.

In a more controlled tone, she continued, "Don't feel bad, Chief. I'm just as surprised as you are that I'm not certifiably insane. Surprised, relieved, and"–her gaze locked onto Jake's– "scared too."

Jake just looked at her. She was relieved, she said. Relieved and scared. That was interesting.

He was knocked flat on his ass. He couldn't deny what had happened any more than he could explain it. He wasn't sure he wanted to understand it. He had never given much thought to life and death, or whatever might exist in between, if anything did. Hell, how could you believe in souls and angels if you didn't even believe in God?

Sensing his confusion, Laurie turned to Hollinger. "Chief, I don't think either of us can give you a logical explanation. Do you think you could take it at face value if Jake just confirms that it's true?"

Hollinger looked at Jake. "I want to hear you say that this woman is a total stranger who found you through some psychic... mental... vision thing. You say it, Jake, or I'll haul her back downtown."

"You arrested her?" The anger in his swollen face would have frightened a lesser man.

"Damn right I did, you stupid son of a bitch!" Hollinger shouted. "What the hell would you have done? You were reported missing to me by your chief, in the strictest confidence. Then I get a call from a woman threatening me, saying I'd better come get her or you were going to die. Of course, I arrested her. She's lucky I didn't throw her in a damned cell. You're going to lie there and tell me you would've believed her story?"

As the logic of it sank in, Jake's anger deflated. He exhaled in a painful gust. "No."

"Well, I guess that just goes to prove that you're both cynical and distrusting."

Uncomfortable, Laurie shifted as she spoke, lifting herself slightly and stretching her neck and back. As she twisted, Jake watched her despite himself. Even as tired as she clearly was, every movement held an effortless sensuality. She had curves in all the right places and a natural grace that made him wonder how she moved under different circumstances. Frowning at how easily she distracted him, he shook his head, only to be sharply reminded of his condition.

He grunted in pain.

At the sound, she was at his side in an instant. "Are you alright?" Concern threaded through her voice.

"He's fine," Hollinger said with a smile. "He's been banged up before." Then he looked back at Jake. "I still haven't heard you say it, old buddy."

Both he and Laurie looked at Jake expectantly again. Through clenched teeth, he replied, "Once and only once. Never again... old buddy."

Grinning more broadly, Hollinger nodded in agreement.

Clearing his throat with effort, Jake continued. "She saw me walking on the beach with Lacayo's thugs. After that, she could... feel me. I could hear her."

The chagrin on Hollinger's face was almost too much. Jake felt an urge to smile. He probably would have, if it hadn't hurt like hell. His lips were still swollen and bruised, and exhaustion was beginning to set in. He could feel the adrenaline rush from waking up to find Laurie there, draining away fast. Pressing his head back into the pillow, his eyes slid shut of their own accord.

Laurie looked at Hollinger with concern. He shrugged and brought his fingers to his lips, signaling her to let Jake sleep. She nodded and began to sit back down in the chair beside the bed. Hollinger rested a hand on her shoulder and whispered, "He'll be out for a while. Let me buy you some coffee."

"I don't want to leave him."

"Brown's just outside the door. We'll grab the coffee and drink it in the waiting room. If he wakes up, we'll know it before his eyes are even open. Come on, lady, you've got to be as beat as I am."

Laurie had to admit the thought of hot coffee was tempting. She hadn't eaten all day. Besides, something told her the Chief had more than coffee on his mind.

"Okay, Chief," she said. "But please, let's make it quick."

"After you, Ms. James."

The hospital cafeteria was nearly empty. Laurie glanced at her watch and saw it was almost three in the morning. She hadn't realized how much time had passed since she'd walked through Claire's door. They ordered coffee and doughnuts, then headed back to the elevator.

After instructing Officer Brown to signal them if he heard Jake move, they went to the waiting room. Sitting in the uncomfortable chairs, they prepared their coffee in silence. Laurie bit into the stale doughnut. It tasted like sugary cardboard, but she was suddenly ravenous and wolfed it down anyway. Hollinger smiled at her with weary understanding and took a bite of his own.

Once they had finished the remaining two doughnuts, they looked at each other. Hollinger appeared ready to speak when Laurie drew a deep breath and plunged ahead.

"It's alright, Chief. I'm ready to tell you anything you want."

"Call me Sam, please." His tone was neutral.

Laurie responded carefully. "I take it this means you no longer think I'm a criminal?"

He shrugged his powerful shoulders, the dark fabric of his shirt stretching briefly. "Like I told Jake, you didn't really leave me much of a choice."

"I know."

"Well, Ms. James, do you want to tell me how you got yourself into this and what you know?"

"Call me Laurie, please." She waited for his nod, then explained how she had seen Jake on the beach that day and about the dreams that followed. She told him about Claire and how she had been an innocent bystander in the whole mess. "You know, you were pretty rough on her."

Frowning, Sam lifted a dark brow. "I was rough? What about her?"

Laurie smiled faintly and steered the conversation back on course. "Anyway, I'm not psychic. The only person I've ever had this kind of… connection with is Jake. I think Claire might be, though–psychic, I mean. She seemed to know what I was thinking before she hypnotized me."

"She hypnotized you? This just keeps getting crazier by the minute." Sam rubbed his eyes in frustration.

Laurie felt compelled to defend Claire. "Without her, I–we–would never have reached him in time." A shiver ran through her as the truth of it settled in. If Jake hadn't died on his own, she knew they would have killed him. She had no doubt the man who tortured him so viciously wouldn't have stopped until Jake was dead. The memory of the pain she had shared with him was still sharp and disturbingly real.

"So you really don't know anything about what Jake was involved in?"

Hollinger's voice pulled Laurie back to the present. "No, I don't. I didn't even know he was a police officer until you told me when you arrested me." She stood abruptly and looked at him. "I want to go back to him now. Is there anything else?"

"No. I'll be here until he wakes up. I need to notify Chief Morris in New York that we've found him." His expression hardened slightly. "Jake still has a lot of questions to answer."

Chapter Four

Three days later, the sunlight streamed through the tiny east window of the hospital room. The rays bounced off the stark white walls, lending an almost blinding brightness to the morning. Still asleep, Laurie turned her head to escape the glare, only to jolt awake when a sharp pain shot through her neck. She lifted her head from her folded arms, rubbed the stiff muscles, and yawned. It took her a few moments to remember where she was. She turned to check on Jake and found him staring intensely at her.

For a moment, she simply stared back. He still looked like a monster in a B movie, swollen and purple. To Laurie, the simple fact that he was alive made him look wonderful. He did not speak. He just sat there, watching her. Self-consciously, she ran her fingers through her hair. She felt the heat rush to her face and knew she must look awful. As usual, when she was nervous, she retreated behind the cool, impersonal voice she had perfected in law school.

"Good morning. How are you feeling?"

"I have to get out of here."

"What?" she asked incredulously, losing her composure at once. She stared at him, her mouth falling open. He must still be in shock, she thought. He had suffered a concussion. Maybe that was it.

"I said I have to get out of here. So do you." His expression was deadly serious.

"You can't leave. You're still hurt. The doctor will be here today to see you. I'm sure he'll tell you when you can expect to go home." Without waiting for him to answer, she continued, her words tumbling out in nervous chatter. "Um... home. I hadn't really thought about it. Is there... um... someone you'd like me to call? Your family? A friend? Your wife?"

A sick dread settled in her stomach as she waited for his response. So much for impersonal. She had assumed he was single. She had been sure of it. But in the bright morning light, everything seemed different. He seemed different, almost unfamiliar.

"I could call her, if you like..."

"Stop it. There's no one. You know that." His voice was edged with impatience. "Now listen to me. We have to get out of here."

In his urgency, he tried to lean forward, and pain exploded through his ribs, leaving him gasping for air. Laurie moved instantly, pressing his shoulders back against the pillows. His hand shot up, gripping her wrist tightly. He pulled her closer and whispered, his voice urgent and low.

"Someone set me up, Laurie. Once they find out I'm not dead, they'll come after me. I'm the only one who can take him down."

"Take who down?" Laurie struggled to ignore what his touch was doing to her pulse. She was almost grateful when he released her.

"Lacayo."

Laurie shivered. The violence he kept so carefully contained vibrated in his voice, twisting something deep in her stomach. She fought to shake the dark feeling creeping over her. "Who is he?"

A deep baritone voice came from behind her. "He's the heavyweight champion of the drug runners, isn't that right, Jake? He moved down to South Beach about a year and a half ago when things got too hot in New York."

Hollinger had entered the room silently, completely unnoticed.

"That's right." Jake's eyes were grim as he and Sam exchanged knowing looks. For Laurie's benefit, he explained, "No one has ever been able to take him down. He's covered his tracks so well that there's never been an opportunity to prove he runs the drug ring. Until now."

"You said it was a setup?" Sam asked.

"It had to be. I was in, Sam. Lacayo was supposed to receive a shipment two days ago. I was in charge of the operation. The delivery was set up twenty miles off the coast. It was ingenious."

Laurie was sure she heard admiration in his voice as he continued. "Instead of speedboats, a Haitian cargo ship was doing the pickup. The coke was supposed to be hidden inside bicycle tires. The tires would be tied alongside the delivery boat. The Haitians would just pick up the net and float into the river as usual. You know the Coast Guard has a hard time inspecting them. The boats are always loaded down with junk."

"Junk that helps their families back in Haiti survive," Laurie said sharply. Irritation edged her voice. She had worked with many Haitian immigrants and knew the crushing poverty they had left behind. She also knew most of them worked two or three jobs to make sure the families they had left behind did not starve.

Jake grunted his agreement.

Sam let out a low whistle. "Shit. The tires? You're right. Those boats are hanging all over the Miami River with mountains of bikes piled on their decks." Hollinger shook his head in disbelief. "It's still risky, though. The Coast Guard's still going to board them."

Warming to his subject, Jake leaned forward slightly and continued. "That's the beauty of it. Lacayo's men are already on board before the ship ever really docks. Divers accompany the ship down the river. The stuff is slipped out of the nets little by little to the divers. Once each man's sack is filled, he heads for shore, where I would have been waiting to take delivery."

"Where was the DEA?" The question came from Laurie.

Without thinking, she placed her hand over Jake's. When she tried to withdraw it, he held on, his fingers sliding through hers. Laurie's heartbeat quickened, and a flush crept up her neck.

Jake didn't seem aware of what he was doing, but Sam noticed. His gaze lingered on their entwined fingers. He studied his friend for a moment, surprise flickering across his face, before turning back to the conversation. "Well, where was the DEA? And how come I didn't know this was going down?" He crossed his arms over his barrel-like chest and lowered himself into the same uncomfortable chair he had occupied the night before.

Oblivious to Laurie's flushed cheeks and his friend's bemusement, Jake continued to hold her hand, absently caressing her palm with his thumb. His voice slowed as he went on. "My DEA contact is an agent named Linda DeMarco. We've never met face to face. The whole thing was set up through Morris and her agency. DeMarco and I spoke briefly on the phone to finalize the details the day Lacayo took me down. As soon as the entire shipment was in my hands, DeMarco and her team at the docks would have moved in and made the bust."

Needing a distraction from the feel of his fingers tracing slow circles on her palm, Laurie interrupted him. "What about Lacayo?"

“There’s already a warrant for his arrest prepared and ready to be served. He would have been taken into custody two seconds after those other bozos had their rights read.” The thought of Lacayo twisted Jake’s insides with rage. He had almost gotten the bastard. Unconsciously, he tightened his grip on Laurie’s hand.

Laurie murmured a soft protest at the sudden, unexpected pain.

Realizing he was squeezing her hand, Jake looked up in surprise. Beneath the bruises, his face deepened to a darker shade of red as he stumbled through an apology. “I, uh… I’m sorry. I didn’t realize… Sorry.” As if punishing himself, he shoved his hands beneath the bed sheet. Trying to ignore the abrupt emptiness left behind, he turned to Sam, who looked faintly amused. “The point is, there’s no way Lacayo figured this out on his own.”

Laurie noticed the grim looks the two men exchanged. Her thoughts drifted to the betrayal Jake had suffered. She didn’t know many details about Jake North, but she knew who he was. She hadn’t missed the surprise on Sam’s face moments earlier. She understood that Jake was not a man who showed emotion, least of all the softer kind. The man she had awakened beside was hard and impenetrable as steel. She also sensed that this was only one of many betrayals he had endured. A fierce protectiveness surged through her at the thought of how much he had already survived.

She snapped back to the present at the sound of Jake's voice. "I lost one chance to take this guy down, Sam. I won't lose another. I have to know who the leak is."

"How do you intend to do that? Your cover is blown wide open," Hollinger replied.

"I know enough about Lacayo's operation to throw a serious wrench into it. I could probably get him convicted on money laundering, but that's not enough. I have to flush out whoever's feeding him information. Once he's out in the open, the bastard is going to pay."

Laurie felt a shiver of fear slide down her spine. Although she could no longer hear his thoughts, she felt attuned to his emotions. She knew he intended to kill his betrayer. The violence in him hovered close to the surface, palpable and dangerous. She knew she should be revolted. Until now, she had never been able to understand or accept violence in any form. But how could she not understand now? She had felt the same violent craving for vengeance when she had bent over Jake's bloodied body.

Gruber stared at the yellow police tape strung across the cabanas of the Coral Reef Hotel, a sinking sensation settling in his gut. Diaz hadn't lied. The body was gone. Obviously, the smell had led a passerby to call the police. Damn it. Lacayo would lose it over this.

He didn't bother getting any closer to the cabanas. Drawing attention to himself wasn't worth the risk. The area appeared deserted, but there was no sense in taking chances. Someone could still be combing the scene, gathering evidence, or surveying the damage.

He headed back to his car, trying to figure out the best way to handle Lacayo as he walked. It really didn't matter, he told himself. There was no way to prove who had killed the son of a bitch. They had been careful. They had left no trace. He knew there had been no eyewitnesses.

Wrong.

There *had* been a woman on the beach the day they brought North there. The memory surfaced suddenly, sharp and unwelcome. Just as quickly, he dismissed it. She had been too far away to identify any of them and had driven off before they even went into the cabana. She hadn't come back. He knew that for a fact. He had kept watch the entire time. No one else had been on the beach. It had been deserted for years. There was no swimming, no fishing. Hardly a tourist attraction.

As he slid into the soft leather seat of his car, he let out a deep sigh. None of that would matter to Lacayo. He had wanted the body disposed of. The shit was really going to hit the fan. At least Diaz was gone for a while, and for that he felt a flicker of gratitude. He pulled away from the curb and merged smoothly into traffic.

The body.

Where the hell would it be now?

There had been no mention of a dead body in the morning paper or on the early news. Why hadn't it been reported to the media?

He slammed on the brakes as the realization hit him.

What if the cop wasn't dead?

Stunned, he stared blindly at the road ahead. Shrill blasts of car horns erupted behind him, jolting him back into motion. He eased forward again, his hands shaking. Nausea rolled through him. Sweat trickled down his neck and soaked his armpits.

If he wasn't dead, he could tell the story.

Shit.

Gripping the steering wheel so tightly his knuckles turned white, Gruber reeled with the knowledge that his life was suddenly hanging by a very precarious thread.

Amanda slammed down the receiver impatiently. Laurie was still not home. She had tried reaching her at the office, but Dorothy had told her Laurie wasn't in. Dorothy had sounded worried. Not wanting to alarm her any further, Amanda said she had forgotten that Laurie had mentioned a doctor's appointment. Strangely, there had been a note of relief in Dorothy's voice. Amanda then called the hospital, but no one answered in the waiting room. Curiosity and worry gnawed at her.

The beauty salon was busy as usual. Loud music, the hum of hairdryers, and bursts of laughter blended with the sharp scent of hair dye and the rich aroma of dark coffee constantly brewing in the tiny lunch area at the back of the salon. Normally, Amanda would have been clipping, cutting, and setting alongside her employees. Today, she had handed her regular clients over to the other two stylists, much to their disappointment. She couldn't concentrate. Amanda never touched anyone's hair when she wasn't fully focused. Her business was like brain surgery. One wrong move and you could lose a client forever.

Claire suddenly came to mind. She would know what was going on. Grabbing the worn address book from the receptionist's desk, Amanda flipped quickly to Claire's number and dialed.

Claire's smooth voice came on the line. "Hello?"

"Hi, Claire. It's Amanda."

"Oh, hi. I was hoping it was your cousin." Claire sounded utterly exhausted.

"That's why I'm calling." Amanda felt irritation rising at Laurie's silence. She should have called by now. "I'm worried." She tried to keep the complaining tone out of her voice but failed miserably.

Claire debated whether to let Amanda know that she, too, was worried. She hadn't slept all night. Images of Laurie and Jake running in fear had haunted her, keeping rest at bay. A dark circle of corruption and betrayal seemed to surround them both. She and Amanda had been friends for a year now, and she knew her well enough to understand that Amanda would be unable to bear it if her beloved cousin came to harm.

She decided it was best to keep things low-key for now. "Amanda, don't worry too much. They're in the hospital under police guard. I doubt anything could happen to Laurie under the circumstances."

"Yeah… but this guy. You said he was very close to her. How close, Claire? Will he take care of her, or hurt her?"

This, she could answer without deception. "He would never hurt her. He'd die before he'd let anything happen to her." She knew it was true.

Still unsatisfied, Amanda pressed on. "How can you be so sure? I know you're good, Claire, don't get me wrong. It's just that this is my cousin we're talking about." Almost to herself, she added, "Laurie's special. She comes across tough and competent, and she is. But she's also innocent. Romantic, you know? What if she gets in over her head trying to help this guy?"

That was exactly what Claire feared might happen. "Listen, Amanda, why don't we go down to the hospital and check on both of them? After yesterday, we have a right to be concerned, don't you think? That way we can be sure everything is alright."

Brightening, Amanda agreed eagerly. They made arrangements to meet for lunch and then go to the hospital afterward.

As she hung up, Amanda felt the familiar blend of curiosity and worry. She had never experienced any spiritual or psychic connections herself, but she fervently believed in the phenomenon. Claire's reading had been uncannily accurate about Max. All the worries and doubts Amanda had felt before accepting his proposal had dissolved after that session with Claire. At the time, Claire had been genuinely happy for her. She had laughed at Amanda's reasons for hesitating over marriage to the man she loved so deeply. She had practically given her a written guarantee.

But none of that optimism was present in Claire's voice now. She sounded tired and anxious. The fact that she wanted to go to the hospital set off warning bells in Amanda's head. Claire was not someone who involved herself directly in other people's problems. Normally, she avoided doing so with strict discipline. Amanda drummed her nails violently against the desk. There was something Claire wasn't telling her.

As she hung up, Claire once again berated herself for getting involved. She knew it would bring mental anguish. Although not everything was clear to her yet, she sensed that Laurie and Jake North were heading into the most difficult test of their lives. She felt that they would be forced to confront more than the evil pressing down on them. They would have to face the past and their own emotional defenses, or their love would be lost—at least in this lifetime.

She wasn't even certain Laurie would welcome her presence. Yesterday, the young woman had leaned on her. In shock and filled with fear, Laurie had known Claire was the only one who could truly understand the depth of her experience. Today, however, was another matter. Laurie might resent Claire's role in what was probably the most traumatic experience of her life. Claire hoped that wouldn't be the case. In the short time she had known Laurie James, she had grown fond of her. Despite her misgivings, she wanted to help her if she could.

She dressed in a loose, flower-print dress and low-heeled sandals. Her turquoise earrings brushed against her neck as she bent to feed Moses before leaving to meet Amanda. The tomcat purred appreciatively and rubbed against her legs. Stroking the cat's scrawny head absently, she thought about Laurie's hypnosis session. She envied the depth of emotion Laurie had felt for the man in her past and present. She tried not to dwell on the regret that surfaced as the thought crossed her mind that she had never loved that way.

Chief Robert Morris stared at the hourglass on his desk. The sand poured silently into the bottom half of the wooden timepiece. It was the first time he had ever turned the damned thing over. It had been a gift from the officers of the 12th Precinct when he had been promoted to Chief of Police. A small inscription was carved into the base: *To Robert Morris, best wishes from your compadres at the 12th.*

That had been more than six years ago. He hadn't thought about those men in a long time. The inscription had been sincere. They truly had been his friends. They had worked together, played together, and baptized each other's children. They had helped drown one another's sorrows with expensive whiskey through divorces, deaths, and retirements.

Sorrow seeped in through the cracks. He missed them.

From the start of his career in law enforcement, he had risen quickly through the ranks. He had everything the department valued: experience, a college education, good looks, and strong public relations skills. Ambition had never been in short supply, either. He had always known he wouldn't be satisfied walking a beat for his entire career. He liked living well and saw no reason to hide it.

Within the next five years, he envisioned a political career for himself. It was no pipe dream. He was the most popular police chief in the NYPD's recent history. Crime rates had dropped significantly since he had taken over. He had earned the respect of the men and women under his command. They knew he wasn't a bureaucrat brought in to pretend he understood law enforcement.

Yes, everything had been going according to plan—until now.

He replayed the message Chief Sam Hollinger had left in the early hours of the morning. It concerned Detective North. Morris had to decide what to say and what to do. Should he go to Miami? He was sitting on a time bomb, and he knew it. No one else had contacted him besides Hollinger, and he wasn't sure whether that was good news or bad.

Noticing that the sand had finished running, he lifted the hourglass and turned it over. As the grains shifted and began to fall again, he rubbed his temples wearily. This was a terrible time to be thinking about old friends and time slipping away. He needed to think.

He needed to get the hell away from that hourglass.

Loosening his tie, he stood and walked out of his office. As he passed his assistant, Lucy, he muttered something about lunch and forced himself not to bolt for the door.

Agent Linda de Marco closed her office door quietly behind her. She shoved her fingers through her sandy-blonde hair, yanking free the clip that held it back from her face. She had just been chewed out, big time, by her boss.

On her authorization, an entire team of agents had been assigned to cover the Miami River two nights earlier. A speedboat, divers, and even a helicopter had been deployed for the operation.

And no one had shown up.

Not Lacayo. Not the Haitian cargo ship. And most alarming of all, not Detective Jake North.

She and her crew had been stood up. She had been made to look incompetent, and her agency had burned through thousands of dollars in manpower, fuel, and equipment.

Dropping into her chair, she pulled the file on René Lacayo from her desk drawer. The man was scum, but he was smart scum. Either Jake North had sold out, or his cover had been blown. She grabbed the phone and dialed the direct line to Chief Morris's office. A woman with a heavy Brooklyn accent answered and informed her that Chief Morris was out to lunch.

"This is Agent de Marco. Please have Chief Morris call me as soon as he returns. He has the number." She slammed the receiver down.

Everything about Robert Morris irritated her. There was something about him that rubbed her the wrong way, which only made it worse because she couldn't identify a concrete reason for it. He was always cordial, always cooperative. The few times she had worked directly with the New York City

Police Department, he had extended every professional courtesy. Ridiculous as it was, even the fact that he was out to lunch annoyed her. He was notorious for his power lunches with New York's political elite. There were rumors he was considering a run for governor. She didn't doubt it. The man had politician written all over him.

"Damn."

She ran her hands through her hair again and pulled out Jake North's file. The manila folder was packed with facts, cold and clinical, yet it revealed almost nothing about the man himself. His military record was exemplary. His NYPD file was loaded with commendations. No family. Few friends. No one seemed to know anything about his private life.

Could he have sold out? Had he been discovered? Was he even still alive?

Frustrated, she closed the folder and stared at the dingy gray wall across from her desk. She really needed to put something up there. Anything.

With a sigh, she stood and headed for the cafeteria. Something told her Morris took long lunches.

Chapter Five

In the hospital room, the three had fallen silent, each lost in their own thoughts.

Laurie closed her eyes in an effort to shut out the images that had tortured her for days. She didn't want to think about the pain Jake had endured anymore. It still made her ill. A shiver ran through her as the memory of Jake's bloody, seemingly lifeless body snaked its way into her mind. She tried to tell herself it could have been worse. This monster, Lacayo, could have finished the job.

Hollinger was the first to speak. "If what you say is true, I think I might have gotten ahead of myself."

Laurie's eyes flew open. She stared at him, wondering what more could possibly go wrong.

Jake didn't even blink. "What do you mean?" His voice was flat and low. His eyes narrowed imperceptibly, his body tensing. Without seeming to move a muscle, he shifted into readiness. To Laurie's eyes, he suddenly looked like a panther about to pounce.

If he hadn't known him for so long, Sam would never have picked up on it. Most people would never have realized they were in danger, but Jake's voice was a dead giveaway. Sam had heard it before. He knew what it meant. He felt no fear–only a small hurt that Jake would feel threatened by him. He'd been a good friend to Jake. They had been through a lot together.

"I called your chief."

"When was this?" Jake's voice was still tense, but his muscles relaxed.

"Last night—or rather, early this morning."

Worried, Laurie broke in. "Do you think he's the one who set you up?" Unconsciously, she placed her hand on Jake's arm again.

Jake tried to ignore the pleasure he felt at her touch. He needed to focus. He and Sam exchanged a knowing look. Anything was possible. How often had they cleaned up after men the public believed to be beyond reproach?

"How do you figure it?" Hollinger leaned forward in his chair as he spoke, his voice so quiet that Laurie found herself leaning in just to hear him.

In the same low tone, Jake responded, "Not very probable. Morris doesn't seem the type. He's got political aspirations. It wouldn't be very smart of him to get mixed up with the likes of Lacayo." He paused, lost in thought. "On the other hand, money makes the world go 'round, my friend. It could be someone on his staff. Could be anyone involved in the investigation. Whoever it is, they can't afford to leave me alive." His gut clenched at the thought of betrayal by a fellow officer. "What did he say when you talked to him?"

Hollinger grinned. "I didn't. I just left a message asking him to call me back. He's a hard man to get hold of."

Laurie couldn't believe her ears. Both men spoke easily, as if the fact that Jake's life was still in danger was of no consequence. Anger burned inside her. She'd been a victim of the traitor as well. She'd been tortured right along with Jake. She couldn't keep the acid out of her voice. "I'm glad you're both so relaxed. I, on the other hand, think this is a huge problem. For all we know, someone could be coming after Jake any minute now!" Glaring at Jake, she crossed her arms over her chest and hissed, "I, for one, have no interest in finding out what it feels like for you to die!"

She saw Jake's face pale beneath the bruises, but Sam just kept grinning.

"Well, well... I do believe we're annoying Ms. James, Jake." There was a speculative gleam in his eyes.

Jake didn't smile back. She was right. He didn't understand why, but he knew she had felt every blow he'd received. A dark heaviness settled over him. She had no business in the middle of all this ugliness. He looked at her, taking in the soft curve of her cheek, the natural rose of her lips, those beautiful eyes. She was a fine woman. He didn't know how he knew it, but he knew it without a doubt.

Too fine a woman to be mixed up in this mess. Too fine a woman to be mixed up with him.

He had to get her out of it before she became more entangled than she already was. He ignored the emptiness that gripped him at the thought of never seeing her again. He had no choice.

With a coldness he did not feel, he turned to her and said in a rough voice, "You're right. I have no desire to feel what it's like either. I think the best thing for you to do is go home and forget about this whole mess. Get on with your life. This is police business, and as you can see,"–he nodded at Hollinger–"the cavalry has arrived."

Sam Hollinger hadn't held his breath in a long time. He held it now. Jake didn't get it, but Sam had been married too long not to know his friend had just made a major mistake.

Laurie felt as if he had slapped her. Tears stung her eyelids, but pride kept them from falling. She stood and grabbed her purse. She missed the muscle jumping in Jake's jaw as he watched her. She didn't trust herself to look at him.

Facing Sam, she said, "Chief Hollinger, if you need me, you know where to find me. Good luck... to you both."

Sam let his breath out in a whoosh. He hadn't been promoted to Chief because he was slow on his feet. They needed Laurie James. Hell, who was he kidding? Jake needed Laurie James. With all the authority he possessed, he barked, "Not so fast, Ms. James. I still need to question you again. You may have seen something you don't remember offhand."

Disconcerted, Laurie replied, "Fine. You can reach me at my office." She began rummaging through her purse, looking for her business cards. The tears were threatening to fall. How could he send her away so coldly? Desperately, she searched the bottom of the bag. "Damn these bags anyway." Without thinking, she turned and dumped the contents of her purse onto the bed.

As a shower of miscellaneous items fell on him, Jake grunted. His body still felt like one big bruise.

When Laurie realized what she had done, she began stammering. "Oh... oh my God! I'm sorry... so–so sor–oh!" She couldn't contain them any longer. Tears spilled down her cheeks. Mortified, she babbled as she tried to scoop up the mess she had made. "Why don't you just jot down my number, Chief? I'm certain I don't remember anything else, but–"

Her tears were his undoing.

Jake felt like the world's biggest ass. This woman had risked so much without having to. All for him–someone she didn't even know–and he was sending her away as if she didn't matter. He hadn't even thanked her. He realized she had been fighting to keep her composure and understood that kind of pride.

He had made her cry.

The realization tightened his throat. He hadn't known this woman for one week , and twice she had brought him dangerously close to tears. He heard her going on and on to Hollinger as she tossed her belongings back into her bag. He reached out and closed his hand over hers, stilling her jerky movements.

She fell silent, staring at the large, scarred hand covering her smaller one, refusing to look up at him. With a painful grunt, he lifted his other hand and wiped the moisture from her cheek. Fascinated, he watched another tear form and slide down her dark lashes, suspended there like a liquid jewel. For a moment, he was transported back to his dream that morning. There had been no sadness in her sea-green eyes then. They had sparkled with happiness.

He knew he would give anything to see them sparkle that way again.

"I'm an ass. I'm sorry." He couldn't remember the last time he had apologized to anyone. Keeping his hand on hers, he added ruefully, "Haven't even thanked you, have I?"

She gave him a watery smile that made it hard to breathe. "I'd like to say it was my pleasure, but I'd be lying to you."

He laughed, even though it hurt. "No, I guess not."

They had forgotten Sam was there. He didn't mind. Sam Hollinger realized three very important things as he watched the two people on the other side of the room. He realized he had to get Jake the hell out of this hospital. He realized Laurie James might truly be in danger. And he realized that both those facts gave him a golden opportunity.

Gruber finally arrived at Diaz's girlfriend's apartment. The place always smelled of olive oil and onions. So did the girlfriend. He sat impatiently on a small kitchen stool, waiting for Diaz to get dressed and say his goodbyes. The girl's mother stood with her broad back to him, tossing green peppers into a frying pan. She ignored him, wiping her hands on the stained apron she wore. It wasn't hard for Gruber to see the woman the girlfriend would eventually become.

For now, though, Connie was a hard-bodied young woman in a tight dress, and that was all Diaz required. What the hell was taking the idiot so long? Gruber hated waiting in general. Waiting for Diaz made him furious.

The bedroom door finally opened, and Diaz sauntered out with his designer jacket slung over his arm and his fly open. Connie clung to him, barely dressed. Disgusted, Gruber listened as she whined about her lover's haste. Diaz benevolently patted her backside and ignored her pleas. Gruber watched him hook his tie around his thick neck, standing wordless.

Once they were outside, Gruber tried to ignore Diaz's graphic description of his heroic acts of manhood in Connie's bed and nodded toward the car. He waited until they had pulled out of the parking lot before telling Diaz what he had seen. He allowed himself a moment or two to enjoy the fear contorting his partner's face, then began giving instructions.

If they were going to face Lacayo after this screwup, they would need a plan—a united front.

Diaz nodded dumbly as Gruber explained what they had to do. They needed to talk to their mole in the police department. They had to find out whether the cop was alive and, if so, where they were holding him. They would stop to call their contact before going to report to Rene. Hopefully, they'd get enough information to distract Lacayo from administering punishment.

"Sure, Grub. Anything you say, buddy."

Gruber stiffened at the shortening of his name. Gripping the wheel tightly, he soothed himself by imagining his fist slamming into his partner's jaw.

Claire ate her salad and watched Amanda put away a large plate of bow-tie pasta. She had come to admire Amanda's appetite for food almost as much as she admired her appetite for life. Amanda wasn't heavy; she was voluptuous. It was a word that had fallen into disuse in recent years, but it fit her perfectly. She looked resplendent in a curve-hugging jersey dress in deep burgundy. There wasn't a man in the restaurant who didn't pause to stare at Amanda as they were led to their table.

Of course, Amanda was oblivious to the attention. She had no idea how attractive she was. It was just one more endearing quality Claire loved about her friend.

On Amanda's wedding day, her besotted husband, Max, had told Claire—his face split by a big, goofy grin—that his new wife was the most beautiful woman in the world. With an honesty born of too much champagne, he had leaned on Claire's shoulder as he watched Amanda dance and confided that he could already see his bride full and ripe with his child. In his euphoric stupor, he never noticed the tears in Claire's eyes. It wasn't that she wasn't truly happy for them. She was overjoyed at the union. Her tears were born of regret, of thoughts of her own unfulfilled dreams.

"Claire? Claire! You're not even listening to me!" Amanda sounded caught somewhere between irritation and worry. "What's going on? I know you're not telling me everything."

"Sorry." Pulling her mind back to the present, Claire toyed with the stem of her wineglass. She didn't want to frighten Amanda. She didn't want to lie to her either. "It's just that there's a lot more to this than meets the eye."

Amanda set her fork down. "Laurie's in danger." She wasn't asking. She was stating it, because she knew Claire wouldn't.

Claire spoke quickly, trying to ease her fears. "It's not all clear to me, Amanda. I had horrible dreams all last night. If the danger is real, this man is her only chance."

Amanda pushed her plate away. The sudden fear blooming in the pit of her stomach killed her appetite. "What did you dream? That the guy who beat up the cop wants to hurt Laurie? Why? He can't even know about her. She has nothing to do with whatever was going on."

"I know." Claire shook her head. "I'm not sure he's the only one involved. Whoever it is doesn't really care about Laurie. It's Detective North they want."

Raising her voice, Amanda shot back, "Then how can you say her only chance is this North guy? We have to get her away from him as soon as possible!" As she spoke, she gestured wildly, knocking over her iced tea. "Damn it!"

A waiter in a snowy white jacket hurried over to help. While they were momentarily interrupted, Claire's thoughts drifted back to her dreams. She had hardly slept. Over and over, she had dreamed of Laurie trapped in the grip of giant hands. Blood ran between the massive fingers as Laurie twisted in agony, trying to escape. Just before she was crushed to death, Jake North would appear, frantically trying to pry the gruesome fingers apart. The blood made the hands slick and difficult to grasp. Finally, desperate, he would pull out a long, sword-like knife. One by one, he chopped the fingers away until he could free Laurie.

Each time, Claire had awakened drenched in sweat and screaming, never certain whether he had saved Laurie in time.

The images were grotesque, but one thing was clear to Claire: the message was unmistakable. This man was the only one who could save Laurie. The closer he stayed to her, the sooner he could pull her free from death's grip.

The waiter finished mopping up the spilled tea and disappeared quietly with the dripping towels. Claire noticed that Amanda's hands were shaking. She had to convince her–convince everyone–of the importance of keeping Laurie close to the man she had rescued. She would need Amanda's support to persuade Chief Hollinger and Detective North. Laurie would protest at first, Claire knew that. But in the end, she would agree. She was already bound to this man, even if she didn't want to believe it.

"Listen to me, Amanda." Claire waited until Amanda gave a nervous nod before continuing. "It's vital that Laurie stay with him. Her life depends on it. And it depends on us, too. We have to help him keep her safe. Okay?"

Amanda had absolute faith in Claire's psychic ability, but she also knew Claire couldn't see how it would all end. She loved Laurie like a sister–more than a sister, maybe. Laurie wasn't just family; she was her best friend. There was no time in her life that didn't include memories of the two of them together. She would do anything to keep her safe.

"Please," Amanda said softly, "let's just go to the hospital. I need to see her. I just want to know that she's alright."

Claire squeezed Amanda's hand, trying to reassure her. She signaled the waiter and reached for her purse, dread curling deep inside her. She was doing exactly what she had sworn she would never do again–becoming personally involved in a case she knew would bring nothing but violence to her soul.

◐○◑

Linda de Marco slammed down her receiver. Chief Morris had not yet returned to his office. As soon as he checked in, her message would be delivered. Something was wrong. North's disappearance was no coincidence. The whole thing smelled like three-day-old garbage.

Picking up the file on her desk, she began making phone calls. By the time she was finished, she would know a hell of a lot more about Jake North.

◐○◑

Dorothy was unaccustomed to the silence that had invaded the office. She toyed with the huge amber beads hanging around her neck. It was unlike Laurie not to call. Dorothy had left messages for her at home, but she hadn't called back.

At least she had gone to the doctor. Dorothy tapped her long purple nails nervously against her desk. What if she was really sick? She murmured an *Our Father* and a *Hail Mary* under her breath. She had been a Catholic once and found that she reverted to the old prayers whenever she was worried or afraid. She couldn't bear it if anything were to happen to Laurie. Laurie was the dearest friend she had. She was the daughter Dorothy had always wished for.

She remembered the day she had applied for the job as Laurie's secretary. Laurie had almost fallen out of her chair when Dorothy walked into the office wearing a purple-and-pink silk wraparound dress with matching four-inch heels. Dorothy still chuckled when she remembered how the elegant younger woman had struggled not to stare at her clothes.

Long ago, Dorothy had stopped trying to imitate or impress other people. She had wasted her youth trying to be someone she wasn't. She had been unable to please her ex-husband or his mother, and more importantly, she had made herself miserable. On her forty-fifth birthday, she had left her hometown—and the "domineering duo," as she had always thought of her spouse and mother-in-law. She had left everything she owned behind. She didn't want any of it: not the expensive, demure clothes; not the rigorous diets; not the furniture her husband had refused to let anyone sit on.

She had driven away from everything she wasn't in order to begin a quest to find everything she was. So far, she liked what she had discovered. She liked bright colors, sexy clothes, and rich food. She liked men too—lots of them…all of them. She enjoyed several steady relationships with men she loved and who loved her. They liked her just the way she was, and that was how she wanted it.

Laurie loved her the way she was, too. The young lawyer had looked beyond Dorothy's limited résumé and seen past her colorful exterior to the competent and intelligent woman beneath. Dorothy had offered to dress "down" for Laurie's father's first visit to the office. Laurie had laughed and forbidden it. She'd said she was proud of her and that no one else in all of Miami had as efficient–or as color-coordinated–an assistant.

Dorothy sighed and began organizing the pending files for the third time that day. She bit her flame-red lip and prayed once more that Laurie was alright.

Darlene Williams hung up the phone with a trembling hand. They had never called her while she was on duty before. She glanced furtively around to see if anyone had noticed. Dispatchers weren't allowed personal calls until their breaks or mealtimes. Everyone around her seemed to be working normally. No one appeared to be paying much attention to her.

She wiped the sweat from her palms onto her dark brown slacks. She had always hated talking to that scum Diaz, but the albino was worse. He scared her senseless. She had no real choice. Every once in a while, one of them would call and ask her questions–simple ones, not too hard to answer. She never asked why they wanted to know; they never told her. Simple.

Two days later, she would find an envelope filled with cash tucked beneath her apartment door.

After the first time, she had felt so guilty. When they called again, she told them she couldn't continue to help. It had been the albino on the line. He said he understood her position and thanked her. Two days later, her son's bed was slashed with a knife while she was at work and her boy was at school. None of the neighbors had seen a thing. The next time he called, she gave him what he wanted to know and took the cash without a word.

Shaken, she asked her supervisor to cover for her while she took a bathroom break. Irritated, the woman nodded and snapped at her to make it quick. Darlene almost ran to the restroom. She splashed water on her face and pressed a rough paper towel to her brow. Her hands wouldn't stop shaking.

Something big was going down. A few days earlier, Chief Hollinger had requested that any calls or information about a man named Jake North be directed to him—and to him alone. It was all over the station that the guy had been found a couple of days ago at an abandoned hotel on Miami Beach, beaten to a pulp. Two women had been brought in for questioning.

Now the albino had called her at the station instead of at home or on her cell phone. He wanted to know where the man found at the Coral Reef Hotel was and whether he was still alive. She told him the man had been found, but that she didn't know if he was alive or not. Chief Hollinger had not returned to the station. There had been no further communication, except for his call to the Murphy woman after he had taken the second woman from the station.

Gruber's reaction to the news that two women were somehow involved had terrified her. He remained silent for a moment, then slammed the receiver against something–hard. The sound of the impact made her jump. Luckily, the other dispatcher was too caught up relaying information about a stolen vehicle to notice her reaction. The albino then asked for the women's names.

She hesitated until the image of her son's slashed bed floated through her mind. It took her two more seconds to give him what he wanted. Staring at her pale reflection in the mirror, she told herself it didn't matter. Nothing was more important than her son.

Chapter Six

Amanda and Claire arrived at the hospital at precisely the moment Sam Hollinger began analyzing the options for Jake's safety. Just outside the door, the women were arguing loudly with the guard, who took their verbal abuse stoically. At the sound of the Murphy woman's voice, irritation flared in Sam. What were these two doing here anyway? At this rate, half of Miami would know Jake was here.

Quickly, he opened the door and hustled them into the room. Laurie's cousin continued to complain loudly about the arrogance of the police department as she moved to embrace Laurie. The Murphy woman stood quietly just inside the doorway.

As the women embraced, he broke in impatiently. "What do you think you're doing? This is a police matter, for heaven's sake. No one is supposed to be allowed in here."

Amanda, hands on her hips, turned to retort, but Laurie cut her off. "Amanda, please. Chief Hollinger is right. You could be endangering yourselves by being here."

"What about you, Laurie?" Amanda demanded. "Why do you think we're here? Claire didn't sleep all night. She says you're in danger. What did you expect us to do?" She began tapping one of her beautiful high-heeled pumps impatiently.

Laurie realized Amanda was afraid. Amanda always became belligerent when she was afraid. An icy pulse shot through her veins as the words sank in. Claire believed she was in danger. She looked at her hesitantly. "Claire?"

Before Claire could respond, Jake growled, "She knows you shouldn't be here–that's what." Looking to Claire for support, he continued, "It's Claire, right?" He gave her just enough time to nod before rushing on. "She trusts you. You've got to get her out of this mess. I wasn't doing a very good job of it a few minutes ago, but I was trying to tell her the same thing. Tell her. Tell her she needs to forget this whole thing."

Claire watched him as he spoke. She didn't really listen to his words, but she could feel his fear and his protectiveness. There was also a terrible sadness in him. He didn't want Laurie to leave him. The sadness ran deep–deeper than the moment they were living. There was a great need in this man. An image of a windswept desert came to her. His life was dry like that desert; no one had brought life-giving rain into it for many, many years. She knew Laurie could bring that rain into his life–if they could keep her alive.

The terrible thought jolted her back to the present.

"I'm sorry, Detective North, but I can't agree with you." All eyes turned to her. Uncomfortably, she continued, "That's precisely why I came. You are both in danger. It's too late now. Laurie's only chance is to stay with you."

The words swept through the room like an electric current. Laurie gripped Amanda's hand tightly. Sam Hollinger stared at Claire enigmatically. Jake North looked at her as if she had lost her mind.

It didn't take him long to say it. "Are you crazy?" he rasped. "I'm the reason she's in danger! I'm investigating a killer—a man who wouldn't hesitate to slit her throat. Hell, he'd enjoy it!" Bone-deep fear drove through him as he spoke. She had said it was too late. He told himself the woman was a nut, just some palm reader caught up in the excitement of the last couple of days. He looked at Hollinger. "Sam, tell them." He couldn't keep the desperation out of his voice.

"I'm sorry, Jake, but like I said before, it's the best way. I don't have the resources to watch you both separately. I have to agree with Ms. Murphy."

Even Claire looked surprised.

"You yourself were saying you had to get out of here. I believe there's a good possibility that Ms.—uh—Laurie might be a target. Too many people saw her at the station, and here at the hospital too. It's bound to get out that she has something to do with you. Besides, you need a place to heal that's more private than this hospital room."

For the first time since they had known each other, Sam Hollinger surprised Jake.

"You're as crazy as she is!" Jake said incredulously.

Sam knew he had to make Jake see reason, but the man had never been easy to persuade. He was impossible to manipulate. A man with no weaknesses couldn't be manipulated. But Sam had allies in the two women. They had come here with the same idea that had been slowly germinating in his mind. Laurie hadn't said a word, but her tearful scene just moments earlier had told him she didn't want to walk away and forget his friend. Laurie James. There was the leverage he needed.

He hadn't missed the muscle twitching in Jake's jaw when she had risen to leave. Laurie was Jake's newly discovered weakness.

In a reasonable tone, he said, "Look, Jake, you're no fool. Lacayo is bound to find out about her. They'll go after her if they think she can tell them something. I can have my men watch her for a while, but face it–I don't have the manpower to protect her for long." He saw Jake's fists knot in the sheets. Encouraged, he continued, "It's easier to watch you both if you're in the same place. I'd feel better if you're there with her anyway. No one is going to be more careful with her."

Laurie stared at Jake. Then she looked at Sam and finally turned to Claire and Amanda. Claire was nodding energetically. Laurie tried desperately to grasp what they were proposing.

"Won't they come after him again?"

"They'll track him faster in this hospital," Hollinger replied tersely.

Jake spoke in the same cold voice he had used moments earlier. "I want the bastard to come after me. This time I'll be ready for him. But I don't want to risk Laurie in the process."

Amanda had been fidgeting in the corner for a while now. She couldn't contain herself any longer. She hissed into Claire's ear, "I feel like I've stepped into a James Bond movie!"

Claire caught her arm and put a finger to her lips. She whispered, "Shhh."

As she observed them, an image began to form in Claire's mind. She saw a window lit brightly in the pitch-black night. She heard the terrible shattering of glass and a woman's scream...Laurie's scream. Her heart began to hammer, and her hands started to shake.

Seeing her go pale, Amanda cried, "Claire! Oh, someone help me! She needs to sit down!" She put her arms around Claire's waist, trying to hook Claire's arm around her neck to support her.

Sam rushed over and lifted Claire from Amanda's grasp. He settled her limp form into the recliner next to the bed. "Get water!" he barked. He noticed the fine sheen of perspiration on her face. Her eyes were closed, and she was white as a sheet, his dark hand in sharp contrast against her pale skin. Someone shoved a Styrofoam cup into his hand, and he pressed it to Claire's lips. "Call a doctor, for Christ's sake!" he snapped at Amanda.

Jake reached for the button on the bed rail, but Amanda stopped him. "No! She'll be fine. She saw something, that's all." Her voice was shaky but adamant. "Give her a few minutes."

"Amanda, are you sure?" Laurie asked worriedly, looking at Claire's limp form. "She doesn't look well at all."

"Yes, I'm sure. I've seen it happen to her before. She can't control what she sees. Sometimes it's...too much for her." Amanda stared at her friend, remembering the times she had watched Claire pass out. It never boded well. Amanda had once believed that second sight would be a blessing–until she met Claire. Now she was grateful to stumble through life in the happy ignorance most people were blessed with.

Laurie and Jake exchanged a concerned look. Without a word, she moved to sit beside him on the narrow bed. It felt natural to move closer as apprehension washed over her. It felt just as natural that his hand would rest protectively on her waist.

Slowly, Claire came out of it. She stared up at Chief Hollinger's worried face. The thought that he loved his wife very much flitted through her mind. He should tell her more often. As she often did after a vision, she spoke without thinking. "You need to tell your wife that you love her."

The concern vanished from his face, replaced by exasperation. "Is that what this was all about, Ms. Murphy?"

She shook her head. "No, Chief." She sat a little straighter and looked toward the bed. Once again, she faced the perpetual dilemma of her life: should she say exactly what she had seen or not? From experience, she knew she couldn't stop what appeared in her visions. She could only forewarn. She saw Jake's hand resting on the small of Laurie's back. She knew he wouldn't listen if he believed someone was going to try to kill Laurie, but she was certain her interpretation of the vision was correct. They needed to stay close.

"Detective North," she said quietly, "you're right in your assumption that whoever this person is will make a move. But he'll try to hurt Laurie whether you're with her or not. She has a better chance with you. Stay together—but don't forget for one moment that your lives are in danger."

Gruber stared down at his phone. His search finally led him to Laura James, immigration lawyer. He searched his memory, trying to recall the name, but drew a blank. He'd never heard of the woman before and had no recollection of Rene ever needing an immigration lawyer.

He tucked the phone back into his pocket. Walking back to the car slowly, he mulled over the new development. When he opened the car door, he was blasted by rap music at full volume.

Damn it!" He reached over and switched off the radio. Turning angrily, he faced Diaz. "Don't play that shit in my car," he said through gritted teeth.

"Take it easy, Grub. Just take it easy, man." Diaz shifted uncomfortably on the leather seat.

"Take it easy? You idiot! You don't get it, do you?" He could feel hot fury pumping through his veins. "We are this close"–he held his fingers inches apart under Diaz's nose–"this close to having our asses handed to us in a sling! Who do you think Rene is going to hold accountable if this guy is alive and well? And the women! What are we going to tell him about the women? Who the hell are they?"

"I don't know, man. I don't know." Diaz dropped his head into his hands like a football player who'd fumbled the ball. "Did you find a number?"

"I couldn't find a home address for but I did find her office information." He spoke while driving, without looking at Diaz. Right now, the urge to kill him was too strong to risk it.

"Where did you find it?"

Gruber took a deep breath. "She's a lawyer. I Googled her."

"Oh."

Gruber wondered if it were possible for anyone to be that stupid. He glanced at the clock on the dashboard. Four o'clock. He'd have to wait a while. First, he had to get rid of

Diaz. What he needed to do would require a finesse far beyond his partner's capacity.

He considered reporting to Rene. They'd better call in. Rene would be expecting a report and would be twice as angry if he had to track them down to get it. Gruber had his cell phone, but he never used it to call Rene. You never knew who might be listening in on those damned things.

He turned the car back in the direction of Connie's. She'd keep Diaz out of his hair for a while. It was on the way anyway. He'd stop to call Rene before dropping Diaz off. He wanted Diaz to hear the conversation so he wouldn't have to explain it to him again later.

Robert Morris returned to his office to find several urgent messages. Two were from Agent Linda de Marco. One was from Chief Hollinger of the Miami Police Department. The last was from an Antonio Sosa. The pink slips seemed to burn in his hands.

He had spent the last few hours perched on a barstool at the Up Wind, a local bar in his old neighborhood. His lunch had consisted of beer pretzels and three whiskies, straight up. He knew his hand wasn't shaking from the alcohol.

He sat at his polished desk and stared dully out the window. Feeling sick, he wondered what had been done to Jake North. "Goddamn it." He laid his hands flat on the desk and stared at them. They were softer than they used to be. Suddenly, the manicured fingernails repulsed him. Swearing, he closed his hands into fists.

Against his will, his gaze drifted to the hourglass. The sand had finished running. Time had run out.

To comfort himself, he thought about everything he had accomplished–his beautiful house, his boat, his children, and the expensive private schools they attended. They deserved the best. He deserved the best. He turned back to the hourglass and stared at it with intense hatred. He picked it up and held it in his palm. Looking out the window again, he told himself it was nothing but glass, sand, and wood. Nothing more.

A sharp pain made him look down in surprise. Blood oozed from his hands. He forced them open. They were filled with small shards of glass and bright red sand. He had crushed the hourglass without even realizing it.

Shaking, he rushed to the wastebasket and tried to pick the glass from his flesh. Christ. He gave up and punched a button on his phone. "Lucy, get in here!"

His secretary bustled in. He never barked at her like that. Her shock was evident as she looked at his hands.

"It's nothing. Bring me a towel so I can wash up." She reached for his hands, trying to examine the damage.

"How did this happen, Bob?"

"Lucy, just get the towel," he snapped.

She gave him a strange look but hurried out of the office.

Half an hour later, he sat staring at his bandaged hands, trying to forget the foreboding image of blood staining them.

◐◯◑

Here's your revised paragraph with the requested change:

Linda de Marco hung up the phone gently this time. She read the email on her screen. Jake North's life was captured in the five short pages she pulled free. Putting her feet up on her desk, she leaned back and began to read.

Jake North had been born thirty-five years ago in Reno, Nevada. He had become a ward of the state at the age of four. Apparently, his mother had abandoned him in the waiting room of one of the local hospitals. There was a small notation from the caseworker stating that the boy had cried almost nonstop for over a month—and then, one day, he had simply stopped. No one was sure what had happened, but he had seemed to finally accept that his mother wasn't coming back. He refused ever to speak of her again.

The woman in Linda felt a twist of pain for the little boy. How could a woman just leave a child that way? She forced herself back to the papers in front of her, reminding herself that many hardened criminals had similar sob stories. That didn't make them any less dangerous.

North had gone from foster home to foster home, never adopted because of his aggressive behavior. His rebelliousness didn't sit well with prospective parents. He had aged out of the system at eighteen. He had barely graduated from high school, although most of his teachers agreed he was highly intelligent. He'd been arrested–but not charged–for disorderly conduct. There was a brief mention of a brawl in a local bar related to the arrest. Apparently, the bartender had refused to press charges.

Days later, he had enlisted in the Marines. Linda was mildly surprised by the long list of commendations. Apparently, Jake North had found a place where he fit. He had risen through the ranks and eventually commanded one of the Corps' most elite secret units. The end of his military career had come voluntarily. He resigned.

Now she was more than mildly surprised.

Why would he quit the one thing he did well?

There was no mention of the circumstances surrounding his unexpected exit from the military. The absence of information alerted her immediately. She would have to dig deeper.

She read the final section of the report quickly. It held nothing she didn't already know. He had joined the NYPD. They had offered him an administrative position, but he had turned it down in favor of joining the narcotics unit. Although the report didn't say so, Linda suspected he had been involved in anti-drug operations during his time in the

Marines. The last two administrations had had no qualms about using the military in the war on drugs.

What didn't fit was his refusal of the administrative post.

Why?

And where the hell was Chief Morris?

Claire and Amanda drove Laurie home. An unmarked police car followed behind them. In the back seat of the second vehicle, a bruised Jake North lay huddled low. It had taken every ounce of strength he had left to climb in when they had snuck him out of the hospital.

He would heal at Laurie's house. Jake had tried to talk Sam into taking him home instead, but his friend had refused. Trish was already furious that he hadn't been home for more than five minutes over the last two days. Dragging in a wounded Jake North would only make things worse. Besides, Sam reminded him, it was easier to watch one location than two. Laurie would have to be under surveillance anyway, and keeping them together meant fewer officers involved.

Claire and Amanda had agreed without hesitation. Only Jake and Laurie seemed to have any reservations.

As the car rolled along, Jake tried to straighten his legs, but he was simply too long for the back seat. His entire body throbbed. With a sigh of resignation, he hoped she didn't live very far away.

To kill time, his thoughts drifted to the fact that Laurie hadn't been overjoyed at the prospect of taking him into her home. She had been strangely quiet—almost distant—when Sam and the other two women made the decision. He didn't understand why that bothered him. After all, he was the one who had wanted her out of it. He still believed it was crazy to involve her further.

So why did it irritate him that she hadn't jumped for joy at the idea of taking him home?

◐○◑

"Signal him to drive in ahead of us, Claire," Laurie instructed wearily.

"Sure." Claire nodded and slowed the car. She stuck her arm out and pointed toward Laurie's driveway. Understanding, the officer pulled in and drove toward the back of the house. Once both vehicles were parked, Claire cut the engine. The three women climbed out of the tiny sports car quickly. Claire and Amanda moved to help the officer with Jake while Laurie hurried to unlock the back door. Within seconds, they were all inside.

Jake looked as though he might pass out. Laurie would set up the sofa bed later, but he needed to lie down immediately. The painkillers the doctor had prescribed were in her purse. She stepped closer and slipped her arm around his waist. She could barely support his weight.

"Put your arm around me," she said gently.

He didn't argue. She could feel how weak he was.

Leaving Amanda and Claire in the kitchen with the young officer, Laurie half-walked, half-dragged Jake down the hallway to her bedroom. His eyes were closed against the pain; he simply followed her lead. She didn't bother turning on the light. It wasn't quite evening, and soft daylight filtered through the sheer curtains.

Breathing hard from the effort, she turned them both and helped him sit on the edge of the bed. His groan hit her like a blow to the stomach. Carefully, she eased him back until he was lying down. Tightening his hold, he pulled her down with him.

Lying beside him, the heat of his body pressed along the length of hers, dizzying her. For a moment, she let herself savor the feel of him—wanted nothing more than to stay there forever. The thought startled her. She pulled away as if burned.

His groan of protest made her feel guilty for letting her thoughts wander at all.

She tried to pull him up, so his feet weren't hanging off the end of the bed, but he was too heavy for her. "Come on, Jake–slide up a little, okay?" She wasn't sure why she was whispering. Something inside her didn't want to disturb the quiet of the room. He muttered something she couldn't understand and made a feeble attempt to pull himself farther up the bed. His feet were still over the edge, but at least they weren't dragging. She pulled the pillow from beneath the comforter and lifted his head as gently as she could.

As she leaned over him to plump the pillow, he reached up and grabbed a fistful of the silky, long brown hair that had fallen over her shoulders. She froze. His eyes were closed, but he brought her hair to his nose and breathed in deeply. Mumbling, she heard him say, "So good... bed smells just like you." Then he let go and didn't move again. By the time she closed the door gently behind her, he was snoring softly.

Laurie slipped quietly back into the kitchen. Amanda was leaning over the counter, her perfectly manicured nails drumming rhythmically on the bright tile.

The policeman stood rigidly in the center of the room, looking decidedly uncomfortable. He was a handsome young man–over six feet tall and lean–with nice brown eyes and an earnest air about him. His sandy hair seemed to stand at attention, as military in its stiffness as the young man's posture. Laurie mused that most women would find him very attractive. *His eyes will never flash silver fire at a woman, though.* She thought of the man lying sprawled across her bed. Without meaning to, she envisioned his body sprawled quite differently, covering her own… pressing her down into the mattress with his weight. A slow heat climbed from her lower body to her cheeks, staining them red.

"Ma'am, are you alright?"

Abruptly, Laurie landed back in reality. She had been having a sexual fantasy in the middle of her kitchen. Embarrassed, she pressed her hands to her hot face. "Yes—yes, I'm fine. I guess it's all been a bit much." She smiled weakly at Amanda, then looked over at the young man. "Would you like some coffee?"

Encouraged by his eager nod, she busied herself preparing it and began chattering nervously. "Where on earth is Claire?"

"She was tired and went on home. I'll have Max pick me up as soon as you're settled."

"Oh. I'm sorry I didn't get to say goodbye." Distracted, Laurie turned back to the officer. "Please sit down. This will be ready in a minute." Glancing over her shoulder, she saw Amanda straighten as if to speak. Not ready to talk about it all, she added brightly, "Amanda, can you get the cups, please?"

Mumbling under her breath, Amanda rose and reached up to the cabinet where she knew the coffee cups were stored. She had to stand on the tips of her toes to reach them, her dress riding up her hips as she strained. To Laurie's amusement, the officer's eyes widened in appreciation.

Suddenly, it was all too much–the fear, the pain, the uncertainty. Unable to contain herself any longer, Laurie burst out laughing hysterically.

Alarmed, Amanda asked, "Are you okay, Laurie?"

"I'm sorry, Amanda. I guess I'm just a little hysterical. I don't know what got into me." Turning her back on them both, Laurie lowered her head into her hands and sighed as she leaned against the counter.

Amanda went to her and wrapped her arms around her. "Honey, you need to rest. Just sit down here." She guided Laurie to a stool and sat her down. "I'll finish the coffee."

Settling onto the stool, Laurie smiled at the officer. "What's your name?"

"Julian Brown, ma'am."

"Can I call you Julian?"

A grin appeared, bringing its boyish charm with it. "You bet, ma'am."

"Laurie–call me Laurie."

"Okay, Laurie."

Grinning ruefully, she said, "I'm sorry about this craziness." The words died in her throat as a fissure of heat traveled down her spine. She knew before he spoke that Jake was in the room.

"I'm glad to see everyone is having a good time."

The tingling sensation continued through Laurie's body. Sarcasm weighed heavily in the gravel of his voice. She looked up to find Jake hunched in the doorway, one arm wrapped around his ribs, the other braced against the doorframe to support his weight.

She felt his pain again, but this time it was laced with anger. Her eyes widened when she realized the anger was directed at her.

◐◯◑

Shaking off the disturbing sensation, Laurie rose quickly and slipped beneath his upraised arm. "What are you doing?" she scolded. "Are you trying to hurt yourself? You shouldn't be out of bed!"

Her breath left her in a rush as Jake's arm came down, crushing her to his side with surprising strength.

Leaning down, his eyes bored into hers, and Laurie was momentarily distracted by the image of silver fire. As she stared into them, she felt no fear. He was furious–she knew because she felt it. She also knew he was capable of great violence. But even as he held her tight, even as he stared at her with white-hot anger, she knew he would not hurt her.

She smiled as he scowled blackly, her arm tightening around his waist, turning his angry grip into an embrace. She twisted her body into his, taking his heat and anger completely into herself. She lifted her left hand to caress his cheek, as if to cool his flesh with her touch.

"Come on," she said softly.

His scowl remained, but the feel of her hand against his face seemed to drain the anger from him. He had jerked awake in pain and in desperate need to relieve himself. The thought of asking for help was almost as unbearable as the pain itself. He had dragged himself off the bed and out of Laurie's room, but once in the hallway, the sound of her voice had drawn him like a magnet. Besides, he didn't know where the bathroom was anyway.

When he reached the kitchen, he saw Laurie sitting close to the handsome young policeman. He saw them exchange smiles. A black rage tore through him so violently that he became momentarily oblivious to the pain in his side. He had wanted to wrap his hands around the kid's neck and squeeze until that besotted smile vanished.

But somewhere in the back of his mind, he had felt Laurie's awareness of him. He had felt her shake off her fear. That sliver of connection–of Laurie inside him–stopped him from lunging at the man sitting so close to her. That, and his condition, he admitted ruefully to himself. Then she had touched him, and the fury had drained away, leaving only the feel of her body against his and the soothing caress of her hand on his face.

Without loosening his hold, he allowed her to guide him back down the hallway, both of them oblivious to the consternation on the faces of the two people left behind in the kitchen.

Laurie led him into the bathroom. Neither commented on how she had known what he needed. His scowl deepened when he realized she had no intention of leaving him alone.

"I'd appreciate a little privacy," he ground out, trying to pull free of her grip.

"No way. You're in no shape to stand." There was iron in her voice.

"Goddamn it! I won't. I will not–" His anger flushed his face a dull red beneath the bruises.

"Yes, you will! I'll turn around, okay?" Impatiently, she turned her body away from him but kept her arm firm around his waist. Their bodies touched from shoulder to hip, suspended in what felt like an ancient, intimate dance.

"Laurie..." There was a warning in his voice.

"Forget it. I'm not leaving you alone. You could fall and hurt yourself." She punctuated the statement with a sharp stamp of her foot.

They scowled at each other fiercely. Finally, Jake's physical need overrode his pride. He would not humiliate himself by having an accident in front of this woman. He remembered the horror in her voice when she had found him in the cabana, covered in his own filth.

"Dammit. Turn around, then," he growled.

Laurie turned her head away but kept her arm around his waist. She hid her small smile of victory. It faded quickly as she heard the rustle of fabric sliding over skin and felt the tension of the tight muscles in his abdomen beneath her hand. An image of his body—bare and rough—slipped treacherously into her mind's eye. The heat she had felt in the kitchen returned tenfold, tightening the muscles low in her body.

He relieved himself as quickly as possible. His groan of relief shattered her wandering thoughts. Belatedly, she wondered if he would know what she had been thinking. The connection between them felt different now, changed since the separation after his rescue. Even if he couldn't hear her thoughts, she realized with mortification that one look at her flushed face might tell him everything.

She squeezed her eyes shut, as if that could hide her from him.

She heard the sound of the zipper, then felt him turn in her hold, his hands settling on her shoulders. She kept her eyes tightly closed.

"Laurie."

She couldn't bring herself to look at him.

"Angel," he said softly, "look at me."

Feeling foolish, she opened her eyes to find the silver gleam of humor in his. "Are you done?" she snapped.

"Why?" Some of the humor faded from his eyes. "Are you in a hurry to get back to your friend?" Turning away, he washed his hands quickly.

Laurie blinked at him owlishly in the mirror. "Who?"

"Your friend–the pretty boy. You two looked cozy. I guess I should apologize for interrupting." His scowl returned full force as the scene in the kitchen replayed in his mind.

Indignation flared in Laurie. "Why, you overgrown ox! What do you mean, cozy?"

Ignoring the pain in his side, Jake turned and bent so close their foreheads nearly touched. "You seemed mighty friendly with him," he snapped. "You don't even know him, and you were all over him!" He couldn't understand why the thought of her smiling at another man filled him with such fury. He knew it should mean nothing–that he was being ridiculous and insulting–but it was driving him insane.

She was his.

He shoved the thought away as quickly as it came, rejecting its meaning.

"All over him?" she sputtered, incredulous. "All over him?" Understanding suddenly lit her narrowed eyes. "You're jealous," she hissed.

Jake jerked his hands back to his sides as if burned. "Jealous!" he sneered. He was so angry he didn't realize his cracked lower lip had split open again. Blood began to ooze from his mouth.

Horrified, Laurie forgot her anger at once. "Oh, Jake–your mouth!" Her hand flew up, pressing gently against his broken lip as if to stop the bleeding.

Disconcerted by her sudden change, Jake stood staring at her, dumbfounded.

"Ven, amor." She lowered the toilet lid and gently pushed him down, then stood over him, her face inches from his, worry in her beautiful eyes.

Come, love.

He knew enough Spanish to understand. The words pleased him absurdly, even as he told himself they meant nothing–nothing more than an endearment she might murmur to an injured child. Without quite knowing why, he adopted a look of misery, groaning softly as he shifted on the cold toilet lid.

Laurie's hands seemed to be everywhere–his face, his shoulders, his chest–as if mapping his pain. He nearly expired when her breast brushed his shoulder. To his great disappointment, she decided he was alright and withdrew to open the medicine cabinet. A moment later she returned, holding a small tube and making soft, murmuring sounds that made him wonder if she would sound like that in bed.

She squeezed a gel-like substance onto her fingertip and bent close, smoothing it over the broken edge of his lip with the lightest touch. It was too much. Being touched, standing so close–it was too much. When she lifted her eyes from his mouth, she found herself caught in a silver flash of desire. He was so close. Without thinking, Laurie tilted her head and lowered her lips toward his. She heard him groan as she closed her eyes. Her only thought was that this was what she had been waiting for all her life.

Jake could no more have stopped himself from kissing Laurie than he could have stopped breathing. His mind shut down as a force more powerful than anything he had ever known drove him to claim her mouth with ravaging need.

There was no gentleness in the kiss—only a raw, driving hunger that threatened to swallow them both. He tasted his own blood and knew she did too; the knowledge brought a strange, savage satisfaction. Despite the pain, he pulled her down, aware he might frighten her but beyond caring. For three long days he had believed he was going to die. The woman in his arms had been his only connection to life in that death trap. Now, in the strangest twist of fate, she was real—warm—and giving him exactly what he needed.

Hungrily, he slid his right hand down her side and cupped her head with his left, deepening the fierce kiss. The taste of her nearly sent him over the edge. He tried to pull back, suddenly afraid of the raging need consuming him, but Laurie clung to him, dragging his mouth back to hers and lifting his hand to her breast.

The feel of her in his palm undid him. *I'll lose myself in her.*

"Yes!" she panted, digging her nails into his bruised flesh. He was far beyond feeling such small pain.

It took several moments for either of them to hear the knocking on the bathroom door.

"Uh, ma'am? Are you two alright? Do you need some help?" Officer Brown's concerned voice froze them both.

"I'll strangle him." Jake's chest heaved as he pressed his forehead to Laurie's. "I'll kill that dumb kid with my bare hands."

◐◯◑

Heads pressed together, both breathing raggedly, Laurie and Jake sat, trying to regain their composure. Not underestimating Jake's wrath, Laurie straightened and addressed the locked door. "We're fine." She winced at the breathless sound of her voice. Clearing her throat, she tried again. "Just fine. We'll be out in a minute."

Jake stared up at her as she stood and hurriedly straightened her blouse, running a hand through her thick hair. She looked flushed and soft—achingly appealing. For a moment, he forgot where he was and, more importantly, why he was there. Then the truth came crashing back, more effective than a stream of ice-cold water.

He had no right to this woman. No right to want her, or to be jealous of anyone who smiled at her. Because of him, she was in danger—caught innocently in a web of corruption and betrayal. He had to stop this before it went any further, he told himself sternly.

Groaning, he pulled himself to his feet. He swayed with the effort and reached for the sink to steady himself. He watched her eyes—still soft with passion—cloud again with alarm.

"Let me help you," she said softly, reaching for him.

He forced himself to push her hands away, ignoring the confusion in her eyes. *Steady, boy, steady. It's for her own good.* Coldly, he said, "I'm sorry. This was completely out of line. It won't happen again. It must be the medication." He knew the last remark would offend her. He kept his eyes down, coward that he was, unwilling to witness the hurt he knew would cross her face. Then, running a hand through his hair, he snapped, "Let's get out of this damned bathroom!"

Confusion and hurt mixed with a full measure of a woman's pride inside Laurie. One minute he was wild for her; the next, he dismissed her coldly. She couldn't read him now. Angry as hell, she drew herself up and opened the door for him. "After you," she said stiffly, standing motionless as he shuffled past.

She walked by him in the hallway, ignoring his hesitation at the bedroom door. Opening the linen closet across the hall, she grabbed sheets and a blanket, her movements sharp with anger. Without looking back, she marched through the kitchen, unwilling to face anyone. Entering the living room, she began making up the sofa as a makeshift bed.

"That will be fine, thank you."

Her back stiffened at his formal tone. Irritated, she thought it ridiculous that he could move so quietly given his condition. Equally impersonal, she replied, "I'll sleep here. You won't be comfortable." Almost accusingly, she added, "You're too big for the sofa," managing to make his size sound like a character flaw.

"I'll be fine. I won't take your bed," he argued.

His choice of words only fueled her anger. "Don't be stupid! You won't be able to rest here. Now leave me alone!" Furious, she snapped the sheets in the air before laying them over the cushions.

Just as Jake was about to snap back, Amanda stomped in. "What is the matter with you two? Honestly!" She crossed her arms and shot a look of exasperation at them both. Jake stood like a bent tree. Laurie continued beating at the sofa. When neither responded, Amanda turned to Jake and scolded, "She's been through a lot for you. Let's see some cooperation." His jaw jutted out further, but a flicker of guilt slid across his face.

Sensing he would behave–for now–Amanda called for Officer Brown to help Detective North to bed. When the young man reached for his arm, Jake shook him off and growled, "I can walk, damn it!" To Jake's extreme irritation, the kid walked beside him anyway, arms half-raised as if ready to catch him at any moment.

Laurie's unladylike snort made Jake grit his teeth. He fought the urge to turn around and continue their battle, feeling a childish satisfaction at Amanda's next words.

"And you, Laurie! What on earth is with you? You're supposed to be taking care of him. Lord knows you went to enough trouble to save his ass!"

Amanda's words knocked the wind out of Laurie. Exhaustion washed over her. For days she had felt like Alice in Wonderland, tumbling down the rabbit hole. What had happened with Jake in the bathroom was just another violent swerve on the crazy ride her life had become. She looked at her cousin, who stood scowling, arms crossed.

"You're right, of course." She sat on the rumpled couch. Head tipped back, eyes closed, she missed Amanda's worried look.

Trying to be companionable, Brown lowered his voice. "You should have seen the little one at the hospital, sir. These two are something else." He whistled softly under his breath.

The admiration in the other man's voice only darkened Jake's mood. Before he could stop himself, he snarled, "You're on duty, kid. Don't forget it."

The young man fell silent as they entered Laurie's room. He stayed until Jake lay down, then turned at the door. "You know, sir, some jobs are more pleasant than others." He smiled as he closed the door behind him, pretending not to hear the expletives coming from the bed. Who did this guy think he was, calling him *kid*, anyway?

Later, Laurie sat alone in the darkened living room. Her head rested against the cushions as she slowly twirled a glass of merlot between her hands. Julian Brown had been relieved by an undercover officer stationed in an unmarked car across the street. Before heading out, he had explained that the officer would be checking the grounds regularly throughout the night. He had also asked her to secure the house and set the alarm once he was gone.

Amanda had left earlier. She had embraced Laurie on her way out, murmuring that everything was going to be fine. Laurie knew she was trying to convince herself as much as Laurie. Her cousin had done a poor job of hiding the worry in her eyes.

Laurie sipped the mellow wine and wondered why she wasn't afraid. The events of the past few days made no sense. Objectively speaking, a stranger slept in her bed. Her home was under police guard. A psychic had declared her in mortal danger. And yet, she felt no fear.

Because he is here with me.

She lingered on the thought, tempted to deny it. She couldn't. It was the truth. Her world had been turned upside down; she was in danger, and yet everything felt as it should because Jake North was snoring in her bed. Shaking her head, she set the wine glass aside and prepared for sleep.

When she lay down, she was surprised to find she couldn't keep her eyes open. She had forgotten how long it had been since she'd last slept.

◐◯◑

Two nights later, Laurie was awakened by a muffled sound that seemed to come from far away. She sprang up from the couch, momentarily disoriented. A soft groan came from the direction of her bedroom.

Jake.

Angry with herself, she realized she had forgotten to give him his medication before turning in. Heedless of her half-dressed state, she grabbed the pills from the side table and went to the kitchen to fill a glass with water. Quietly, she slipped into her bedroom.

It took a moment for her eyes to adjust to the darkness. After a minute, she made out Jake's restless form on the bed. *How thoughtless,* she scolded herself silently. She moved to the side of the bed and sat down. Setting the water and pills on the nightstand, she laid her hand gently on the hard muscle of his arm.

"Jake," she said softly.

She never saw the arm that shot out and dragged her down, clamping around her neck like a vise. Choking and struggling, she realized he had no idea where he was. "Jake!

Jake—it's me!" Her voice rasped as she clawed desperately at his forearm.

As suddenly as it began, it was over. He released her so quickly that she tumbled off the edge of the bed, gasping for air.

"Shit! What are you doing?" His voice was sharp—furious.

Indignation flared inside her. "Me? What am *I* doing?" Laurie rubbed her throat with one hand and tried to push herself upright. The lamp beside the bed snapped on, momentarily blinding her and causing her to fall back onto the floor.

As Jake stared down at her, he was a man in pain in more ways than one.

She had no idea of the sensual picture she made sprawled on the floor in nothing but a small pink tank top and black panties. His body reacted instantly. Shifting the sheets to conceal the undeniable response, he thought wryly that it was good to know the important things were still working in spite of Lacayo's sessions. The memory sobered him. Frowning, he reached down, grabbed her shirt, and hauled her up like a scraggly kitten, setting her back on the bed. Just thinking about Lacayo was enough to cool him considerably.

Livid, Laurie turned on him like an enraged lioness, batting his hands away and shoving him back onto the pillow. He grunted as a sharp pain stabbed his side. Staring up at her in the dim light, he took her in slowly. She was furious—there was no mistaking it. Sparks flew from her beautiful green eyes. Her chin was lifted like a prizefighter's.

In spite of the pain, he couldn't help smiling in admiration as he watched her erupt.

"How dare you? How dare you manhandle me that way?" Leaning forward, she pointed a finger menacingly at him. "I come in here to give you your medication because you're groaning and moaning—out of the goodness of my heart." She stopped abruptly, eyes narrowing dangerously. "Are you laughing at me?"

Trying to bite it back, he couldn't help himself. Something about seeing Laurie in the half-light—angry and yelling—brought out the devil in him. Reaching up, he slid his hands up both her arms, slowly, savoring the softness of her skin. She was warm from sleep, and he couldn't help wondering what the rest of her felt like. He grinned as he watched her mouth snap shut and her eyes widen, then saw her turn the sweetest shade of pink he'd ever seen. She didn't pull away—just leaned over him, as still and nervous as a deer caught in oncoming headlights.

His brain ordered his hands to release her. His mutinous hands refused. She was soft but strong. Of their own accord, his fingers slipped into her hair, pulling locks through them, enchanted by the silk against his rough skin. He lowered one hand and traced a thumb across her lower lip, back and forth in a hypnotic rhythm.

Laurie had felt many things in her life, good and bad, but nothing had prepared her for the onslaught of sensation at Jake North's hands. This was slow and tender, filled with excruciating white fire. Heat coiled through her belly, then slid into every part of her body. Without thinking, she turned her face into his hand, kissed his thumb, then slowly drew it into her mouth.

Yes. Every nerve ending screamed. She wanted to taste him…all of him.

Jake drew a sharp breath, struggling not to embarrass himself. He was rock hard, and all she had done was suck his finger.

"Laurie," he whispered, his voice deep and dark in the low light.

She looked at him then, and he knew he would never forget the sensation of drowning in those deep green eyes.

He didn't know who moved first and didn't care. All he could feel was Laurie–on him and over him and in his mouth–filling him with warmth and desire and…intense pain!

In her ardor, Laurie had leaned into him, her elbow digging into his bruised ribs. He tried valiantly to hold back the gasp, but it escaped in a hiss.

"Oh my God! Oh, Jake! I'm sorry…" Laurie jumped off him the instant she heard it. He cradled his side, watching desire vanish from her eyes, replaced by worry. She fumbled for the medication on the nightstand and brought the pills to his mouth, slipping them gently between his lips.

"Here," she said softly as she reached for the water. "Drink these. They'll make you feel better and help you sleep."

"Sleep is the furthest thing from my mind, angel." Still, he took the damned pills. He hurt all over again. Damn.

Flustered, she lowered her eyes and blushed again. She made to leave when his hand shot out and caught her wrist. "Stay."

"You're in no condition–"

"Some parts of me are debating that, but you're right. I need to sleep–and so do you." He smiled forlornly. "I promise I'm not going to jump you. I just... I just want you to lie down next to me, even if it's just for tonight."

Nothing else could have touched Laurie the way that did. *Even if it's just for tonight.* She had just found this man, just discovered what it felt like to be touched by him, and she knew he wasn't hers to keep. This was not a man to be held by anyone. She hesitated, knowing it would break her once he was gone. As he released her wrist and turned his head away in silence, she knew it would hurt even more not to have him–even in this small way...even if only for one night.

Carefully, she slipped into the bed beside him. At the feel of her weight on the mattress, Jake turned, pretending it wasn't joy leaping in his chest–pretending it hadn't mattered as much as it did that he thought she might deny him.

Gingerly, he turned to face her. "Turn off the light."

Laurie reached up and switched off the lamp, regretting the darkness that hid his face, yet relieved it hid what she knew was plain to see in her eyes. She wanted this man—more than she had ever wanted anything—and not just in her bed. She wanted to feel his thumb lazily caressing her mouth every day of her life. She wanted to stare into those silver eyes and let them consume her forever. Squeezing her eyes shut, she tried to fight the yearning.

"Come closer." His voice was growing groggy now; the medication was taking hold. "Wanna feel you against me. So beautiful...so fine, baby..." He brought his arm around her and tried to pull her to his side. When she resisted, afraid of hurting his ribs, he tightened his hold, whispering again, slurred and sleepy, "Please...just wanna hold you. Just tonight. Just one time...something right and good...don't leave me, please, love..."

She told herself it was only the medication—that the pain and longing in his voice weren't real. She repeated it over and over as her tears fell silently onto the pillow. *Don't leave me, please, love...*

He had died sometime during the night. There was no other explanation.

Cautiously, Jake took in the bedroom—the sheer curtains, the softness of the sheets, and finally the heat of the woman wrapped around him like a second skin. Laurie lay with her head tucked into the hollow of his shoulder, one arm draped possessively across the bandages on his chest. One silky thigh lay across his. Afraid to break the spell, he remained still, listening to her breathing and feeling her heartbeat against his battered side.

Turning his head slowly, he buried his nose in her hair and breathed her in. She smelled of soap and something uniquely Laurie. As he had since childhood, he committed it all to memory. Good things, he knew, rarely lasted or repeated; they had to be savored when they appeared. Thinking back over the last few days, he decided that if there was a God, He couldn't be all bad to allow him to wake in Laurie James' arms.

He was almost accustomed to the thought when she shifted, her leg brushing across his groin. All thoughts of God vanished as his body snapped to attention. Instead of moving away, Laurie unconsciously slid farther over him, the vee of her thighs pressing down on what had become rock hard. Sweat beaded on Jake's forehead. "Okay, Jake, old boy, take it easy. She's asleep, for Pete's sake." He hadn't realized he'd spoken aloud until he heard a sleepy murmur from beneath his chin.

Instinctively, Laurie burrowed closer to his warmth. Still asleep, her body responded to skin on skin, liquid heat blooming deep in her center. With a will of its own, her leg rubbed softly against the solid flesh beneath it. A groan of pleasure escaped her lips.

In a very different agony from the days before, Jake watched as Laurie pressed her mouth to his chest in a warm, wet kiss. All bets were off. Ignoring the excruciating pain—and so consumed with desire he barely felt it—Jake lowered his head to take what he knew he had no right even to dream of.

◐○◑

Heat and pleasure seemed to seep into every inch of Laurie's skin. Even through her t-shirt, she could feel the exquisite touch of the big, rough hands on her breasts. Eagerly, she opened her mouth to receive her lover's kiss.

Her lover? Slowly, Laurie's mind struggled to focus.

Tangled so tightly against Jake's body that she could hardly tell where she ended and he began, Laurie's heart hammered as if it would leap from her chest and be swallowed whole in Jake's demanding kiss. Desire snaked through her, arching her body in desperation against his. Need—like nothing she had ever known—squeezed her heart almost painfully. She understood now. She knew why no man had ever been right before. *This* was what she had been waiting for...this man, this embrace.

A tear escaped along with her moan as she gave herself to Jake and to her destiny.

She bucked wildly when she felt Jake's hand slip down her stomach and slide into her silk panties. His blunt fingers pushed aside the scrap of fabric to bathe in the dampness between her straining legs. His thumb found the center of her womanhood and circled.

Laurie came apart in his arms. His fingers urged her on as he watched the beauty of her release and felt it throb against his hand.

In a red haze, Jake tried to slow down, tried to breathe. Touching Laurie–tasting her–was driving him mad. He needed to be inside her. *Now.* Desperately, he lifted himself–and this time he could not contain the scream of agony.

"Jake!" Legs still trembling from her intense release, Laurie could only manage to get to her knees on the bed. She paled at the sight of his ashen face and the cold sweat slicking his neck and brow. Shaken, she realized yet again that neither of them had stopped to think about his bruised body.

"Oh, love, I'm sorry–I'm so sorry!" She leaned over him, kissing his clammy forehead, murmuring apologies. "Let me get your painkillers."

She started to slide off the bed, only to feel Jake's hand clamp around her wrist like a vise. Startled, she looked at him anxiously. "What is it? Should I call the doctor?"

"No...stay." As waves of pain washed through him, Jake fought to regain control of his body—and his emotions. Christ. Laurie was like a drug in his veins. He had forgotten everything, even his injuries. He knew he should stop this now, before it went any further. But he was too weak. Right now, he needed her like he needed air.

More gently, he tugged her back to his side. Through clenched teeth, he murmured, "I'm sorry. I lost my head. Just lie down here with me—we don't need to do anything. I won't touch you, I promise. I just... I just want you here. You were so beautiful to watch."

Looking down at him, Laurie felt her heart shatter. There was so much pain, so much need in this man. *Her* man. She no longer bothered denying it to herself. Tears threatened again. Blinking rapidly, she slid down beside him, careful not to touch his bruised side.

Propping herself on one elbow, she looked into his pale face, his eyes nearly closed against the pain. She smiled when his arm curved around her, breaking his promise not to touch her. Even in pain, he needed the reassurance that she was really there. Gently, she bent and kissed his beard-roughened cheek, then lifted her head to meet his gaze.

"Are you okay?" she whispered.

"No." His voice was deep and rusty, like an old, bent nail.

Guilt stabbed through her. How could she have forgotten his injuries? In her need, she had forgotten everything but the delicious heat between them. Worry shimmered in her voice. “Let me get your pills.”

“Don’t want them.”

“Jake…”

Silver flashed. “Want you…I need you.”

Laurie’s eyes widened as she searched his face. The desire in his gaze was bone deep. An answering need slid along her spine. “I don’t want to hurt you,” she whispered huskily.

Jake reached up and cupped her chin, watching her sea-green eyes widen. Unable to control the hunger in his voice, he asked, “Do you want me?”

Unexplainable joy surged through him when he saw the answer in her eyes before she whispered a shaky, “Yes.”

“Kiss me, angel. Just a kiss.” Another taste of her was worth it, even if his hard-on hurt more than his ribs.

Laurie lowered her mouth to his and gently brushed her lips against Jake’s. With a tenderness that made his hands shake, he lifted her silky hair, stroked her cheeks and the graceful arch of her neck, then cradled her face as he deepened the kiss slowly. *Open up to me again, angel. I need to taste paradise one more time.*

His gentleness undid Laurie completely. She wanted to give him everything. Opening to his sweet invasion, she returned each touch, each stroke, pouring every emotion she felt into him again and again. Without knowing why, she understood that her touch could heal this broken man. Murmuring incoherent words of love against his mouth, she smoothed her hands over his face, his chest, his arms. With butterfly-soft touches, she willed his body to feel her warmth, to draw comfort from her care, her need to give.

Jake was drowning. As wave after wave of Laurie's touch pulled him into a place, he had never been, he thought of heaven—and for the first time, knew it existed here, in this bed, flowing from this woman.

When he tried to move, Laurie gentled him. "Stay still…let me love you."

The sting of tears burned like hot coals as he closed his eyes. *Let me love you.* He knew she meant it. There were no lies in this woman. He knew it as surely as he knew he didn't deserve her—or her love. But how does a starving man walk away from a feast? He could no more push her away than tear out his own heart.

"Laurie…" He barely recognized the tenderness in his own voice.

Feeling his surrender beneath her hands, Laurie slid her mouth away from his despite his protests and traced a warm trail of kisses down his throat to his chest. She tasted his skin—salty, rough—then kissed the dark bruises edging the bandages one by one, smiling against him when she heard his soft gasp.

Never lifting her mouth from his body, she explored farther, down to the soft black patch of hair above his groin. When his hands tangled in her hair to pull her back, she lifted her head and met his eyes. “Let me... I want to. Please, Jake.”

“I want it to be good for you too, angel,” he whispered, his hands massaging her scalp through the heavy waves of her hair.

Smiling like a siren, she answered, “Just being able to touch you, taste you–it’s heaven, Jake.” His groan was all the answer she needed. Turning her head, she took his rigid manhood in her hand reverently. With a woman’s appreciation, she smiled. Bruised or not, Jake was a well-built man in every way. As she caressed him, she bent to kiss the velvet tip of his desire.

Jake nearly came off the bed. If he didn’t know the pain that would follow, he would have lifted Laurie and dragged her beneath him, burying himself so deeply inside her he’d never find his way out. He gritted his teeth as she continued her sweet assault. *Hang on, boy... just hold on,* he ordered himself desperately.

Laurie closed her eyes and took Jake into her mouth slowly–and heard her lover moan as he thrust against her mouth wildly.

For the second time in just a few hours, Jake found himself at the gates of heaven. His last conscious thought was that this time, his angel had taken him through them and into paradise.

Chapter Seven

Gruber watched as the light from the second floor of the shabby office building was suddenly extinguished. He stood against the iron security gates protecting the furniture store behind him from people just like him. The store was located across the street from Laura James' law office. He had waited for two hours in the shadows, not wanting anyone on the busy street to notice him. He knew how memorable his pallor was to most people. He had waited and watched as the fruit stand and the local bank finally closed.

He waited a bit longer until he saw a fat woman in ridiculously loud clothing step out onto the street and walk with a surprising lightness of foot toward the nearby parking lot. Once she was out of sight, he pulled the baseball cap he wore lower onto his head and casually crossed the street. He did not head for the doors of the building but rather circled the block to the back alley that provided passage to the city trash collectors twice a week.

It took him a moment to be sure which building he wanted. Once he determined that the chained doors to his right were his target, he hunkered close so that, if he were spotted, it would be plausible that he was simply a drunk taking a leak. Carefully, he slipped the slim metal tool out of his pocket and went to work on the deadbolt holding the rusty chains together. In seconds, he caught the chains before they could hit the cracked asphalt beneath them. With swift, silent movements, he expertly disarmed the basic alarm system and slipped into the building.

Using his pinpoint flashlight, he found his way through the electric and storage rooms into the main lobby of the building. Careful not to flash the small light toward the glass doors at the front, he scanned the directory next to the elevators. Laura James had her office on the third floor. Noting the number, he headed for the stairwell.

Holding the massive metal door until it shut with a quiet click, he climbed the stairwell, arriving at the third floor with his usual quiet efficiency. It was pitch black in the cool hallway. The pinpoint of light swung left and right, shining on the numbered doors. Finally, in front of the door he was looking for, he went about breaking in with the same ease he had downstairs.

Once inside, he slipped to the window and slowly closed the blinds of the front office. The light was so small it would be almost impossible to detect from the street below, but he took no chances. He stepped into what he knew to be the lawyer's private office and closed those blinds as well. Then he got down to business.

Methodically, he went through every shred of paper in the office. Case by case, file by file, he scanned everything, looking for any reference to Lacayo or any of his activities.

He searched every drawer, careful to leave no trace. He found absolutely nothing to tie the woman to the cop or to Lacayo. He clenched his jaw and slammed a gloved fist onto the polished surface of the lawyer's desk.

Somehow this woman was involved in this fiasco, and he was going to do whatever it took to find that bastard cop, dead or alive. Like a shadow, he slipped out of the building, knowing that he would be paying a visit to Ms. James again very soon.

Once again, in the space of hours, Jake awoke wrapped around Laurie. By the brightness of the light streaming through the sheer curtains, he figured it to be sometime around nine in the morning. He couldn't even begin to contemplate looking around for the alarm clock. He imagined it was on the nightstand somewhere behind the curvy shape huddled under the comforter. Laurie's leg was once again tangled in his. Though he would have enjoyed having her more fully in his arms, he was grateful that she lay at his side with only her hand resting on his arm. He imagined he would be immobilized completely if he kept abusing his ribs the way he had last night.

He stared at the beautiful woman sleeping sweetly next to him and remembered her lovemaking during the night. He had never had a woman give herself so generously. She had consumed him with a gentleness so sensual that he had surrendered, helpless in her hands.

He shut his eyes as images of the last few days of his life swam through his mind. The only relief from the bitterness was the image of Laurie. It would kill him when he had to leave her. The thought seemed to echo in his mind. Many years ago, he had sworn he would never again let anyone matter that much. But it was too late. This delicate, brave woman had saved him only to kill him, one day at a time, one memory at a time, for the rest of his life.

When he had composed himself, he opened his eyes to find her staring at him. She looked rumpled and sexy, her hair spread across the pillow beneath her. They stared at each other for a moment, each searching for something to say.

"Good morning," she finally whispered, giving him a slow, devastating smile. "How are you feeling?"

His misery of a moment before faded like morning fog under the warmth of the sun. He cleared his throat and tried to smile, trying not to imagine how ghastly the effort might seem to her. "Very... alive..."

Her smile widened, and she leaned up to press a soft kiss to his cheek. Stretching gently, she giggled. "Very much alive, if my memory serves me correctly!"

Before he could respond, she gave a squeal and shouted, "Oh no! What time is it?"

Turning quickly, she threw a pair of very sexy, very naked legs over the side of the bed, jumping off before he had a chance to stop her. His reflexes were definitely slow. Regretfully, he watched her rush from the bed to the bathroom, admiring her firm, round bottom that was conveniently at eye level.

He heard the water start running and thought about Laurie standing beneath it. With a painful grunt, he began easing his beat-up carcass off the bed. Once the room stopped spinning, he began his slow journey across the bedroom with the look of a man on a mission.

◐○◑

Laurie let the hot water pour over her, standing motionless under the strong stream. She knew she was running late, but she'd start rushing in a minute. Right now, she just needed to compose herself before she faced Jake again. She didn't question last night. She knew now that she was meant to find him and meant to bring him into her home, into her bed, and ultimately into her heart. Loving him last night had been as natural as the breath she expelled slowly now.

She loved him. She had known him for just days, really, but she loved him. It was real and bone-deep. She had no doubts remaining.

What will I do when he leaves? I'll die a slow death every day, remembering what it was like to hold him in my arms. The thought seemed to knock the breath from her like a body blow. Her tears disappeared into the water rolling gently down her face. Until now, she had only been alone. She would now learn what loneliness was.

She lowered her head against the tile of the shower wall. Suddenly, a draft of cool air hit her, making her shiver. Turning swiftly, she found herself facing a very naked, very out-of-breath Jake.

"Are you crazy?" she asked in shock.

He looked like a gladiator she had seen in a movie once, beaten up but standing proud. She stared dumbly as he stepped into the cascade of warm water. She watched the water rush over the bandages around his chest and down the line of his beautiful torso. A flush crept up her skin as she saw that he was ready for more than a shower.

Raising her eyes to his, she licked her lips and whispered, "I could always take the day off."

He gave her a wicked, ghastly grin and opened his arms to her.

All thoughts of loneliness fled as his hands slipped down her slick back to cup her bottom. With a moan, she closed her eyes and lifted her face to him. Opening to him completely, she let him plunder her mouth and her body.

"I want to be inside you," he ground the words against her mouth.

She was on fire. "How? I don't want to hurt you again," she murmured against his lips. "And you're ruining those bandages."

"Turn around."

She protested weakly as he tore his mouth from hers. He gripped her hips, turning her to face the shower wall, and braced her hands on the wet tile. Instinctively, she pressed back against him, feeling him straining between her thighs. She smiled in victory at the sound of his desperate growl and felt him grip her waist, grinding her against his pelvis.

Jake laid the palm of his hand on the small of her back and pushed her gently forward, bending her until he was positioned to do what he'd been dreaming of doing. He clenched his teeth, trying to hold on to his self-control. At another time in his life, he would have thrust in and taken his pleasure, but this was Laurie. He wanted to take her with him; to give her the same mind-blowing pleasure she had given him last night.

Slowly, he eased into her, feeling her clench around him like a silken fist. It took everything he had not to come right then and there. He entered inch by inch until he was so deep, he could feel her womb. Her cries of pleasure echoed in his head, making his body tighten fiercely. His pleasure mixed with the pain in his ribs, but he didn't care.

Laurie couldn't bear the pleasure of it. She felt herself shatter into a million pieces. Crying out, she began to thrust back against him, faster and faster, her world spinning out of control.

Jake could feel Laurie coming apart beneath his hands. He heard her scream out his name and allowed himself to give in to the vicious need clawing at his gut. Throwing his head back, he drove into Laurie and let his world explode.

Half an hour later, Laurie called Dorothy to let her know she would be taking the day off. She did her best to assure her that everything was alright but knew that she had failed to ease her friend's worry. The twinge of guilt about Dorothy and the clients she knew would be inconvenienced dissolved at the sight of Jake sound asleep in her bed.

Dorothy banged the receiver back into its cradle. What the hell was going on? Laurie had never taken a day off without notice. She didn't sound sick, but that didn't mean a damned thing. Frustrated, she picked up the phone and began calling the clients on the day's agenda. Of course, she thought, now she'd have to hear the bitching all morning long.

Sam Hollinger waited patiently for Robert Morris to get on the line. The secretary had sounded a bit nervous, asking him to hold while she transferred the call. Suddenly, Morris' tense voice came on the line.

"Hollinger, it's Morris. What's going on?"

"We found your man." Sam left it at that, waiting to gauge the man's response.

Morris closed his eyes, swallowing back the bile. Jake North had been a good cop. He'd deserved better than this. Feeling ill, he replied, "We'll be expecting the body sent back to New York, Chief."

Sam's eyes narrowed in suspicion. He replied carefully, "I never said he was dead, Morris. He's alive. Barely, but alive."

Morris held the receiver in a death grip, oblivious to the pain in his hand. Stupid. How stupid could he be? Forcing elation into his voice, he responded, "Thank God! Your men have done a great job, Hollinger! Where is he?"

"He was discharged from the hospital this morning. He won't be able to travel for a while yet. Rene Lacayo and his goons worked him over pretty well." He felt grim satisfaction in the knowledge that a warrant for Lacayo's arrest was being processed as they spoke. The charge was attempted murder.

Robert Morris broke out in a cold sweat. "L...Lacayo?" He could not control the slight stutter.

Sam began to get a very bad feeling. Morris hardly seemed like the same person who had called him days ago asking him to search for Jake. There was more here than met the eye.

"Yes, Lacayo. I believe Jake was working undercover here for you, building a case against him, right?" His tone was impatient and borderline sarcastic.

"Yes, of course." Regaining his composure, Morris continued in a steadier voice, "Where can I contact North?"

Cautious, Sam gave as little information as possible without revealing his suspicions. "He's staying with a friend. I'll have him report to you as soon as possible. I'll have to get back to you, Morris." He hung up quickly before Morris could pressure him further. He pulled the scrap of paper with Laurie's number on it and punched in the numbers forcefully.

Things had just gotten a lot murkier.

Morris bit back an oath as the phone clicked in his ear. The bastard had cut him off again! He dialed the Miami Police Department but was informed that Chief Hollinger was on another call. He practically barked his request for a call back as soon as humanly possible.

What a goddamned disaster! Jake could now testify against Lacayo about the drugs and the attempt to kill him.

Once in custody, Lacayo could offer up New York's Chief of Police in order to broker a better deal with the feds. Panicking, his breathing became agitated. He could not let this happen. Nothing could destroy his carefully constructed plan. Not even Jake North.

Making an effort to calm himself, he tried to clear his mind. He had to warn Lacayo and get him to leave the country. If he avoided custody, there would be no reason for the scum to give up any information.

Breathing deeply, he picked up the message from Antonio Sosa and dialed with shaky fingers, trying not to look at the newly oozing bandages wrapped around his hands.

Dorothy nearly jumped out of her skin when the shadow crossed her desk. The man had entered so silently that she had not even heard the door. His appearance was also disconcerting. Pale as a ghost, she thought. Maybe that's why she hadn't heard him come in, that and Mr. Abad's tirade on the other end of the phone line, she mused. She signaled the stranger with her hand to have a seat. The man eased himself gracefully into a leather chair and picked up a magazine.

Returning her attention to the ranting coming from the receiver, she sighed. She didn't really understand most of the words, but she got the message loud and clear. Mr. Abad was irate because he had taken the day off to see Laurie, and now the appointment was being canceled. She didn't blame him, but there was nothing she could do except apologize again and offer to reschedule at his convenience.

Finally, Mr. Abad stopped long enough to catch his breath, so she quickly jumped in, asking if next Tuesday at the same time was acceptable.

"Mr. Abad, I promise she'll be here for the appointment. It's very rare for her to miss a day of work." She raised her eyes to the ceiling as she continued placating the man. "Yes, yes sir, you have my word. Thank you."

Now that the client had been rescheduled, she caught her breath and turned toward the strange man lounging in the waiting area a short distance from her desk. He seemed to be engrossed in the magazine he held, but something told her that he was not an avid fashion magazine reader.

"May I help you?"

The man put down the magazine and stood. He stepped soundlessly toward her. When his shadow again crossed her desk, she found herself looking into the coldest eyes she had ever seen. Dorothy shivered involuntarily.

"I'm here to see Ms. James." The voice was deep and just as cold as the face that went with it. There was a slight trace of an accent she couldn't quite pinpoint. Maybe German, she thought.

"I'm sorry, but she's not in. Do you have an appointment?" She knew full well he did not, as Mr. Abad had been her last appointment to reschedule.

He smiled slightly and replied, "No, I'm sorry, I don't. It is a bit of an emergency, though." He leaned down a little closer, making her lean back uncomfortably. "Do you expect her in later?"

Rolling her chair back further to put more distance between them, Dorothy replied in an irritated tone, "No, I don't, Mr…"

"Mr. Anderson."

"Well, I'm sorry, Mr. Anderson, Ms. James won't be in today. May I make an appointment for you sometime next week?" Dorothy picked up her pencil and held it expectantly over the agenda. She was eager to get this strange man out of the office.

"No, that won't do. You see, this won't keep until then." The man moved his hands on the desk. Focused on his pale face, Dorothy missed how he covered her scissors with his right hand.

His voice was calm, but there was no mistaking the threatening tone. Alarmed, Dorothy suddenly felt compelled to stand and walk over to the door. Holding it open, she gestured toward the hallway and said in what she hoped was a calm, professional voice, "I apologize, but there's nothing I can do. Ms. James is ill today and won't be coming in, as I'm sure you overheard while you were waiting. Please take a card from my desk and feel free to call tomorrow. Perhaps she can fit you in since it's so urgent."

Gruber slipped the scissors into the palm of his hand, holding them at his side. He walked toward the door slowly. Glancing beyond it, he smiled. He had come during lunchtime, knowing that few people would be in the offices. The lawyer's office was at the end of a long hallway, with the restrooms and stairwell between it and the next office. Across the hall there was only a storage room for the maintenance crew.

As he approached the large woman, he calculated that she would not be easily carried. Too bad she had stepped so far away from her desk. He didn't want anyone looking through the frosted glass to see the figure lying behind the door. He would need to move quickly.

"Let me leave you my card. Perhaps Ms. James would be kind enough to call me." He slipped his left hand into his suit pocket. The woman's eyes followed his movement, as he knew they would. She had only a second to register her surprise before the scissors were lodged violently into her neck, severing her jugular. Jerking violently, she slammed back against the door and then slid slowly to the floor, holding her hands to her gushing neck and staring at him in disbelief.

Gruber jumped back, but not in time to avoid some of the spray of blood. Locking the door, he quickly dragged the woman across the floor and laid her behind her desk, still gasping for life.

He glanced regretfully at the blood smeared all over the floor. He usually avoided such messy killings, but he could not afford for a gunshot to be heard, and the woman seemed too strong to be strangled without great resistance. He had decided upon entering the office that she was a fighter. Meek people never dressed so flamboyantly.

He tucked the scissors into his pocket and stepped into the private office behind the woman's desk, barely registering her desperate final breaths. He walked to the adjoining bathroom and began to wash the blood off his face and hands. Once he had cleaned up and wiped everything down, he pulled on his gloves and went back to the woman's desk to search her handbag. Dumping the contents onto the desk, he fished out the small red address book.

There was no entry for the James woman under J, but he did find an entry for "Laurie." Grabbing a Post-it and a pen off the woman's desk, he wrote down the address in his neat, careful handwriting.

Stepping over the prone woman without even a glance, he pulled off the gloves and tucked them into his other pocket. He decided to use the stairwell. He wore a dark suit with a dark shirt, but there was no reason to take a chance on anyone noticing him or the blood on his clothes on his way out. He had parked in the alley with just that in mind.

For the second time in two days, Gruber let himself out of the building with the ease of a ghost passing through a wall.

During her last moments, Dorothy was excruciatingly aware of every sound and every smell around her. She could hear her killer moving around the office. She could smell the rusty odor of her own blood as her life gushed away, pooling beneath her. She'd always imagined that she'd die of a heart attack and hoped that it would be during sex. It had never crossed her mind that life would be stolen from her so violently or so inexplicably.

Why?

Tears streamed from her eyes, rolling down the sides of her face as she heard the door close with an ominous click behind the stranger. The man had wanted to see Laurie. Fearing for her friend and knowing that she would be unable to warn her, Dorothy tried to move. Her left hand was lying in the bright red blood pouring from her neck. Moving her fingers an inch at a time, she tried to write her last words.

As her eyes closed for the last time, her hand smeared the last letter she had tried to write. With her arm outstretched, she resembled the Michelangelo masterpiece as she pointed to the letters "pale ma."

Lacayo snapped the phone shut. Fury left him momentarily unable to speak. Breathing like a thoroughbred after a long race, he threw his champagne glass across the room, watching it shatter against a priceless painting.

The son of a bitch was alive. That traitorous dog North had escaped him. Grabbing the bottle of champagne, he hurled it at his own image in the gilded mirror above the antique console. The shattering glass sounded like thunder in his ears. The sound of objects breaking and his screams of frustration brought the uniformed maid rushing into the room.

"Señor!"

Spinning toward her, he screamed, "Get out! Get out, you bitch! Puta!" He searched for something else to throw at her.

The woman's face contorted in terror, and she raced from the room without another word. A priceless Oriental urn hit the door just as she slammed it behind her. He began to breathe more slowly.

That coward Morris had sounded near tears as he recounted his conversation with the cop in Miami, he thought viciously. That piece of shit thought that he, Rene Lacayo, would simply put his tail between his legs and disappear, leaving the pompous cop to go on with his farce of a life in New York. Morris would pay for his arrogance, as would North.

He surveyed the damage around him as he fought to regain control. His hand itched to stick a knife into someone. But he knew better than to give in to the rage that consumed him without thinking things through. The last time he had let his fury loose, he had narrowly escaped life in prison in the shitholes of Brazil. Only his money had saved him.

Money would not be enough this time. The cop had tricked him, made a fool of him, and he could not bear it. He would finish what he had begun. He would have his vengeance.

If only he had not been distracted with the arrangements for the drug shipment that had been held up due to the cop's interference. He would have enjoyed torturing the traitor and finally finishing him off. He would not have to leave his beautiful home above the water to run again. Damn Gruber and Diaz. Idiots! He would take care of them soon.

But for now, he still needed them.

He crossed the room and reached through the shattered glass of the mirror to turn the dial of the safe hidden behind it. A man like him knew that you had to be ready to move at a moment's notice. Pulling the small duffel bag out of the deep safe, he headed for the garage, where one of his many cars was packed and waiting for just such a trip.

He grabbed his phone and dialed Gruber. Gruber answered immediately.

"Gruber."

"You listen to me, you dumb shit! That bastard cop is alive and well! He's fingered me!" Lacayo's screams were so shrill that he sounded like a woman.

Gruber had never heard so much emotion in Lacayo's voice. His entire body clenched in fear.

"I'm on it. I got the address of the bitch he's with."

Lacayo screamed into the phone, "You knew? You knew he was alive? I'll rip your heart out! You get him, if you want to live. You get him and bring him to me. You call me at this number when you have the son of a bitch, and not before. You screw this up again and you're dead!"

The line went dead. Sweat rolled down Gruber's back, making him recall Diaz as he had cowered before Lacayo the other night. Lacayo's shrill screams echoed in his mind. He knew the only chance he had to live was to get that cop back into Lacayo's hands.

Grimly, he pulled the Post-it from his pocket. This shit was going to end tonight. Then he was getting the hell out of Miami.

It was late afternoon. Laurie puttered around the house, humming to herself. Jake had fallen asleep after another session of the best sex she'd ever had in her life. There was definitely something to be said about experimenting, she thought with a grin. She blushed a little as she recalled how they had explored all the possible positions that would give them both pleasure without hurting Jake's bruised body. She hadn't minded being the one to control the movements at all.

She could just imagine what it would be like once he was healed. As soon as she had the thought, it brought her mood crashing down like a two-hundred-pound rock rolling down a hill. Once he was well, she might never see him again. The sudden ache in her heart was so strong that her eyes filled with tears. How could she possibly go back to life before Jake?

The phone rang suddenly, making her jump with a curse. She didn't want anything to wake him. He was exhausted and needed to rest.

"Hello," she said breathlessly into the receiver.

"Hey, cuz."

She should have known that Amanda couldn't go long without being updated. "Hi there."

"Well?"

"Well what?"

"Well what! What do you think? What's going on?" Amanda's impatience was humming through the phone line.

"He's asleep." Laurie wasn't about to volunteer any more.

"Did you do him?" Amanda's voice was excited and expectant.

"Amanda! That's none of your business!" Laurie snapped indignantly.

"You did him." There was smug satisfaction in her cousin's voice.

"I can't believe you! I'm hanging up now!"

"Wait, Laurie, wait! I'm sorry!" Amanda pleaded. "Don't hang up. I'm dying here. You can't just leave me halfway through the story!"

Laurie couldn't help but smile. For Amanda, nothing mattered but getting the scoop. Affection for her cousin made her smile warmly. She whispered into the phone, "Okay, okay, I did him."

Amanda's screams were worthy of a thirteen-year-old girl and made Laurie hold the phone away from her ear. "Shhh! Cut it out."

Suddenly serious, Amanda answered, "Oh Laurie, if I weren't so worried for you, I'd be so happy for you."

Laurie frowned and bit her lip. "I know. Oh Amanda... I love him."

Silence hung heavy on the line.

"Amanda, are you there?"

"I'm here." Her voice was laden with misgiving. "Laurie, I love you. Please be careful. Claire says he's a good man and that you belong with him. He seems to care for you." There was a hitch in her voice as she continued. "But I couldn't bear it if something happened to you, Laurie. I couldn't bear it if he hurt you."

For a second time, tears filled Laurie's eyes. "I know. I love you too. I don't know what's going to happen, but he'd never hurt me, not willingly. Please believe that." She knew in her heart that was true. He'd never want to hurt her. He'd never know that he could destroy her just by leaving her side. He'd think he was protecting her.

Sam Hollinger sat in his driveway staring at his house. It was a nice house, nothing fancy, but well taken care of. He saw the bikes his children had left leaning up against the garage door. He'd given up any hope of ever actually parking inside it. There always seemed to be something blocking his car's path. He smiled ruefully at the sight.

Sighing tiredly, he opened the car door and stepped onto the driveway. The wild barking warned him that Cujo, the mutt his kids had begged him to let them keep, was charging up behind him. Knowing what the impact would do to his back, he quickly spun and sidestepped the furry giant. The dog tried frantically to brake, stopping just short of smacking into the car door.

"Gotcha, sucker!" Sam patted the dog's head, happy to have outsmarted the beast. Whistling, he walked toward the front door with the dog, who held no grudges, following cheerfully behind him.

Letting himself in, he allowed himself a moment to absorb all the different sounds of his family and his home. He could hear his wife calling to the kids to come in and wash up for dinner. He could hear the muffled laughter of his kids coming from the backyard. The old grandfather clock was just striking the half hour. It occurred to him that he was truly a blessed man.

Trish came through the kitchen doorway, mumbling to herself as she rifled through the day's mail. She was as beautiful to him today as she was the day they'd met.

You need to tell your wife you love her.

The so-called psychic's voice echoed in his head. How long had it been since he'd told Trish that he loved her? When was the last time they had made love? He was shocked to realize that he didn't remember. How the hell did that happen?

"Hey you! You're home!" Trish gave him an absent smile and a peck on the cheek and went on checking the mail.

Oh no, he thought. It's happening. That awful place in a marriage where the people in it stop seeing each other. No way was he going to let that happen.

He reached for his wife of fifteen years and pulled her against his chest. Surprised, she asked, "What's gotten into you?"

"I just remembered that I love you." He said it the only way he knew how to say it, simple and straightforward. He was horrified to see her eyes well up. "Hey, what's the problem? Do you want me to take it back?" he teased nervously.

His wife looked up at him and smiled. "No. I just missed hearing it."

You need to tell your wife you love her.

"I'm sorry," he said as he kissed her gently. "I didn't realize how long it had been. The job, the bills… I'm sorry, sugar." He spoke between kisses.

"I love you too, honey." She wrapped her arms around his neck and deepened the kiss.

"Check Mom and Dad out! They're making out!"

Grinning, Sam whispered in her ear, "Do you think your sister would mind sitting with them tonight?"

Trish's eyes shone with promise. She laughed gleefully as she raced to the kitchen phone.

Sam shook his head in wonderment. He'd never be that stupid again.

Gruber had tried to think of a way to do this without Diaz but came to the conclusion that two guns were necessary. He had driven past the James woman's home earlier and had picked out the unmarked police car in a matter of seconds. It was too risky to go it alone.

Resigned to his fate, he had contacted Diaz and asked him to meet him on Lincoln Road. As always, the coolness of the evening brought people out in droves to the trendy strip of restaurants and boutiques on Miami Beach. They huddled over drinks as Gruber filled Diaz in on the events of the day. He had confirmed with that twitchy bitch dispatcher that North was holed up at the lawyer's home.

"We have to finish this tonight." He gazed at Diaz, who sat with his brow furrowed as if he were trying to figure out a difficult riddle. Diaz had extensive experience in breaking and entering. It would be best for him to slip into the house. He warned that he could not be sure the woman didn't have a dog. They'd have to take precautions.

He thought again of his conversation with Lacayo. Either way, he knew he had to cut his losses and get out of town, but perhaps if he gave Lacayo the cop, he wouldn't bother to come after him. It was his only chance. He kept that thought to himself. He could not care less what Lacayo did to Diaz.

They would have to kill the woman. There could be no loose ends.

Once again, he leaned in and went over the plan with Diaz.

◐○◑

It was getting close to dinnertime, and Laurie was finishing up some homemade chicken soup. She imagined that he'd probably have preferred one of the T-bone steaks in her freezer but figured this would be easier on his stomach for now. She was slightly flushed from the heat coming off the stove and from the glass of wine she had just polished off.

Jake hadn't stirred in hours. She'd checked on him every so often, worried that something was wrong, but he seemed fine and even grumbled in complaint when she'd woken him to make sure he was okay. She wished she didn't have to disturb his sleep, but he hadn't had anything to eat in far too long. They didn't need anything else weakening him.

Once the soup was ready, she reluctantly tapped on the bedroom door. "Jake?" She spoke softly, not wanting to jolt him awake. She stayed a safe distance from the bed, as she didn't want to end up flat on her butt again.

"Jake?"

He turned slightly, mumbling in his sleep.

Even with the ugly bruises, he was beautiful. He was so perfectly male in every way. She kept her distance but said a little more firmly, "Jake."

One silver eye opened.

"What are you doing over there?" he mumbled against the pillow.

She smiled and said, "Just being careful. No more startling you awake, mister."

"Sorry about that." He didn't look the least bit contrite.

"No problem, considering the end result," she smirked. "I have some homemade soup for you."

Both eyes opened. "You made it?" He sounded surprised.

"Yes," she replied with slight indignation. "I can cook, you know."

A slow smile eased its way across his features. "I think I'm going to become religious."

She raised a brow and asked, "What?"

Chuckling, he answered, "I'll explain later."

He eased himself up slowly and started to try to get out of bed.

"No, stay there. I'll bring it in to you." She didn't give him a chance to answer before she'd popped into the kitchen and was back carrying a tray loaded with a bowl of soup, some bread, and a glass of water.

"I would share the wine, but I don't think it will mix well with your pills."

He looked at the tray. She'd put a small daisy in a tiny vase on the top corner. It touched him that she'd bother with something like that for him.

She laid the tray across his lap. He patted the bed next to him and said, "Sit."

Happily, she accommodated him, careful not to move the bed too much as she scooted over next to him. She watched him begin eating and knew complete contentment when he turned and said, "This is the best soup I've ever had. I usually just open a can."

He ate in silence, enjoying the food and the warmth of her shoulder against his arm. He glanced at the digital clock on the nightstand. It was past six. He'd slept for a long time. That worried him. He knew he couldn't let down his guard. It wasn't only him on the line this time.

"Hand me those pills."

She reached quickly across the bed and plucked them off the nightstand. "Does it hurt?" she asked worriedly.

"I'm fine. I just need you to do something for me."

"Anything."

He knew she meant it. That touched him, too. "Take them and flush them down the toilet."

"What?" she exclaimed in alarm.

"Just do it." He saw that she was ready to protest, but he cut her off. "I can't be out of it, angel. It's not safe. I don't want you tempted to give me the pills, no matter how uncomfortable I get." He put the bottle into her hands. "Please, just do it."

She stared at him. She knew he still had to be in pain. What if it became too much?

Firmly, he hammered home his point. "Laurie, I know what I'm doing, and I know why I'm asking you to do this. If someone comes after us, I need to have a clear head."

If someone comes after us.

She had almost forgotten that they were in danger. In the safe cocoon of his arms, within the familiar walls of her home, she had temporarily blocked out all that was happening from her mind. He could see it in her eyes. It pained him to bring back the fear into them, but he would take no chances with her.

"Come here." His voice was gentle. She brought her face up to his and accepted his soft kiss. "Please, angel."

She could not deny him. "Okay," she replied with a small, tight smile, "but don't bitch when your ribs hurt."

He grinned. "I won't." God, he loved this woman. Shit. He loved her. It shouldn't have come as such a surprise, given all that had happened, but it did. He hadn't loved anyone since he was a child. He had stopped believing that he could a long time ago.

He heard the toilet flush and watched her walk back to the bed.

"Mission accomplished, Mr. Macho Man." Her smile faltered as she took in his glazed expression. "Don't tell me you changed your mind!" she cried.

"No. You did fine. Thanks." His voice was a bit mechanical.

"What's the matter?"

"I..." He didn't know how to say it. He didn't even know if he could say it. What could he offer her?

He looked around the beautiful room, taking in all the genteel details a woman like Laurie always managed to carry off flawlessly. There were lovely floral prints on the pastel walls and family pictures in delicate silver frames. In one of them, she stood at the center of a big group of people at what had to be a family barbecue, based on the physical resemblance of many of the faces. He didn't know the first thing about gardening or barbecues. She was obviously a woman who enjoyed both. How could someone like him possibly make her happy?

Yet how could he possibly live without her, knowing she'd be doing those things with some other man? The thought brought a grim scowl to his face.

No way.

"I don't garden and I don't barbecue," he said defensively, as though she'd asked him to.

Confused, she replied, "Okaayy..."

"I don't have a family." The words seemed to be spilling out of their own accord. "I don't even know where my parents are or if they're still alive. I don't want to know." He couldn't believe he had said that. He hadn't spoken of his mother or his anonymous father since he was a child.

Laurie sat in dazed silence. What could she say to him? Her heart ached with the pain of what he had just revealed to her. Kneeling on the bed, she put her arms around his neck and bumped her nose softly against his. With her face close to his, she whispered, "I don't care if you don't garden or barbecue. I can do that. I have plenty of family, and I'm happy to share them with you."

Looking into her beautiful, honest eyes, he found the strength to say the words. "I love you. If I had any decency, I'd walk out of your life and let you make a life with someone good enough for you, but I'm a selfish bastard, Laurie. I don't think I can live without you."

Laurie felt as though the whole universe had somehow just shifted. Tears stung her eyes, and a wild joy filled her heart. He loved her. He would stay with her. Nothing else mattered. Nothing.

"I love you too." She didn't give him a chance to respond or to argue with her. She just kissed him. Her whole heart was in that kiss. She hoped that somehow, he'd feel that the way he'd felt so many other things.

He felt it, and his heart knew. There was no going back. He would never leave her. He'd die first.

Chapter Eight

Night fell over the peaceful residential neighborhood. The officer watching Laurie's house yawned and shook himself like a wet dog, trying to wake himself up. He had four more hours on his shift and couldn't afford to be caught snoozing. Besides an occasional stray cat, nothing had moved on the street for a couple of hours.

He decided to walk around the property to check out the perimeter, so to speak. At least it would get his blood circulating again. Stepping out of the dark sedan, he started to lean back into the car to reach for his flashlight. He never saw it coming. The dull thump of the bat crushing his skull was heard by no one.

After making sure the cop was dead, Gruber pushed the unlucky man back into the patrol car and positioned him so that his silhouette appeared normal from the street. Silently, he motioned to Diaz, giving him the go-ahead.

Diaz nodded and moved stealthily toward the house next door to Laurie's. He had already made sure there was no dog or alarm system on the property. Dressed completely in black, with a mask covering his face, Diaz seemed to disappear into the night.

Gruber silently moved back to his car, which sat halfway down the block. Crouching down, he began the interminable wait for Diaz.

Diaz slipped over the fence dividing the two properties with the ease of experience. He'd already scoped out the backyard. No dogs and no alarm system here either. People were so stupid. With a small thud, he landed in the shadows close to the fence. He checked his side for his gun. It was still snug inside his waistband. He took his time, making no noise as he checked each window and door, careful not to step close enough to cause his shadow to be seen from within. The cop and the broad should be asleep, but he took no chances.

When he came upon the kitchen window, he saw his opportunity. It was an old jalousie window. If he was careful and took his time, he could slip the panes off, giving him plenty of room. Pulling his tools from his back pocket, he got to work.

Jake tried to get comfortable. He reminded himself that he was the one who made Laurie flush the pills. His side hurt like hell. Laurie was curled up against his hip. She had scooted down there against his protests. She'd kissed him senseless and promised to make it up to him when he felt better. She'd put pillows against his ribs in case she moved around too much in the night. Fat chance. Despite his discomfort, he grinned as he heard her soft snore. Smiling, he thought she looked like a curled-up kitten.

It still amazed him that she loved him. He thought about everything that had happened between them and knew there was no way he could doubt it. No one put themselves through the hell she'd gone through unless they did it for love. Anyone else would have bailed. Just like his mother had.

He had told her about his mother. He had gone on to tell her about himself. About the small boy who simply couldn't cry anymore. She had cried for him. She'd cried and kissed him and told him that she loved him. She'd promised him that love forever.

Forever. He tried to wrap his mind around the concept. He knew she meant it. He wanted that too. He wanted to give her forever. How to give it to her was what scared him senseless. The military and police work were all he knew. Laurie's roots were here in Miami. He could always apply for a position on the force here, he supposed. Sam would help him. In truth, he didn't care, as long as they were together. Hell, he'd learn to knit for a living if that's what it took.

He laid a hand on her head, caressing her gently. She burrowed her bottom further against his leg, almost pushing herself underneath it. Grinning, he pushed the worries from his mind and closed his eyes. He knew Hollinger's man was outside. At least tonight he could try to get some sleep.

Claire woke to a scream. The darkened window had haunted her dreams again. Sweat made her silk nightgown cling to her body and trickle down between her breasts. Shaking, she stepped out of bed and made her way into the kitchen. She poured herself a shot of whiskey and drank it down in a gulp. If this kept up, she'd turn into an alcoholic, she thought ruefully.

Something was happening. The fear wasn't fading.

Laurie and Jake were in trouble. She knew it.

Steadier, she rushed back into her bedroom and began dressing without regard for what she was tossing on. Something bad was about to happen, and she had to try to stop it.

Diaz crouched with his feet in the sink. He took a moment to orient himself. Once his eyes had adjusted to the darkness, he was able to climb down silently and step carefully across the kitchen. He saw the dining room to the left and assumed the bedrooms must be in the opposite direction. Heading into the dark hallway, he reached the first door. Grateful that the door was ajar, he slipped inside. It took him only a few seconds to see it was an office.

Continuing across the hall, he passed the bathroom; that door was also ajar. There was only one door left. It was almost completely closed. Grateful he wouldn't have to turn the knob; he placed his left hand on the door.

With infinite care, he pulled his gun. He'd have to take the woman out first. The cop was beaten to a pulp, so he figured he'd offer little resistance. A gun barrel to his head should convince him to move along quietly. Taking a deep breath, he began easing the door back one centimeter at a time.

It took Jake a moment to make out the tiny squeak over the sound of Laurie's soft breathing. In that second, he came wide awake.

Someone was entering the room.

Where the hell was his gun? Sam had given him a gun to replace the one Gruber had taken from him once they entered the cabana. He had no idea where the damned thing was. Idiot! He never let it out of his sight, but Laurie's lovemaking had made him careless. He figured she had probably put it away. His carelessness could cost them both their lives.

Years of military training kicked in. He knew that he probably only had a few seconds to make a move. Carefully, he reached his hand over to the nightstand, praying that the intruder wouldn't see the movement in the darkness. Thank God Laurie had pulled the shades down beneath the sheer curtains. The light from the street would have made every movement visible.

His hand closed around a cool object. The glass of water Laurie had brought for him earlier. He prayed his aim was as good as it used to be. If he could catch the intruder by surprise, he might have enough time to launch himself at him and knock him off balance. He knew his injuries would slow him down terribly.

Please God, let me protect her.

It was the first prayer he'd ever said.

Gripping the glass, his eyes strained to make out the bulky shape slowly entering the room. Taking a deep breath, he threw with all his might. As he threw, he half-kicked, half-pushed Laurie further down the bed with his left hand. If the son of a bitch took a shot, instinct would make him shoot higher than the foot of the bed.

Laurie grunted in pain as Jake's rough shove connected with her shoulder. Immediately terrified and fully awake, she heard glass shattering and a muffled curse. She thrashed around and realized that Jake was no longer in bed with her.

Oh my God, there was someone in the room!

Struggling, Laurie tried to pull the comforter off her head. Where was Jake? "Jake! Jake!" she screamed, clawing at the bed sheets.

A gun went off just as she dragged herself out from under the tangle of sheets.

"Jake!" Her scream pierced the darkness. Terrified, Laurie tried to focus her eyes. "Jake!"

"It's okay, baby. It's okay." Jake's gruff voice came out of the darkness. Blinking rapidly, she finally made out his shape in the shadows and rushed into his arms.

"Are you okay? Laurie, are you okay?" He sounded scared.

Crying uncontrollably, Laurie kissed him anywhere she could reach. Tiny, desperate kisses of relief and fear showered his chest and his arms. She was even more terrified when she felt the fresh blood on his bandages.

"Are you alright? Oh my God, Jake, you're bleeding! What happened?" Her eyes, finally fully adjusted to the darkness, looked up to see the fury in his eyes as he stared at the dark form on the floor of her bedroom.

Jumping back in fear, she asked, "Is he dead?"

Instead of answering her, Jake planted a hard kiss on her mouth. A cold rage built and crested within him as he realized how close he had come to losing her. The son of a bitch was dead, alright. Somehow, he'd managed to connect with the killer's gun hand when he landed on him. In the struggle, he was able to turn it on the intruder. In his rage, he emptied the damn thing into the son of a bitch. He could feel his wounds bleeding from the impact, but the bandages had helped keep his side together.

Thinking of what could have been, he let loose a savage growl as he sat Laurie on the bed and turned to brutally kick the motionless form on the floor. It was wasted energy, but it made him feel better for some stupid reason.

Grunting, he realized he couldn't bend down. "Laurie, listen to me. I need you to come here. Don't be afraid."

Laurie eased off the bed. She understood what he wanted. He was mistaken if he thought she was afraid. She felt neither fear nor pity for the bastard on her floor. He had come here to kill them. To kill Jake. Hot anger and adrenaline rushed through her system. She reached for the light.

"No, baby. No lights. I need you to remove his mask."

Nodding, she obeyed and walked over to the man on the floor. She bent over the immobile form and pulled the man's mask up over his head.

"Diaz!" Jake practically spat the word.

Laurie felt the same violence come over her that she had felt when she had found Jake in the cabana. Looking down at the dead man, she felt nothing but glad that he was dead. Without stopping to think about it, she raised her foot and, as Jake had done, kicked his face as hard as she could. She yelped in pain when her bare foot connected with the man's stone-hard jaw.

The silliness of the act made the violence ebb away.

Stunned by her action, Jake grabbed her to him. "Come on, baby. It's over."

"No! It's not over. Jake, he could have killed you!" She felt a white-hot fury as she looked down at the hulking shadow on the floor.

Jake stared down at her. He would have thought she'd be in tears. Instead, she looked ready to kick the guy all over again. All to defend him. Damn, but she was one hell of a woman, he thought, shaking his head in amazement.

Pulling her with him, as if afraid to let her out of his sight, he dragged her to the bed and picked up the phone. He dialed Sam Hollinger's home number as he held Laurie close to his heart.

Gruber was beginning to get anxious. It was taking too long, even for that dolt Diaz. Something was wrong.

Swearing under his breath, he pulled out his rifle and headed toward the woman's house.

◐○◑

"Sam's on his way." Jake stayed on the edge of the bed and tightened his arm around Laurie. She was still shaking. Adrenaline was coursing through her system, making her edgy.

"Can we put on the lights now?" she asked in an anxious voice.

Kissing the top of her head, he whispered, "Once Sam and his people get here, angel. I don't want to take any chances. That albino son of a bitch could be out there."

She breathed in deeply. "I'll get your gun." Her voice was calm now.

"You know where it is?"

She stuck her face into the crook of his neck and mumbled something.

"What?"

Slowly, she dragged her head up. "It's under the kitchen sink." Her lower lip seemed to stick out farther than usual.

"How did it get there?" Jake asked incredulously.

"I hid it there."

"Why?" His voice rose an octave.

Her lip stuck out farther. "Because it's loaded. Someone could get hurt."

They stared at each other in the semi-darkness.

He started chuckling as the absurdity of it all struck them both. "Can I have it back now?" A bit more somberly, he finished, "I emptied the bastard's."

The laughter soothed her. She whispered, "I'll be right back."

"No, I'll get it." Worry was back in his voice.

"I'll find it quicker, and besides, you can't bend down."

"Stay down and be careful." He couldn't deny that he was in no condition to bend down and rummage through the cabinet.

Nodding, Laurie began to feel her way into the darkened kitchen. She made her way toward the sink. Grimly, she noticed some of the panes on the window above it were missing. She bent over and felt around for the gun in the cabinet underneath. All she could find were bottles of cleaning supplies. She bit her lip. She couldn't turn on the lights, but she needed to find the gun. She remembered the flashlight in the kitchen drawer.

She slid out the flashlight and turned it on.

Gruber had been circling the house, trying to hear a noise or see movement that would tell him if something had happened to Diaz.

The small light came on suddenly and flickered erratically through the kitchen window. Diaz didn't carry a light, so he knew it had to be one of them. That meant Diaz was either caught or dead. This goddamned nightmare just kept getting worse.

Biting back a curse, he swore to himself it would end tonight, one way or another. With grim determination, he snapped the night scope into place and took aim through the window, waiting for the light to swing around again.

Claire's car turned the corner with a squeal of rubber worthy of a hell-bent teenager. Honking her horn like a madwoman, she peeled into Laurie's yard. A muffled shot sounded, and her heart stopped in her throat as she heard a scream from inside the house.

"Laurie!" Heedless of the danger, she yelled as she ran out of the car and toward the house.

Jake died a thousand deaths from the moment he heard the muffled shot and Laurie's scream to the moment he reached her on the floor of the kitchen. An anguished cry ripped from his throat as he saw the woman he loved lying prone on the floor.

Frantic and ignoring his own pain, he knelt down and grabbed her shoulders. Turning her gently, he called her name, "Laurie!"

Groaning, Laurie looked up at him. "I'm fine, love. I'm fine." Slowly sitting up, she gasped, "Ouch!"

Jake's gut tightened in fear. "Were you shot?" Gently, he felt for blood on her.

"No, but I've got a piece of glass in my hand."

Relief coursed through him like a flood. "Jesus, Laurie! I don't think I can take much more tonight. Thank God you're alright. Stay down, okay, baby?"

Nodding, she produced his gun and handed it to him.

"I found it."

He didn't know whether to laugh or cry.

Sirens sounded louder and louder, and someone was banging on the front door.

Instinctively, Laurie started to get up, but he held her down. He didn't care if the hounds of hell were bursting through that door; he'd face them all to protect her.

In the end, the door was smashed in by Hollinger and his men, with Claire Murphy hot on their heels. Nothing seemed strange to Laurie and Jake anymore. It seemed to make perfect sense that Claire would fly into the kitchen at that moment.

She hugged Laurie tightly and smacked a tearful kiss on Jake's mouth. He kissed her right back. The way Jake figured it, she had probably saved Laurie's life. The colossal noise she made had probably caused the shooter to hesitate and screw up the shot.

He had no doubt the shooter was Gruber. He knew the man would have killed Laurie easily if he'd had half a shot. Closing his eyes, he tried to rid himself of the "what if" scenarios running through his mind.

Hollinger was already radioing the albino's description into headquarters. When he came back to the dining room table, he had a grim look on his face.

"What else is wrong?" Jake's senses were still on high alert.

Hollinger motioned him into the other room with a curt nod.

Jake followed him, grunting a little in discomfort as he moved. "What is it, Sam?"

"My man outside wasn't the only victim." He rubbed his hands over his face before continuing. "Her assistant was murdered earlier today. The lady's boyfriend called 911 when she didn't make it to dinner. Normally, we would have waited twenty-four hours, but since it was related to your case, we checked it out immediately." Sam looked ready to punch someone.

"Jesus!" Jake couldn't believe what he had just heard. Damn it. That poor woman. He thought of Laurie's affectionate description of the colorful Dorothy as they had lazed in bed earlier. He knew this would be unbearable for Laurie. Bitterly, he thought of how she was continuing to suffer because of him. And it wasn't over. After tonight, there was no doubt they were tracking her to get to him.

Feeling sick, he looked at Sam. "How'd she die?"

"Stabbed to death with a pair of scissors. Wrote the letters 'pale ma' in blood before she died. Seems she passed before she could finish. He just left her there, bleeding out." Sam looked as ill as Jake felt as he described what they had found.

"Shit." Jake dragged his hand through his hair.

"You want to be the one to tell her?"

Jake gave Sam a hard look. "Give us a moment."

Hollinger called his men out of the kitchen as Jake sat down next to Laurie at the kitchen table. For a moment, he felt as though he'd aged twenty years.

"Jake, what's wrong?" Laurie looked up at him with concern. She'd put on a silk robe, and it made her seem even more feminine and fragile to him. Clearing his throat, he tried to find the words to tell her what had happened.

"Laurie." He looked down at her, wishing he could make it all go away, knowing that he couldn't. "Baby, I have some bad news."

Laurie paled. "What is it? Is there something wrong with you?"

He grasped her hand and tried to continue. "Laurie, it's about your assistant."

"Dorothy?" She looked confused.

"Laurie." His voice was as gentle as a spring rain. "Dorothy is dead." He sat across from her and waited a moment for his words to sink in. "I'm sorry. I'm so sorry, angel."

Laurie gripped his hand like a lifeline in a storm. Dorothy, her wonderful friend, so full of life, just couldn't be dead. It was impossible to think that she was gone. There had to be a mistake.

"How can that be? There must be some mistake!" She uttered the words with desperate hope. Her hands began to shake, and she felt a clammy coldness on her skin.

He could feel her hand trembling in his. There was no easy way to say it. He owed her the truth, but each word burned his throat like acid. "She was stabbed to death. Sam's men found her in your office after a gentleman friend called to report her missing."

The jagged sound of pain that escaped her twisted in his heart like a knife. Looking at the pain in her eyes made a terrible guilt and a hot rage seethe through him simultaneously. He was responsible for bringing this horror and pain into her life. And now she wouldn't be able to escape it. Unless he finished it. He had to find Lacayo and Gruber and end this. He had to kill them both, or she'd never be free.

Tears ran down Laurie's face as she looked at him helplessly. His heart broke at the sight of her trusting eyes. Putting aside his rage and numb to the aches of his body, he knelt before her and bowed his head on her lap. Holding her hands to his face, he struggled to beg for her forgiveness.

"I'm so sorry, angel. I'm so sorry. It's my fault, it's all my fault. Please, forgive me. I swear, I'll make it right!" he cried, wrapping his arms around her waist. "I'll make it right."

They held each other tightly, with only Laurie's soul-ripping sobs breaking the silence. Laying her cheek against his bent head, her tears washed over them both.

Once her sobs had subsided, she slowly lifted her head. His words began to sink in. He blamed himself. She wondered how much pain a man could take before he broke. Love for him filled her heart with compassion.

"Jake," she whispered, stroking her hand through his hair.

Finally, he lifted his red-rimmed eyes to hers. Placing a hand on each side of his face, she kissed his mouth gently. "It's not your fault. Do you hear me, love? It is not your fault."

He stared at her in disbelief. How could she hold him blameless? Humbled, he rested his forehead against her chest for a moment. Raising his head to her again, he waited for her to finish.

"The only people at fault are these evil men. Do you understand what I'm saying, Jake?" She looked at him with an intensity that made his skin prickle.

He nodded slowly.

"We are going to stop them," she whispered fiercely.

She didn't hold him responsible. Her forgiveness washed over him like balm. Relief and admiration coursed through him. But fear tore at him, too. He had not missed the "we" in her whispered promise. Staring at her beautiful face, he saw strength and honor. He understood the need for justice she was feeling; it coursed through his veins as well.

"Yeah, angel," he replied quietly. She had a right, he supposed, to see it through. She'd sure come through tonight like a warrior. "We're going to stop them. I promise." He meant it. He held her tightly as he swore to himself that he'd see her through this safely somehow.

Claire and Sam sat across from each other in the living room. The silence was uncomfortable for them both. They had heard every word exchanged between Laurie and Jake in the next room. Claire rubbed her arms as if to warm herself.

"I want to thank you," Sam said suddenly.

"What?" Claire asked.

"Thank you for your advice in the hospital."

Understanding dawned, and she smiled weakly. "You're welcome."

Clearing his throat, Sam asked, "How did you know to come?"

Looking at him tiredly, she replied, "I had a nightmare. The same vision I had at the hospital." Laughing shakily, she added, "At least this time it ended a little better."

"Thanks to you. I don't know that we would have made it in time. If the guy's as good a shot as Jake says he is, she'd be dead right now if you hadn't barreled your car into the yard that way." The words were said quietly but with conviction.

"I used to work for the police sometimes, back home. Cardozo, New Mexico." Claire didn't know why she told him but felt the need to make him believe she wasn't a lunatic. "I just couldn't do it anymore. There were so few happy endings."

Sam understood her more than she knew. He knew the bitter taste of bile each time he found a dead body instead of a live victim. He knew how that could wear a soul down. If it hadn't been for Trish and the kids, he'd probably have found his way to the bottom of a bottle or worse years ago, like so many police officers did. He could imagine what actually seeing the crimes in her head must have done to her.

"I understand," he said gently. "I'm sorry I didn't believe you at first."

Claire smiled wider this time. "It's okay, Chief. I know how it must have sounded." She sighed wearily and nodded toward the kitchen. "They have to leave this house. He'll come for them."

Pressing his fingers to his temple to ease the pressure in his head, Sam grunted his agreement.

"I'd like to help, Chief," she said.

His head jerked up.

"Let me see the man in her bedroom. Take me to her office. I can help you find him." Her voice was urgent and pleading.

How would he explain this to his superiors? Even as he asked himself the question, he knew he would lead her into the bedroom where the corpse lay over a pool of blood that was already congealing. He knew she could help them find the albino and Lacayo. The cop in him itched to find the scum. The friend in him realized that the sooner that happened, the sooner Jake and his woman could get on with their lives without fear.

"Okay, lady. Follow me."

Several people were crowded into Laurie's bedroom. One man shot pictures of the body and the room as others dusted for prints and rummaged through the space for bullet casings. What she knew to be blood stained the floor beneath the body of a large man. The mask he had worn was pulled back over his head. Claire stared at the brutal face. Not even in death had the features softened.

The officers in the room looked at Hollinger questioningly. They were unused to having civilians at a crime scene.

"She's okay." His tone dared them to question him. The officers quietly resumed their activities.

"Any identification on him?" Hollinger directed his question to the officer who carried a plastic bag containing a vicious-looking automatic handgun with a long silencer attached to it.

"No, sir. Nothing."

Sam nodded to Claire to go ahead with whatever it was she needed to do.

Claire bent over the body and hovered motionlessly for a moment. After taking a deep breath and closing her eyes, she reached down and placed her hand on the man's chest.

She jerked back as images of violence surged through her. It took her a moment to get a grip on herself and control the images, shrinking them in her mind to the size of a small screen. She had to pull back, removing herself from what she was doing, or it would make her ill.

Once she had herself back under control, she laid her hand back down and began seeing flashes of the man's life, little bits and pieces from the mundane to the violent. She caught a flash of a sterile white room hovering over the ocean and evil black eyes boring into everything they surveyed. She knew true evil and recognized it immediately. She had no doubt that this was the man after Jake and Laurie.

Moving her hand slowly over the body, she caught another image of a dark-haired, voluptuous young woman dressed cheaply but wearing an expensive diamond bracelet. The name Connie came to her.

Opening her eyes, she asked, "Does Jake know him?"

"Yeah, he says his name is Diaz. One of Lacayo's thugs."

"Well, I can tell you that he's got a girlfriend named Connie who's sporting one hell of a bracelet." She spoke quietly so as to avoid being overheard by the cops milling about.

"I'm sure he's got a record a mile long. We'll pick him out from the mug shots and then run him through the computer for the last known address and take it from there. I'll bet this Connie can help us find the albino." Sam felt better knowing there was something concrete he could do, finally. He strode from the room, then hit the brakes in the hallway.

Leaning back into the bedroom, he barked, "Well, what the hell are you waiting for, Murphy? Get your ass in gear!"

Relieved that he was still including her and feeling a familiar surge of adrenaline, Claire got her ass in gear and ran to catch up.

Gruber raced through the streets of Miami, cursing and pounding his fist against the steering wheel. Even if he had killed the bitch, it meant nothing. He had failed. The cop had eluded him again.

He had heard the sirens as he sped away. The cops would be swarming the house. There was no chance now. If Diaz was still alive, he would point them to him eventually. If he was dead, his corpse would do the same once they figured out who he was and who he worked for.

He had to get out of Miami. He had to get out now, before Lacayo came for him. There was no time. Decided, he turned the car and headed home. All he needed was his passport and the cash stashed in the safe beneath the closet floorboards.

He'd be gone before Lacayo found out about the failure. Screw the cop. Let Lacayo go after him himself. If it hadn't been for the sick bastard, none of this would have happened.

Regaining his composure, he drove into the night.

Chapter Nine

Later that morning, Sam called Laurie and asked her and Jake to meet him at police headquarters. He wanted Jake to see if he could pick Diaz and Gruber out of the mug shots on file and hopefully find whatever additional information might be in the system. Jake agreed. The house would be safe for now. Sam's men were in place and the splintered front door was being replaced as they spoke. The officer assigned to duty with them offered to drive, but Laurie asked him to follow them instead.

"I need a little privacy, officer. You understand, don't you?"

Jake just shook his head as the guy totally melted under her watery gaze and gave in.

"Sure, ma'am. Just follow behind me, please."

They headed out to the garage to get Laurie's car. Jake gave a long, low whistle when he saw the Corvette. "Wow! If I didn't already love you, I'd fall in love with you right now."

Laurie laughed at the look of admiration tinged with a little envy in his eyes. Some of the sadness she felt eased just a tiny bit.

"Are you in any shape to drive?" Yeah, like she needed to ask, she thought. She had to smile at the joy that lit his eyes when she tossed the keys across the hood to him.

Jake's grin was a delight. For a moment she could see the boy he once was, and she wondered if he had had many pleasures in his youth. She climbed into the passenger seat and leaned over to kiss his cheek.

Wrapping his hand around the back of her neck, he pulled her back for a proper kiss. "Hey," he whispered, "I love you." He kissed her deeply again and released her. He shook his head and wondered at how easily the words came when he looked at her.

Laurie's heart tightened painfully in her chest. She still could not believe she had found love and lost her friend all so suddenly. As if sensing her sadness return, Jake reached for her hand and tucked it into his.

"Stay with me, angel. It's going to be okay."

They arrived quickly at the station and were ushered into Hollinger's office. He and Claire were waiting for them in front of a computer screen containing pictures of known criminals. It took about an hour and forty-five minutes before Jake found Diaz among the thousands of photographs and files.

"Joe!" Hollinger yelled out as soon as they found the right mug shot. A plainclothes detective came in and took the information down. He stepped back to his desk and got to work on the information.

"I was right. The bastard has a record a mile long," Sam said with satisfaction.

In no time, Joe returned with a last known address.

"Joe, you and Brown follow me." Sam was all business as he strapped his holster on and swung his jacket over his arm. Glancing up at Claire, he snapped, "Murphy, you coming or what?"

Laurie and Jake shared a look. Laurie whispered, "I guess he believes her now."

"I would say so," Jake smiled.

Glaring down at them, Sam replied, "Don't be smart asses. You two stay put until I get back."

"Listen, Sam…" Jake started to protest.

"Stay put! That's an order!" He did not even bother waiting for Jake's answer.

Claire waved goodbye as she ran after him. "Damn man has legs like a giraffe," she mumbled under her breath as she raced down the hall.

Hollinger pulled up to the curb in front of the Ashton Apartments. He and Claire stepped out of his car as the two other officers pulled up behind them.

"Joe, you and Brown take the neighbors. Murphy and I will talk to the building manager." Hollinger took the steps that led up to the large glass lobby doors of the building two at a time.

Holding one of the heavy doors open, he motioned Claire through. They came to the security guard seated at a small marble counter in the middle of the lobby. Sam flashed his badge and asked for the building manager. The guard motioned them down the hall toward another set of smaller glass doors. The wall next to the doors displayed a sign with the word "Office" on it. Sam hoped the manager would be cooperative. They had no time to waste.

They saw no one at the desk located in the small front office, but there were noises coming from the back area.

"Hello?" Claire called out.

"Be right there!"

After a moment, a small, balding man with thick glasses stepped out from the doorway behind the desk. Wiping his hands with a paper towel, he took a look at them and said, "Can I help you?"

Hollinger spoke as he took out his badge. "We're here on official police business."

The small eyes behind the thick glasses widened.

"We're here to ask you some questions about Tony Diaz, one of your tenants."

Claire noted the man's look of distaste when he heard Diaz's name. Stepping in, she asked, "Are you a friend of his, Mr...?"

"Rosenblatt, but call me Herb. God no! That bully? I do my best to stay out of his way." Herb's voice reflected his disgust and an underlying fear of the tenant.

Herb sat at the desk and motioned them to sit down. "Has he committed a crime?" His voice was hopeful.

"Well yes, but actually... he's dead." Claire doubted that the news would affect Mr. Rosenblatt negatively.

"Dead! Oh my!" Herb wiped his hands with the paper towel a bit more vigorously. "He still owes this month's rent!"

"Mr. Rosenblatt..." Hollinger's voice was impatient.

"Herb, please."

"Herb, what can you tell us about Mr. Diaz?" Sam was full of authority and impatience. He had no time for this little man's nonsense.

"Well, he was a bully for one." The note of indignation was not lost on Claire. She imagined the countless times the brute had probably terrorized the small, nervous man before her. Allowing herself a moment to delve into the man's thoughts, she felt his shame for not finding the courage to stand up to Diaz on a myriad of occasions.

"I can only imagine, Herb." She sounded extremely sympathetic. "People like that are very difficult to deal with. Did he have any family?"

"None that I know of. Not many people ever came to visit him."

"How do you know that?" The question came from Sam.

"Well, visitors need to check in with the guard. Everyone signs in and notes which apartment they are visiting. I keep the logs back here." Herb gestured toward the room behind him. "In the two years he has lived here, only his girlfriend came to see him occasionally."

"Do you know the girlfriend?"

"Oh no. I saw her a couple of times, though. Quite attractive, if you know what I mean." Herb wiggled his eyebrows at Sam.

"May we see the records, please?" Claire asked before Sam could make the demand.

"Well, I'm not supposed to show them to anyone, but you are the police, and it's not like he's going to have a beef with me over it!" Herb sounded profoundly relieved that Diaz was dead.

"Come this way."

They left with an address from Consuelo Rivera's driver's license taken from the logs in Herb's files, as well as a description of the woman from the security guard. Claire shook her head ruefully as she remembered the man's gesture to describe Ms. Rivera's most attractive attributes. Apparently, he was a breast man.

Gruber entered the underground parking garage of the elegant condominium on Brickell Avenue after nodding to the security guard at the entrance. He slipped into his parking space and took a deep breath before stepping out of the sleek black car into the smothering heat and humidity of the underground garage. He walked quickly toward the steel gray doors that led to the stairwell. He never took the elevators. He felt no need to bump into any of his neighbors unnecessarily.

After swiping his access card to gain entrance, he took the stairs at a run without breaking a sweat. He worked out diligently for two hours every day and was in excellent physical condition. His line of work demanded that he be able to handle any situation with ease, and that meant being in top form.

After a few minutes, he pushed through the door onto the eleventh floor. Without making a sound, he reached the door of his apartment and entered quickly. The entrance was dark and cool. He could make out the shape of his furnishings from the light that entered through the giant windows that faced Biscayne Bay. Without bothering to turn on the lights, he stepped through the living room and into his bedroom.

The room was so sparse that it could have been mistaken for a cell. The only hint of luxury in the room was the collection of black-and-white photographs that were beautifully framed and hung on the wall opposite the plain bed.

Gruber did not spare the photographs a look, but instead headed into the walk-in closet across from his bathroom. Even in his haste, he did not fail to notice that the bathroom door was ajar. He was meticulous about closing all the doors in each room. It was a compulsive habit from his childhood that he had never been able to shake.

The sight of the open door froze him in mid-step. His heart raced as he understood what the open door meant. Someone was in his home. Lacayo! Anger and fear made him shake like a crazed, cornered animal. Pulling his gun suddenly, he ran into the bathroom screaming as he switched on the light, "Come out, you twisted son of a bitch!"

Swinging wildly, he braced himself to feel Lacayo's knife slice through his skin. As his eyes adjusted, he stared at the empty bathroom in confusion. Beyond reason, having lost all of his self-control, he turned and raced through the apartment, yelling at Lacayo to come out and fight like a man. Nothing.

Could the bastard have come and gone? The closet!

He ran back to the closet. Maybe he could still get away. Lacayo must have tired of waiting for him. There was no way he could know that the cop had gotten away again. Not yet. Maybe he had left the bathroom door open himself. He had never been careless before, but he had been unwinding slowly in the last two days, losing his usual steely composure.

Yes, he could have missed the door in his haste to get Diaz, he thought.

Reaching the closet, he ripped the carpeting from the back corner off the floor, heedless of the designer shoes that toppled over each other. The floor safe was as it always was, unopened with the dial set at the number one. Trying to calm his breathing, he spun the lock forward, then backward, then forward again. The familiar click soothed his frayed nerves.

The safe opened with a small click. The small leather satchel was there as it had always been. Reaching down, he pulled it up and out of the crevice in the floor. Still kneeling, he opened the bag. Several passports and five hundred thousand in cash lay inside its soft leather folds. Relieved, Gruber stood and kicked the carpet back into place.

He turned to find himself staring at the vicious end of a stiletto knife. He felt ill as he looked up into the eyes of death.

"Where do you think you're going?" the question purred out of thin lips.

Too late.

The thought ran through his mind as Lacayo thrust the knife into his chest. He did not even attempt to reach for the gun he had tossed on the floor next to the safe. As his blood began pouring out of him, he could hear Lacayo's giggling from a foggy distance as the knife sliced into him again and again.

Claire stared out the smudged window of Hollinger's car as they neared what they hoped was Connie Rivera's current address. After running the license, the computer confirmed the address of a duplex in Coconut Grove. Apparently, she lived in the rear unit. The computer also produced a record of two arrests for soliciting and one conviction for carrying narcotics. Nice, thought Claire, as she read through the printout.

She looked over at Sam. His profile was as grim as his mood. She knew that he realized every moment that passed was a chance for these killers to get away. He had no real interest in the albino. He wanted Lacayo. With Jake's testimony, he could convict the criminal not only of drug trafficking but also of attempted murder. If they could get to the albino and convince him to testify against his boss in exchange for a lighter sentence, they stood a chance of locking the psychopath away for life.

She had been unable to pick up anything else about the man Jake had killed at Laurie's or about his woman. She had been so emotional in her haste to get to Laurie before the second killer took a shot at her that she had not stopped to try to sense anything about him. They only had Jake's description of the man. He would be easy to recognize. His size and coloring were unique, to say the least.

She sighed as they pulled into the driveway of the duplex. The yard was overgrown with weeds. A shiny new red tricycle sat under a palm tree that stood awkwardly in the center of the yard. Claire felt a slight melancholy as she took it all in. She sensed that the people who lived here had lost all aspiration for anything more for themselves.

She stepped out of the sedan and stopped for a moment to brush her hand over the handlebars of the tricycle. The image of a pretty, dark-eyed little girl came to her. The tricycle had been a gift from her mother's boyfriend. Claire lifted her hand away and wondered if the child had any affection for Diaz. Hopefully, she would not be present when they gave her mother the news that her lover was dead.

"Claire," Hollinger's voice was softer than usual. He had not missed the sadness that crossed her face. "Come on. There's nothing you can do."

"You're right." She shook her hands a little, as if shaking off the images that had distracted her. "We don't have much time. Let's hope she's home."

Hollinger did not bother asking why time was short.

Together they walked past the front of the duplex to the door of the rear unit. Christmas lights were still hung across the edge of the roof above them. Hollinger rang the doorbell and stepped back a pace with his hand over his gun.

After a moment, the door was opened by a middle-aged woman in a stained floral print apron. Claire imagined she had looked that tired for years.

"We are looking for Consuelo Rivera." Sam showed the woman his badge. "Is she here?"

"What's she done?" There was little emotion in the question. The woman seemed simply vaguely interested rather than concerned.

"She hasn't done anything that we know of. We just need to ask her some questions. Is she here?"

The woman considered them both for a moment and then stepped aside to let them in. Without asking them to sit down, she turned and yelled in the general direction of a darkened hallway to the right. "Connie, the cops are here and they are looking for you!"

Without sparing another glance at them or the hallway, she returned to the kitchen and went about her business. There was a strong smell of cooking onions in the house. Claire felt her eyes water a bit.

There was a rustling sound from the hallway, and moments later a woman in her late twenties emerged. She was attractive in a hard kind of way. She wrapped a short black robe around herself as she walked toward them.

"What do you want?" There was disdain in the question, but her eyes betrayed a barely controlled nervousness.

Claire decided it would be more productive if she took the lead on this one.

"Consuelo, we're not here for you. Can we sit down?" Claire's voice was polite and soothing.

"Sure… whatever. Sit down, and it's Connie, by the way. I hate Consuelo." Connie sat on the worn armchair and pointed toward the equally worn sofa. "Is this about Tony?"

"Actually, it is." Claire paused for a moment, feeling a bit of compassion for this brittle woman. "He broke into someone's house last night…"

"No way, lady. He was here with me all night long. He just left a few minutes ago." Connie stared Claire in the eye with steady defiance. "I'll testify to that!"

"Well, that would be a fricking miracle, considering…" Sam looked ready to reach across the coffee table and choke the woman.

"Chief, please." Claire laid a hand on his arm. "Let me."

Sam glared back at her and shrugged his powerful shoulders. "Knock yourself out, Murphy." He leaned back and crossed his arms over his chest. His eyes bored into Connie's with no compassion.

Claire cleared her throat and turned back to the defiant woman. "Connie, Tony was killed last night." She said it gently. The man had been a cold-hearted killer, but she knew that this woman loved him. She could not help but feel some compassion for the defiant young woman.

"What?" Connie shot up from the armchair like a rocket. "That's not possible!" Her eyes filled with tears as she backed away from them. Shaking her head in denial, she cried, "You must have the wrong man."

Claire squeezed Sam's arm, silently begging him to let her handle it. "Connie, I'm sorry, but it's true. He broke into someone's home and tried to kill them."

"No!" Connie screamed and covered her ears. "He's not dead!"

The older woman came out of the kitchen yelling, "I told you he was no good! He was always a bum! Now he's a dead bum! I told you so!"

Connie spun around toward the older woman and, before anyone could stop her, slapped her hard. The crack of her palm against the older woman's face seemed to echo in the cramped room.

Sam shot up from the sofa and grabbed Connie's hands, holding them behind her back. "Do not touch her again! Do you understand me?"

Connie simply crumpled in his hold, hanging limply back against him. "We were gonna get married!" she wailed. "We were gonna get married!"

"He was never gonna marry you! Puta! God will punish you for striking your mother!" the old woman screamed bloody murder.

"Both of you shut up!" Sam roared over the screams and wails.

The women reacted immediately. Except for their sniveling, they were silent. So much for compassion, thought Claire.

◐○◑

It took them twenty precious minutes to calm Connie and her mother down. The women ended up embracing each other. It was difficult to tell whose wails were louder.

Once the sniffling Connie had calmed down, Claire began the questioning. "Connie, did he say anything about where he was going yesterday?"

"No. When... Gruber... called, he just said... that he had... to go."

"Who's Gruber?" Sam cut in.

Connie eyed him vindictively. "Some guy he worked with."

"Where can we find him?"

"How should I know?" Her voice was watery but defiant.

Claire decided it was best to intervene. "Connie, I think it's in your daughter's best interest for you to cooperate. You and your mother want to be here when she gets home from school, don't you? Trust me, you don't want Chief Hollinger to have to drag you downtown, do you?"

At the thought of her daughter, Connie began crying again. "Tony was good to us, you know? He was good to Jennie. She liked him!"

"I'm sure he was. But he's gone now and you need to think about Jennie. Just tell us what you know about Gruber. Do you know where he lives?" The tone was gentle but firm. Claire knew they were wasting precious time. The dying wasn't over yet.

"I don't know..." Connie sniffed and wiped her nose with the sleeve of her robe. "He's weird. All white like a ghost. He doesn't like me. We never talk much."

"Did Diaz... did Tony ever talk to you about him?" Claire began sounding a bit more urgent.

"Sure. Tony thought the guy was real smart. Tony wasn't the brightest, you know?" She looked at Claire for understanding.

Claire nodded and asked, "Did Tony ever mention where Gruber lived? Did he mention who they worked for?"

"He never talked about his boss. It was like he was afraid to or something. I asked him plenty, but he would just tell me to shut up and mind my own business." That seemed to start her crying again.

"How about Gruber?"

Sniffling, she replied, "I don't know the address, but I overheard Tony say once that he had to pick him up at a place called The Ambrose near downtown on Brickell."

Claire looked at Sam but found only an empty couch. He was already walking out the door.

"Do you think we'll find him there?"

Hollinger glanced over at Claire and then focused back on the highway. After a moment he replied, "If we don't find him, maybe we can find something to help us nail the piece of shit."

"You don't have a warrant." Her voice was low but firm. She didn't want anything to blow the case.

Picking up his radio, Hollinger answered, "I will before we go in."

Jake listened quietly as Laurie made arrangements for Dorothy's funeral from Hollinger's office. His hands fisted when he heard the break in her voice as she explained to the person on the phone that there were to be no carnations in the floral arrangements. Apparently, her friend had absolutely hated carnations.

"Roses... roses and orchids, that's what I want. Yes, that's right... all different colors." Laurie struggled to control the urge to sob. "No, she has no immediate family. Just me..."

She could feel herself breaking into a million pieces. She was all Dorothy had in this world, and because of her she was dead. Her hand began shaking so hard that she dropped the receiver as a sob escaped her.

In a flash, Jake's arms were around her. He held her to his chest as he picked up the receiver. "Hello. Yes, I'm sorry. Ms. James will have to call you back. Yes, thank you." He laid the receiver gently on its cradle, keeping his other arm around Laurie's shaking shoulders. She felt so fragile in his arms. He had no words to console her. He was afraid that he would say the wrong thing and that she would completely fall apart.

For some reason, as he held her, he suddenly remembered the despair of finally understanding that his mother was never coming back for him. He remembered the desolation that had filled his young heart. He had felt so alone from that day on, bitterly alone, until Laurie had come to him in another moment of dark despair. He suddenly realized that he had not felt that loneliness again. He tightened his hold on her, bending his head down to shower her hair with gentle kisses.

"I'm here, angel. I'm here." How could he put into words what he was feeling? How could he make her understand that he wished he had the power to carry her pain for her? "Give it to me, Laurie… let it go, baby…"

Laurie heard him through her tears. As it had been from the beginning, she understood what he was trying to say, what was twisting his heart so painfully. He could not bear to see her this way. A soft, warm sensation flowed through her. Her sobs eased slowly until her tears flowed gently down her cheeks without the terrible shakes that had overcome her just a few moments before. This is what it means to be loved, she thought.

She held onto him tightly. Lifting her head, she raised her lips to his. Gratitude and love overflowed in her heart. She hoped that he could feel what she knew she could never put into words. Giving herself over to the kiss, she prayed he would.

The building was in a very exclusive part of downtown Miami. Beautifully landscaped, the place exuded an understated elegance. Claire and Sam had been taking in the details from the car for over half an hour. They were both feeling antsy and impatient.

"Where the hell is Ramirez?" Sam growled for the fourth time. He kept drumming his blunt fingers on the steering wheel, beating out the rhythm of his impatience.

A beat-up Ford Mustang pulled slowly around the corner and parked across the street. It was so dirty that she could not tell what color the car was. The next thing Claire noticed was the scuffed boot that eased out of the driver's side, followed by a pair of very long blue jean-clad legs that eventually brought her eyes to a very hard, sexy male body. She felt a sliver of heat snake up her center. She gave herself a mental shake. It was hardly the right time for her long-dormant libido to suddenly wake up.

"There he is. Let's go." Hollinger stepped out of the car as Claire slid out of the passenger seat and came to stand next to him.

As the man neared, Claire realized that she too was being scrutinized from behind a pair of mirrored aviator sunglasses. Her body seemed to have kicked into high gear without her consent. Irritation made her frown.

"Here you go, Chief." The man handed some papers to Hollinger. His loose stance told Claire that this officer was familiar and at ease with his superior.

"Thanks, Ramirez. All the i's dotted and the t's crossed?" Hollinger did not even glance at the document, keeping his eye on the building's entrance.

"Yep. Judge Goldberg was pissed as hell, though," Ramirez chuckled without looking away from Claire. "I had to go into the sauna at the Biltmore to have him sign off on it. You don't even want to know what that guy looks like in a towel."

Hollinger turned and laughed. He slapped Ramirez on the back. "Just make sure he doesn't hold it against you when you're in court."

"Are you kidding? It'll be hell keeping a straight face knowing what awful things lay under that robe!" Still chuckling, Ramirez gave a lazy salute, then turned back to look Claire up and down slowly.

What the hell was this guy's problem? Claire was really irritated now. "Is there a problem, officer?" Sarcasm dripped from her voice.

Ramirez heard the Chief clear his throat and knew there was no time to play, but he could not seem to stop himself. He slid his glasses down on his nose and stared at her for a moment. He could almost see the sparks shooting off her. Ben Ramirez felt a tightening in his belly that he knew spelled trouble. Baring his teeth in a killer smile, he thought, what the hell?

"No, no problem at all. Everything is just fine, ma'am." He stretched out the word fine, just knowing his drawl would only irritate her more. Still looking her over as if she were an apple, he was about to bite into, he lowered his voice. "Fine as can be."

When he saw her eyes narrow, his smile widened. He was suddenly grateful that he had been the only one available to get the warrant for Hollinger. Turning back to his boss, he said, "Do you need me to stay, Chief?"

"No, I've got men covering all exits. Take the rest of the day off. I know you must be exhausted. Congrats on the Foley case. Job well done."

Ben turned after a flippant salute and headed back to his car, thinking to himself that he would have to corner the Chief later. God, he loved redheads.

Just for fun he watched her through the rearview mirror as he gunned the engine and drove away. She looked ready to take a knife to him. He suddenly felt better than he had in a long time.

"Who the hell is that jerk?" Claire was almost growling. The memory of eyes as black and deep as night laughing at her over the sunglasses made her even madder. The man smiled like a damned shark.

Hollinger raised his eyebrows at her. He had been surprised at Ramirez's behavior. The man was usually a charmer, a real gentleman with the ladies. He had never seen him act so brazenly toward a woman. And Murphy was absolutely seething, he mused. A little stronger reaction than warranted as far as he was concerned. Interesting...

"Ramirez is one of my best detectives." He kept his voice neutral.

"Best? The pickings must be slim, Chief." She did not notice that her hands were fisted.

Sam suppressed a smile and got back to the business at hand. Tapping the search warrant against her shoulder, he said, "Come on, Murphy. You can give me your opinions on Ramirez later. We've got bigger fish to fry."

Claire followed him across the street. She had almost forgotten why they were here. Shrugging off the lingering irritation, she focused her mind on what they were here for. Something told her the visit was not going to be easy.

Lacayo felt much better. Giggling, he reached into his glove compartment. He pulled the airline ticket out and fingered it before slipping it into his jacket pocket.

It was time to tie up loose ends.

Chapter Ten

Claire and Sam waited impatiently as the building manager, a well-dressed young woman who obviously had other things to do, knocked briskly on the door of apartment number 1104.

"It doesn't seem that Mr. Gruber is home, officer." She hesitated before putting the key in the lock. "Do you mind if I take a look at that document? I don't want the management company embroiled in a lawsuit." She held out her impeccably manicured hand expectantly.

Hollinger handed her the search warrant. He never really expected to find Gruber home. Things were too hot for Lacayo and his crew right now. They would be lying low for a good while. He would settle for searching the place on the slim hope of finding something. If nothing else, it would rattle their cages to know that they were closing in on them.

Once the young woman convinced herself that all was in order and that she would not be held responsible for any legal problems, she opened the door and stepped back to allow them in. She could not wait to get out of there. Mr. Gruber always gave her the creeps. He was always polite and he certainly knew how to dress well. But the man's eyes were so cold, almost dead. She shivered at the thought. Hopefully these two would be quick about it.

Sam pulled his gun out before entering the apartment. Holding it before him, he cautiously stepped into the austere living room. "Murphy, just stay here, okay?"

Claire knew it was not a request. "No problem." Her eyes searched the perimeters. He was here; she could sense it. "He's here. I feel him."

Sam felt the hair on his forearms rise. "Just keep back, and keep her out of the way, Murphy."

Claire practically shoved the young woman out the door and into the hallway.

"Hey! I have to be present while you're in there..."

Claire clapped a hand over her mouth and whispered, "Shut up!" She saw the woman's eyes widen and knew she would be still, at least for now. She removed her hand and murmured, "Please, just stay out here out of sight."

Understanding began to dawn and, instead of obeying, the woman high-tailed it to the elevator. Relieved to see her go, Claire headed back into the apartment.

She could not see him, but she knew Hollinger was moving into the bedroom. Steeling herself, she followed.

Sam eased into the bedroom, gun first. He immediately recognized the rusty smell of blood. With his senses on high alert, he slipped quietly toward the bathroom. The door was ajar. He positioned himself to glance at the mirror. The bathroom seemed to be empty. A weak gasp had him spinning with his gun outstretched.

"Jesus! Claire, what the hell! I told you to..." Anger fell away as he saw behind her into the walk-in closet. The back wall was splattered bright red with blood and other matter that he did not want to think about. On the floor was another bloody mess in the shape of a body. "Oh shit..."

Looking back at Claire, Sam could see the horror on her face. "Claire," his voice was gentler now, "Claire..."

Claire forced herself to turn away from the bloody pulp on the floor. It was Gruber. She did not need a vision to know it. The shock of white blond hair over the blood and the pale arms confirmed it. She felt immediately that this was the man who had murdered Laurie's assistant. She had no doubt, just as she had no doubt that the same man who had tortured Jake had stabbed this man mercilessly and enjoyed it. She shuddered at the images invading her mind but found it difficult to find any pity in her heart for him. She, better than most, understood what a monster the man on the floor was.

"I'll call the coroner's office..." Hollinger's voice was strained.

Claire raised her eyes to him. "Sam, he's not dead yet."

"What?" In an instant, Hollinger was on his knees trying to find a pulse. A thin gasp escaped from the bloody mouth.

"La..."

Sam knelt closer. "What? Who did this to you?"

"Lacay..." A violent fit of coughing interrupted the feeble voice.

"Where is he?" Sam was almost yelling now. He needed something, anything to go on. This was his only lead to Lacayo. If the man died before giving him a lead, he knew all could be lost. "Come on, Gruber! Where is he?"

Choking on his own blood, Gruber had his revenge. "Morris... New York." The words escaped on his final breath.

The words had Sam rocking back on his heels. He looked to Claire, whose eyes were burning into his.

"What was it he said?" she asked urgently.

Grimly, Sam replied, "Morris. He said Morris."

"What or who is that?"

Sam rose. "I need to talk to Jake. Let's get this called in. This just got a lot more complicated."

Claire stared at his broad back and wondered just how much more complicated things could possibly get. Glancing back down at the now dead murderer, she cringed. Christ! She needed some fresh air.

◐○◑

The Ambrose was soon overrun with police and staff from the County Coroner's office. It did not take long for the press to show up. Having regained her composure, the building manager stood next to the police department's spokesperson, looking elegant and appropriately subdued. Cameras flashed as the reporters shot out questions they knew could not be answered yet.

Sam hustled Claire into his car as quickly as possible. They headed downtown with sirens blaring and lights flashing. When Gruber had uttered the name Morris, he left Sam with only one plausible scenario. Robert Morris had set Jake up. Rubbing his tense neck, Sam knew all hell was about to break loose again.

Darlene Williams sat at her workstation with sweat running down her back. She had received the first call from Chief Hollinger himself. He would never know the effect his words had on her. The albino was dead.

Oh God! Could it be true? Could her nightmare be over? She breathed deeply and tried to think clearly. She knew the albino worked with a partner. She had to cover her bases. With a shaking hand, she picked up the phone and made what she hoped was the last call she would ever have to make to that number.

When she was done leaving her message, she leaned over and picked up the framed picture of her son that she kept on her desk. A tear slid down her cheek as she held the frame to her heart. The overwhelming feelings of relief and guilt made it difficult to breathe. Nervously, she glanced around the dispatch office. Her coworkers were all busy with calls and no one seemed to notice her. Clutching the photograph, she shut her eyes and tried not to think about the poor woman who had been found dead at the law offices of the James woman.

She would bear the weight of that death her whole life. The noise of the dispatch operators around her made her feel dizzy. There were so many crimes, so many accidents, so much horror. She just could not stand it anymore.

Desperately, she reached for her purse from inside the drawer of the scarred old desk. Slamming it shut, she bolted for the door. She could hear her supervisor yelling at her that she was not due for a break yet.

She never looked back.

The plane landed smoothly at La Guardia Airport. The flight had been smooth and without incident, but he had been unable to relax. He knew he would not return to Miami, at least not as Rene Lacayo. He had already assumed another identity, traveling as Pedro Gonzalez, a man as generic in appearance as his name was in Miami. He traveled only with the bag he had pulled from his safe. It had all he needed. In the end, he mused, money was the one thing that opened every door.

It was not the first time that he had been forced to run. The difference this time was that he had been made to run after failing. His men had failed him. That was no longer a concern since they were both as dead as they deserved to be. His only regret was not killing Diaz personally.

Gripping the arms of the leather seat, he raged silently as he thought of Jake North. The cop had escaped again, and that was unacceptable. Fury seethed in him. He took another drink of the complimentary champagne and soothed himself by imagining the many ways he would hurt his prey once his plan was put in motion.

Once the plane was stationed at the gate, he was out of the airport and in a taxi within minutes. After jotting down the address he was heading to, the cab driver tried unsuccessfully to engage him in conversation. The man finally gave up when his passenger would not even make eye contact.

Lacayo leaned back and closed his eyes. He began to fantasize about the many ways that he would make Morris scream in pain before he finished tying up this particular loose end.

Jake and Laurie had been sitting together for what seemed like an eternity when Sam and Claire finally returned. Judging by the grim looks in their eyes, Jake figured the news was not good.

Sam wasted no time. "Gruber is dead. Lacayo stabbed the living shit out of him."

Laurie took Jake's hand. "What does that mean? Does that mean that monster gets away with it all?" Anger made her hand tremble in Jake's.

Raising a hand as if to ward off an attack, Sam continued, "Before he died, he named Lacayo as his killer. Apparently, Lacayo likes to have his victims die slowly." He stared pointedly at Jake. "That's been our good luck so far."

Jake's eyebrows rose sardonically. "Well, why aren't we out arresting the bastard?"

Sam rubbed his big hands over his face in exhaustion. Finally, he looked at Jake and said, "There's more."

Jake knew he was not going to like it. He squeezed Laurie's hand a little tighter.

"He said the name Morris before he died as well, when I asked where we could find Lacayo." Sam stared at Jake with sadness in his eyes. "He said the words Morris and New York. I'm sorry, brother."

Jake held Laurie's hand in a death grip. The rage boiled up black and bitter. Each blow, each cut he had received at the hands of that son of a bitch Lacayo had been with the knowledge of his superior, a man sworn to uphold the law and to protect the innocent.

Chief Robert Morris had faced many dangers on the streets of New York as a cop when he began his career in law enforcement. He had never let fear grab him by the throat as he crashed through doors, even knowing that death could well be on the other side of each one. He had thrived on the thrill of adrenaline rushing through him as he chased fugitives through the dangerous streets of the city. He had been young and brave and stupid. He had relished living on the edge.

But that was then and this was now. Now he had everything to lose. Now he had the weight of his own misdeeds crushing him into the ground with fear and guilt. He knew better than to believe that Lacayo would simply get on a plane and disappear conveniently into South America. No matter what the little bastard said, deep down in his gut Morris knew that Lacayo would come for him. Not because it was smart, but because the son of a bitch was too arrogant to let the whole fiasco go. Morris wiped the sweat from his brow as he imagined the hell that Lacayo would try to bring to his door.

It was all falling apart. He could feel his future slipping away from him. *No!* He had worked too damned hard to build the life he deserved and he was not going to let a slime like Lacayo destroy it. An image of his lovely wife, their children, and their elegant home flashed in his mind. Jesus! Lacayo was such a twisted bastard he would enjoy going after them just to make him suffer more. Sweat began to roll down his body. What had he done?

As he fought his way through rush hour traffic, Robert Morris prayed for the first time in years.

Lacayo kept his eyes on the elegant brick two story house across the street as he trimmed the hedges along the side of the neatly manicured lawn owned by the recently deceased Mrs. Myrna Goldman. A giggle escaped as he repeated the words "recently deceased" under his breath. The old bitch was probably still bleeding out underneath the stairs in the foyer of the old house. He had butchered her with the very same shears he was using to trim the hedges. He had pulled them out of the tool shed before grabbing the old woman as she gardened in her backyard.

Dragging her indoors had been easy enough. The old hag was nothing but skin and bone and weighed about as much as a child. She did make good lemonade though. He had helped himself to a glass as he stood over her tortured body, cooling off from his exertion as he watched her bleed onto the Oriental rug that ran the length of the hall. She had looked confused, as though she had expected a quite different death. He laughed again as he recalled the old bitch's gurgling breaths as she fought to hang on to life.

Shaking himself out of the pleasurable memories, he once again peered at the house across the street from beneath his baseball cap. The house had no fence, just a wide, perfectly manicured lawn. He could hear Morris' children playing and splashing in the pool behind it. He began whistling as he snipped the deadly shears along the tall green hedge.

He smiled as he saw the rusty red smears of blood along the leaves.

Just a few minutes later, a black sedan pulled into the street suddenly and Lacayo pressed himself into the overgrown section of hedge. He knew his dull green T shirt and pants, along with his camouflage cap, would make him disappear into the foliage, but his heart still tripped in nervous excitement as he watched Robert Morris rush out of the vehicle and into the home that Lacayo had helped him pay for.

Black eyes gleamed in anticipation of what was to come.

"Marie! Marie!" Morris yelled for his wife desperately, slamming the front door behind him.

"Rob, what is wrong with you? Why are you yelling like that?" Impeccable in every way, Marie Morris was calm and put together even when alarmed. For a moment he just looked at her and wondered if she would ever forgive him.

Shaking his head, he grabbed her roughly. "Get the kids, you have to leave." Practically dragging her through the house toward the kitchen, he opened the window that looked out upon the pool where his two sons were splashing and laughing.

"Robby, Steven! Come in right now!" he bellowed.

"Aw, Dad! But we just..." his oldest began to protest.

"Now, Junior, I said come in right now!" His voice boomed like a cannon through the house.

Normally Robby Morris would have tried to negotiate a few more minutes, but something in the tone of his father's voice made him pull himself out of the pool and grab a towel. "Come on, Stevie... something is up."

As always, Stevie did exactly what his older brother did. Dripping water, they walked into the kitchen and stared at their wild-eyed father and pale, frightened mother in silence.

Struggling for composure, Morris released his wife momentarily and stared at his family. What a fool he had been! Did he really think he could involve himself with filth such as Lacayo and not have the stench touch his family? He rubbed his hands across his face and tried to calm down.

"I'm sorry that I've frightened you, but the situation warrants it. Marie, I need you to pack up the boys and yourself for an indefinite stay at your mother's. I'll call you when it's safe to come home."

"Rob, what's happened? What is going on?" His wife's voice trembled in fear and he knew shame as he had never before.

"I can't explain right now, Marie. Please, just do as I ask." His eyes begged her to obey.

Gathering her children into her protective embrace, Marie Morris stared at her husband's sweaty, wild-eyed face. Her stomach twisted in fear. She had never seen him lose his composure this way. Never. She suddenly realized that she did not want to know what had turned her cool, debonair husband into a shaking, sweaty mess. Something in his eyes told her that whatever was happening could destroy them. She was not ready to know. Turning without a word, she walked her children up the stairs with quiet murmurs to calm them. At the top of the stairs, she looked back down and saw her husband pull his gun out of its holster and check the clip before snapping it back into the weapon he so rarely carried. She began to shake. Terrified, she raced up the stairs to protect her sons.

Night had fallen on the lovely suburb where Chief Robert Morris of the New York Police Department resided. Lacayo smirked in amusement as he recalled the taxi that had come for Morris' wife and children. It was a shame that he did not have the time or the additional manpower to bring them back. He would have enjoyed killing them before Morris' helpless eyes.

Morris thought he could dismiss him and send him on his way so that he could continue living the good life, did he? Well, at least the cop had realized that his suggestion would not be taken. The coward was probably barricading his home right now. Good, he hoped he was. He would enjoy killing Robert Morris. He could probably make him piss in his pants just by staring into his eyes. Enjoying the thought, Lacayo sat back and waited. Just a little while more and one more loose end would be tied up.

Chapter Eleven

Laurie gripped Jake's hand tightly in her own. She could feel the terrible fury slicing through him. To be betrayed by a fellow police officer, his superior, into the hands of a vicious sadist like Lacayo was unthinkable. The sight of Jake as they had found him in that filthy cabana flashed through her mind. Jake was not the only one enraged. As she had in the interrogation room in this very police station and later in the hospital, she knew without a doubt that she was capable of violence if given the opportunity to face Lacayo. But she also felt an intense need to protect Jake. He was recovering quickly, but he was in no shape to face the danger she knew awaited him if he were to find his enemy.

Sam stood before them both, silenced for a moment by the palpable emotional connection between his friend and Laurie. Jake was rigid. The anger coursing through him was visible. Sam also recognized the shimmer of sadness in his friend's strange silver eyes. Laurie held his hand in hers against her heart. Her big green eyes were stormy with anger and fear. As he watched them, he had a bittersweet feeling. He had never imagined that his friend would ever allow love into his life, and regardless of how strange the circumstances, he was glad that he had been wrong.

Putting aside the sentiment, he cleared his throat. "Jake, you can't just go off half cocked," he began.

"Morris is mine." It was not a question.

"I understand, man. I really do. But we have to do this by the book or it's all been for nothing." Sam knew he had to find a way to reason with Jake or the whole case could go up in smoke. He did not blame him for wanting his vengeance, but there was more at stake than Lacayo's life. Jake North deserved a life once this was over, and going rogue could cost him his career.

"Nothing?" Jake snarled back at Sam. "That bastard knew what Lacayo would do to me. He knew!" Pulling his hand from Laurie's, Jake slammed his fist against the nearest file cabinet. The punch sounded like thunder in the small office, and the impact had him recoiling in pain as his arm and ribs protested.

Worried, Laurie tried to calm him. "Please, Jake, let's think this through. You'll have your justice. We both will." Laurie reached up to touch his shoulder gently. "You're going to hurt yourself. Let's all stop for a moment and figure out the next step." Looking to Claire, she asked, "What do you think?"

Claire had been standing quietly, trying to get an image that might help. The last twenty-four hours had been stressful, and the images of Gruber's bloody body kept intruding into her thoughts. They were all tired and emotions were running high.

"Let's get something to eat. We're all running on adrenaline and coffee. I might be able to see something helpful if we can all sit together and regroup." She looked to Sam for support.

Nodding, he agreed. "We can get something decent a couple of blocks over at Casey's. I'll drive."

Holding his side, Jake took a deep breath and reluctantly nodded his agreement. He knew he had to reel in his emotions. Instinctively, he reached for Laurie and placed his hand at the small of her back. As they followed Claire and Sam out of the office, he leaned into her and kissed her temple. She tucked under his arm as if she had been doing so for years. Her warmth soothed the jagged edges of his anger. Morris and Lacayo would not escape his wrath, he thought to himself, but he would protect Laurie. He would not risk her safety. He would not have his heart ripped from his chest again.

They slipped into a red leather booth at the back of the pub. The perky hostess knew Sam by name and offered them all a bright smile as she took their orders. Once they had settled in, Jake addressed Claire.

"You've been right about everything up until now, Claire, so let's hear it. What do you see?" He looked at her expectantly.

She shook her head and smiled ruefully. "It doesn't exactly work like that. Let's all talk it out, step by step. All we know for sure is that Morris is involved with this whole mess. What will happen next and what should happen next are what we need to get to." Claire felt a familiar tension settle into her stomach. Absently she rubbed her middle and prayed that she would not misinterpret whatever images came to her and make a mistake that could cost someone their life.

Laurie saw the worry on Claire's face. She could only imagine the pressure she must feel. In the short time they had known each other, Laurie had learned that Claire was much more fragile than she seemed. She took a heavy burden of responsibility on her shoulders each time she shared her visions with those who were affected by what she saw. Laurie knew that she had Claire to thank for having Jake alive and sitting next to her in this cheery restaurant. She owed her more than she could ever hope to repay.

Reaching across the table, she grasped Claire's hand in hers and said, "You don't need to be afraid, Claire. You're not responsible for this mess. We are all going to figure this out together." She smiled and gave her new friend's hand a warm squeeze.

Touched by Laurie's understanding and compassion, Claire smiled warmly and felt the tension in her gut ease a little. "I just don't want to make a mistake."

"Trust yourself, Claire. We do." The reply came from Jake. He smiled at her as he said it. The smile changed his face from ruthlessly hard to devastatingly handsome. Claire could see how Laurie would have fallen for him under any circumstances. Warmed by his kindness, she smiled and nodded her acceptance. "You're a good man, Jake. Thank you."

She was not sure, but she thought he might have blushed a little at her words. Laurie beamed.

◐◯◑

Distracted by his own thoughts, Sam rubbed the side of the sweating glass of iced tea that the waitress had set before him. He was no psychic, but he knew Lacayo would go after Morris. Everything they knew about his criminal past told him that the man was a psychopath and a control freak. He would not be able to disappear and reenter the United States easily if Morris was alive to strike a deal and save his sorry ass by offering up the man whom so many law enforcement agencies had targeted unsuccessfully for so long.

With Morris and Jake out of the way, Lacayo could eventually reinvent himself, create a new identity, and return. Many criminals preferred to operate outside the United States, out of the grasp of the FBI or DEA, but in Lacayo's file Sam had seen a clear pattern. Lacayo always came back.

When he had asked for Jake's opinion on the risky behavior, Jake had stated simply that Lacayo believed that the United States was the only place in the western hemisphere where he could truly have the best of everything. The American dream was alive and well even in the dregs of society.

"He is going to New York to find Robert Morris. That we do know. We need to have Morris picked up and brought in quietly as soon as possible. We don't know who else in the department could be involved. These are your people, Jake." Sam looked over at Jake almost apologetically. "How do you suggest we proceed?"

"Linda De Marco," Jake replied. "She's the DEA agent I was working with. I checked her out and she's as clean as a whistle. I'll call her and ask her to pick up Morris immediately. Then he is mine." Grimly, he stared at Sam as if daring him to object.

Sam understood more than his friend believed. "Once the DEA has him, you can't just take him out, Jake. I wouldn't let you do it anyway. You're a cop. I won't let you throw that away." He squared his shoulders and thrust out his chin as if preparing for a brawl.

Jake stared at him for a few moments, looking every bit the street fighter that he was. It was Laurie who broke the tense silence.

She looked at Sam. "Thank you, Sam. You're an honorable and true friend." Before Jake could object, she turned to him and laid a hand on his beard roughened cheek. Her tender smile did not erase the pleading look in her eyes. "I have plans for you. I need you available for all of them. Jail just doesn't fit into those plans. Understand?" Her smile was all sugar.

"Jesus, Laurie." The wind went out of Jake's sails in a flash. What was he supposed to say to that? Plans? He had no doubt she could plan their next forty years without batting an eyelash. Shaking his head, he realized that he was going to make sure each one of those plans happened or he would die trying.

"We'll do this by the book then," he replied grimly, "but if he threatens Laurie, all bets are off."

It was worth it just to see the happiness in her eyes. Looking back over at Sam, he had to laugh. The man was beaming like a proud daddy. Even Claire was smiling, something she did not seem to do often.

"Alright, fine. Just stop looking at me like that, for the love of God." He pulled his phone from his pocket. "Let's get a hold of Agent De Marco."

◐○◑

Rene Lacayo considered himself a genius. After all, no one came from abject poverty and rose to be rich and powerful by being stupid. He had used his powerful intellect not only to shape successful business models for the trafficking of narcotics and prostitutes, but also to create an empire of legitimate business interests in Central America and the United States. Through layers of holding companies and fake identities, he had become a powerful investor in many global companies.

But he had also learned along the way that certain smaller businesses were just as lucrative, if not more so, than these huge conglomerates for someone like him. One of his many local businesses in New York that had proven to be a true gem was Guardian Security Systems. A home security company that had started small, Guardian had grown exponentially in the last ten years.

The clients of Guardian Security Systems believed that the owner was a nice old Italian man named Vincenzo Russo. They believed Vincenzo operated his family-owned business at his age to help put his grandchildren through college. While Vincenzo was an old man, he was neither nice nor Italian, and he had forgotten his real last name decades ago. He was actually Brazilian. Over twenty years ago, Lacayo had taken him into his organization when the crime boss had bought his way out of a Brazilian jail. Vincenzo had been one of Lacayo's cellmates in that piss hole. He had recognized the drug lord immediately when they brought him in. Anyone who ran drugs or prostitutes in Rio de Janeiro knew Lacayo, though at the time he was known by a different name.

Vincenzo knew opportunity when he saw it. It amazed him that someone so feared was such a physically small man. It did not take a genius to see that he would need protection inside the soiled jail walls that surrounded them. So Vincenzo had offered to provide that service. Lacayo had simply stared at him for a few moments in silence. He seemed to be contemplating whether or not to kill the brawny man before him. Vincenzo felt the sweat run down his back as he waited for what he knew could be his death sentence. Thankfully, Lacayo had accepted the offer. From that moment on, no one dared to get near Lacayo without his permission. Vincenzo was not smart or rich, but his reputation as a vicious killer served him well in prison.

A few days later, the prison guards came to escort Lacayo from the filthy holding cell with great deference. Outside, two well-dressed men awaited to take their boss back to his mansion in the mountains. Before he could step outside the hell of that filthy cell and forget him forever, Vincenzo had yelled out to Lacayo, "Do you forget your friends so quickly?"

Lacayo had turned and stared at him with the coldest, blackest eyes he had ever seen. For a moment, Vincenzo feared he had made a serious mistake.

"Come." That was all Lacayo said. Vincenzo followed him out of that cell and had served him well since. He had also made himself and his family very rich in the process.

While it was true that he did use his share of the profits from Guardian to educate his sons and later their children, he also dictated their careers and their lives. His many children and grandchildren formed a strategic contingent of lawyers, accountants, technicians for the security company, and simple thugs and drug runners. Each was placed in the organization based on their intellectual capacity and talents. Vincenzo was not very educated and could barely read or write, but he was an amazing strategist.

Years ago, on the advice of one of his sons, one of the lawyers, Vincenzo had earned the trust and respect of many of New York's public servants by offering discounts to the police and fire departments of the city, as well as to military families in the area. He gave excellent service and occasionally passed along useful information that his boys picked up while installing alarm systems. He was a model citizen. It all added up to a very useful, growing client base year to year.

Along with the small profit Lacayo received from Guardian, he also had access, via modern technology, to the security systems, property blueprints, and alarm security codes for all homes and buildings that Guardian Security Systems serviced. Vincenzo's boys always installed a few extra surveillance gadgets unbeknownst to their customers. He often logged on and watched video of the private lives of the very cops who were out looking for him. He knew everything about them, how many children they had, whether or not they owned pets, how many times a week they got laid, and all the other dirty little habits they thought they hid from the outside world.

He laughed as he now watched Robert Morris rush frantically through his home, locking down every door and window, setting the alarm system, and finally sitting on his couch with a loaded shotgun in one hand and his automatic pistol in the other. What a loser Morris had turned out to be. He had no clue when or how Lacayo would come for him. Did he plan to sit there for the rest of his life waiting?

He almost regretted that he could not afford to play a longer cat and mouse game with Morris. Bitterly, he reminded himself that Jake North was alive. The DEA would eventually find out who had ratted North out, and that would lead them here to Morris. By that time, he would have taken care of them both and would be sipping champagne in Venezuela.

He shut down the program and closed the laptop. He lay back down on Myrna's flowered, frilly sheets and thought of the fun that awaited him across the street later that night. The images made him hard as stone. Giggling, he began masturbating to the thought of Morris' blood pouring from his body, hot and wet.

Linda De Marco hung up the phone and stared blankly at the empty wall across from her desk as she collected her thoughts for a moment. Her conversation with Jake North and Chief Sam Hollinger of the City of Miami Police Department not only explained the fiasco of a few nights ago, but also revealed who the mole inside the joint agency operation was. She disliked Morris on principle but found no joy in knowing that a cop, any cop, had sold his soul and his fellow officers out for money.

It was a deal with the devil that could cost him his life if North was right. She picked up the phone again and called her counterpart back in the New York office. They needed to pick up Robert Morris before Lacayo got to him and disappeared again.

Laurie was drained. Both she and Jake had spoken little on the ride home. Although they believed Lacayo to be on his way to New York, Jake had insisted that police protection be continued until the case was closed. Sam had given his word, and somewhere out in the darkness his people stood guard over Laurie's house. Once inside, Jake moved with military efficiency from room to room, checking locks and closing curtains to block out prying eyes.

Laurie watched him move around her home and could not help thinking how natural it seemed for him to be there.

It was strangely comforting to see him taking care of her safety. And God, he was beautiful. The dark hair, the strong lines of his body, and those strange, beautiful eyes would make any woman melt, she thought wryly.

He moved a little easier than before, which she hoped meant he was healing quickly. Sam had insisted the doctor come to the police station and bandage him up again. He was smart enough not to ask what had happened to the original bandages, she thought with a slight blush. Jake's face was also less swollen, and she was beginning to see what he really looked like beneath the bruising. He had a strong jaw and a sharp nose. The dark brows above his extraordinary eyes only seemed to make them glitter more. The bruises were lightening to a sickly green color, but even that could not make him unattractive to her.

As if feeling her eyes on him, he turned to her.

"Is anything wrong?" His voice was still rough and low, but he did not seem to have sandpaper in his throat anymore.

When she did not respond right away, he started toward her with a worried look on his face. She met him halfway, stood on tiptoe, and wrapped her arms around his neck, careful not to squeeze him too hard.

"So much is wrong," she sighed.

Jake held her and once again felt guilt wash through his soul. He had brought death and fear into her life, and she did not deserve any of it.

"I'm sorry, Laurie. All this fear and sorrow that I've brought to your door is unfair, and I wish I could take it all away, but I can't." He kissed the top of her head gently.

Laurie pulled her head back and stared into his anguished eyes. She kissed him softly but pulled back again when he would have deepened the kiss.

"I won't lie to you, Jake. I am afraid. I'm afraid for myself, but I'm also afraid for you." She reached up and brushed his midnight hair back from his face. "I am heartbroken over Dorothy. I keep thinking of how much pain she must have felt." Tears welled up in her eyes.

"I promise…" Jake began.

She laid her hand gently over his mouth. "I know. Shut up and let me finish."

He gave her a small smile. "Yes, ma'am."

"All of that is true. But it is also true that I am grateful. Despite this entire horrible, inexplicable mess, I am so grateful because I found you, Jake. I found the love of my life, and I will not have you blame yourself anymore." Her green eyes flashed fire as she buried her hands in his hair and pulled him closer, bringing him nose to nose with her. "You didn't bring this to my life, Jake. We were destined to find each other. I believe that. If Lacayo's men had not taken you to the Coral Reef that day, I believe we would have met some other day, some other way, maybe under more normal circumstances, maybe on a plane or in a restaurant. But he did what he did, and fate bestowed a kindness on us both."

“A kindness? How can you call all of this a kindness?” There was pain in his voice, but he tightened his arms around her.

“Yes, a kindness,” she whispered as her eyes bored into his. “If you had died, our chance would have been taken from us, Jake. But fate took me to a beach in the middle of a workday and woke me up just in time to see you, even if only at a distance. Fate allowed our souls to recognize each other, and under impossible circumstances we found each other and our love again before evil could take you from me. I will thank God every day of my life, of our life together, for that.”

Jake felt an enormous crushing weight being lifted off his heart. He knew in the very center of his being that she was right. Nothing else mattered. After a lifetime of solitude and hurt, God or fate or whatever she wanted to call the divine being that he suddenly found himself believing in, had seen fit to give him the one thing he thought he would never have, love. Whether he deserved it or not no longer mattered to him.

Jake took Laurie’s mouth with a gentleness that made the tears in her eyes fall between their lips. Over and over again he kissed her softly, starting with her mouth and then traveling over to her eyes, cheeks, nose, and back again. Never had she felt so loved and so cherished.

“I love you,” she breathed against his lips.

“I love you, Laurie.”

As he whispered her name, he deepened the kiss, tightening his hold and pulling her flush against his body. She felt the size and warmth of him through her clothes, and her body tightened in response. A passionate heat, wilder than she had ever known, rose in her with a sudden desperation. Pushing him gently backward, she managed to get him sprawled back on the couch without taking her mouth or hands off him.

With her hands tangled in the black silk of his hair, she struggled for control. Her tongue drove into his mouth, and she heard him moan as she straddled him and rubbed herself against his erection. She felt feverish with the need to feel him, to have him inside her.

She tried to remove his shirt, but her hands were shaking so hard she could not get the buttons. "Take it off... now." The order was almost a growl.

Buttons flew as Jake released her long enough to rip the offending shirt open. Her murmur of approval, as her hands met naked flesh, had him pulling apart the pretty embroidered blouse she wore. He heard more buttons hit the floor and, in the back of his mind, promised himself that he would buy her a new blouse soon. He ripped his mouth from hers for a moment and took in the sight of her full breasts covered in sheer black lace. He allowed himself one more second to commit the sight to memory before taking her nipple into his mouth, lace and all, with the hunger of a man starved too long.

At the feel of the wet heat of his tongue on her nipple through the sheer material, Laurie arched back in pleasure. She relished the feel of his large hands molding her breasts to his mouth as he lavished attention on them both. When she felt him remove the bra and take her flesh into his mouth, she was so aroused she almost came.

Jake could feel how close Laurie was to release. Almost regretfully, he released her breasts and brought his hands down to the snap of her jeans. With a quick twist of his fingers, he had them open and unzipped. He wanted her naked. He wanted to be inside her when she peaked. He wanted to watch her when the pleasure washed over her.

"Up, baby... get up so we can get these off you." He gripped her waist and lifted her away from him until she was standing before him. Her face was a study in passion. He took in the sight of her long brown hair, soft and mussed around her face, her full lips red and swollen from his kisses, and her beautiful breasts heaving with desire. It felt like fire was running through his veins as he stared up at her. His erection throbbed painfully in response.

"Now, angel, I can't wait much more." He grunted out the order as he half pushed his pants down. His erection freed, he felt as though he would explode if he did not get inside her right now.

Laurie stared at him with a hunger that made him shudder. There was a wildness in her eyes that he had not seen before. The thought that the fear and pain of the last few days might have something to do with it crossed his mind. He knew what an adrenaline rush could do to you once you came down from it. Feeling a little selfish, he rasped out, "Baby, why don't we go to the bedroom? You can lie down…"

"Do you hurt?" she interrupted quickly. Eyes half shut with desire, Laurie struggled to control her urgency.

"No. I just…" Whatever he had been about to say was cut off abruptly as she began pulling down her pants slowly, revealing a pair of sheer black lace panties that matched the sexy bra he had thrown somewhere. Jake swallowed hard as she kicked the jeans away and slowly lifted the lacy sides of the delicate panties away from her smooth, round hips. He watched as her elegant fingers began a slow, torturous slide down those killer tan legs. Once she had the panties off, she gave them a sassy twirl on her finger and, with a wicked smile, tossed them at him.

Without a word, he caught them, brought them up to his face, and smelled his woman's desire on the damp lace. Never breaking eye contact, he threw them aside and reached out his hand.

Something primitive was let loose inside Laurie as she watched him rub the lace that was still warm from her body against his face. The act brought an almost painful lash of desire that coursed through her, making her tremble. Her breasts ached for his touch.

Taking his hand, she allowed him to drag her back down to straddle him. He was huge and rock hard between her legs. The feel of his body beneath hers was like lightning in her veins. For the first time in her life, she felt completely free. She relished knowing that he was hers to command.

"I can't wait, Jake," her voice low and shaky as she struggled to position him between her legs. "Please, I need you now!"

"Easy, baby, easy." Jake moved his hand between her legs and positioned himself at the entrance of his own personal paradise. She was so tight he almost came there and then. The heat coming from her body burned him as nothing else could. He could feel how close he was, and he tamped down his need with a clenched jaw.

"Don't move. I mean it." His breath was harsh and his heart beat like a drum in his chest. Grabbing Laurie by the waist, he looked up at her. When their eyes met, he rasped, "I love you." Then he pulled her down for a brutal kiss and plunged himself into her silken heat.

As Jake filled her body and plundered her mouth, Laurie came apart. Pleasure snaked through her body in shock after shock of electric sensations. Arching in his hold, Laurie screamed Jake's name as the orgasm tore through her.

Hearing her scream out his name as she shook in his embrace, Jake could not hold back any longer. Grinding her down against him, he felt his release explode from him and rush deep into the woman he loved. Shuddering, he tried to hold on as she milked him with the tiny aftershocks of her orgasm. He held her against his heaving chest as she slowly melted against him.

He knew he needed to get her to bed. She was spent, and tomorrow would be no easier than today for her. But for now, he allowed himself the pleasure of holding his woman, naked and satisfied, in his arms.

Chapter Twelve

Robert Morris sat in his darkened living room with only the muted images of a Yankees game lighting the shadows around him. After confirming that Marie and the boys were safe at her mother's home in Connecticut and the adrenaline rush of bunkering down had passed, semi-rational thought returned. He realized he could not stay here forever, but until he had worked out a plan, he could not go to work. He had called to tell Lucy that he was ill and would be staying home for a couple of days. He asked her not to call unless it was a real emergency. His second in command could handle things until he knew what his next step was.

He had no reason to think that North had a clue about anything, at least not yet. Lacayo was the immediate problem. North could be dealt with once the imminent danger of Lacayo's capture was eliminated. Afterwards, he could find a way to make North out to be the leak in the department. He just needed to think. He just needed to figure things out, that's all.

Loosening the death grip he had on his pistol, he reached over and served himself another shot of whisky. Just to settle his nerves a bit, he told himself. His hands shook as he brought the glass to his lips, so he served himself another one for good measure. The burn of the whisky going down his throat felt good. It reminded him he was alive and, by God, he was going to damn well stay that way!

He looked around his fancy living room, seeing menacing shadows in the gloomy light. Feeling afraid again, he imagined Lacayo looming up from behind every chair and table. "Stop it!" he yelled out loud. The sound of his own voice unsettled him even more. It was too quiet. The silence was making him jumpy. Using the remote, he put the sound back on and felt better.

Hell, he assured himself, he had a top-of-the-line security system, didn't he? That shit Lacayo wasn't just going to walk in on him unannounced. No sir. It had been a while since he had been on a stakeout, but this would do him good. It had been a mistake to let himself get so soft, he realized now. Once this was over, he was going to start riding with his men once a week. Get back to the beginning. That's what he would do. He would put this nightmare behind him and start fresh. Yes sir, fresh!

The tears rolled down his face as he tried to force a grin and served himself another shot.

Lacayo watched Morris on the small screen he held on his lap inside his hiding place. It had been so simple, really. He was able to disarm the alarm from his laptop but program the lights on the panel to remain unchanged. That was a little extra Vincenzo Russo's clients had no idea their security systems came with. A very useful little trick indeed.

All he had to do now was let the miserable son of a bitch drink himself to sleep and the party would begin. He would have preferred to take him down now, but he knew he was no match for Morris physically. The thought irritated him, but he shook it off. The important thing was that he was going to kill the pig the way all pigs deserved to be slaughtered, by gutting him. He covered his mouth to stifle the giggle that rose up. It would not do to alert Morris. Only by making a sound would he give his position away.

Two hours and several shots later, Robert Morris nodded off just as the Yankees won. As the players ran onto the field to swing their pitcher onto their shoulders, a shadow moved silently from the closet beneath the stairwell. An hour ago, the pistol had slipped from his loose grip onto the sofa cushion next to him. As he tried unsuccessfully to keep his eyes open, he had no clue that his enemy was standing behind him, having been inside his home all night, waiting for the right moment to strike him down.

Agents from the New York DEA's office sped through the residential streets of Morris's neighborhood in a nondescript gray sedan. Agent Linda de Marco had given clear orders. They were to get to Morris now and arrest him, but to be low key about their entrance. No sirens sounded. No lights flashed as they drove toward the elegant corner house. The two men inside the vehicle looked at each other as they approached the police chief's home. They parked across the street and waited a moment to scan the area. Nothing moved along the street.

The house was completely dark, but the car registered to the chief was in the driveway. They radioed the team of agents stationed behind the home one street back.

"We're here. No movement on the street and the house is dark. We're going to go ahead and knock, but we'll keep silent radio contact just in case this goes south. Please keep radio silence."

"Roger that." The static-filled voice of their counterpart came in, and then the equipment went silent.

"This must be one major shit-show for us to be arresting the Chief of Police," the agent behind the wheel said as he checked his weapon.

The second agent grunted. "Yeah, well, let's just make sure we don't get splattered." Pulling her weapon, the woman stepped from the car and followed her partner toward Morris's front door.

"Right behind you, buddy."

◐○◑

Lacayo stood silently behind Morris with an evil smile on his face. He had decided to slice his throat, but not deep enough to kill him immediately. He wanted his prey to get a good look at him before he died. He would finish him through the heart, his favorite cut. He knew he would be bathed in blood, but that was part of the joy of the kill. He always took the precaution of wearing protective gear. He was hard just imagining the hot, wet splash of his victim's blood spraying out as he pulled the knife out of the man's chest.

With a manic giggle, he reached over and, in seconds, had grabbed a fistful of Morris's hair and pulled his head back violently. The wicked knife slashed across the pig's thick throat, and the feel of it up his arm was delicious.

Morris instinctively brought his hands to his throat, squealing indeed like a pig. He felt the hot rush of his own blood spurting through his fingers. Wide awake, his first terrified thought was how it was possible that Lacayo was there, inside his house. The second was the horrible truth that he would not live to find out.

Lacayo jumped over the couch and immediately slashed at the slippery hands, cutting deep enough to touch bone and render the hands useless.

Then he allowed himself the luxury of staring into Morris's eyes. The terror he saw there made him giddy. The gasping squeals were music to his ears. The pig looked so shocked to see him there, sitting on his coffee table, ruining the expensive rug beneath his feet with his own blood.

He began giggling uncontrollably as he raised the knife again, this time aiming for the gut. He knew Morris would be in excruciating pain from the blow but would not die immediately.

Before he could strike the blow, a loud rapping came from the front door. Distracted, he did not see Morris raise his foot in time and was rammed back by the large man's desperate kick. The table flipped beneath him and he crashed to the floor.

"No!" he screamed. He jumped unsteadily to his feet.

Morris stood before him, bathed red in blood, looking like a demon from hell. But terror still shone on his face. He turned and tried to stumble toward the door.

Lacayo started to go after him when he heard the voice on the other side of the door yelling, "Chief Morris, DEA, please open the door!"

Rage boiled up in him. If he stayed, he would be caught. Once again, he had let his taste for blood deny him the opportunity to watch the final kill. Almost blind with hate and fury, he turned and headed for his escape route. Even the pleasure of watching Morris bleed out was not enough to risk capture. As he ran, he tried to console himself with the idea that Morris would bleed to death in minutes.

◐◯◑

It was three in the morning when Jake's phone started vibrating on the night table. Awake in an instant, he grabbed it, hoping to avoid waking Laurie. She was sleeping peacefully in his favorite position, with her adorable backside pressed up against him. He saw on the phone's small screen that it was Linda de Marco calling.

"North here."

"Detective North, de Marco here. I'm sorry about the late hour, but I figured you would want to know immediately." She was all business as usual.

"Yes, thank you. What happened with Morris? Do you have him in custody?" The need to confront his former boss was a raw burn in his gut.

"When the agents arrived at Chief Morris's home, they had to break down the door. They found him bleeding out on the floor."

"Lacayo got to him first. Shit!" He knew Lacayo's work firsthand and could imagine the scene the agents had found. "Any chance I won the lottery and you're going to tell me you got Lacayo?"

After a moment of silence, Linda responded, "Morris was still alive, just barely. That seems to be an issue for our man. He never quite finishes, if you know what I mean." It was a rare flash of humor.

"Huh." The grunt was all Agent de Marco was getting from him. He could not find any humor in the situation.

"Anyway, Morris confessed, in very few bloody words, before he died. Apparently, as our guys were breaking down the front door, Lacayo slipped through a window and got away before the second team swung around from the back street. We followed a trail of blood to the neighbor's house across the street. We found the poor woman butchered and stiff as a board. We have locked down the area, but nothing yet." There was a grim tone in her voice now. Lacayo had escaped the clutches of the DEA on more than one occasion. That was what had brought the multi-agency operation about in the first place.

"Thanks for letting me know. I'd fly up now, but you and I know that if you don't have him in the next few hours, he will be long gone. He and I have unfinished business. I'll be in touch later today, Agent." He snapped the phone shut in anger.

"What happened? Did they arrest Morris?" Laurie's voice was groggy with sleep.

Turning back to her, he lay down next to her and wrapped his arms around her waist from behind. Spooning her small shape, he debated for a moment whether or not to tell her the truth. He could always tell her tomorrow and let her sleep in peace.

Sensing the tension in him, Laurie came wide awake. She turned her face and saw the emotions flickering across his face. "Tell me. I need to know. We're together now." Reaching back to stroke his cheek with her hand, she repeated, "Together."

He stared down at her lovely face. She was a tough broad, his Laurie. That was good because she was right. They would be together until death did them part as soon as he could get a ring on her finger, but he could not watch her night and day. He was a cop, and if they were going to share a life together, he knew he could have no secrets from her. It was secrets that destroyed many of his fellow officers' marriages.

"Morris is dead. Lacayo got to him first. He got away for now." Short and sweet. There was no reason for her to have to imagine how Morris had died. He felt no pity for the son of a bitch. It was nothing short of what would have been his own fate if Laurie had not found him. That did not mean he wanted her to have those terrible images in her mind, though.

"What do we do now?" She sounded calm, but he could hear the fear in her voice and feel the slight tremor that went through her body.

"If we are lucky, they will have the bastard in a few hours. If not, if he is smart, he will try to leave the country. I wish I could promise you that they will get him, Laurie, but the truth is the man has several identities and is a true chameleon. It would not be the first time he slips out of the country." He did not give voice to his belief that Lacayo would come back for him, regardless of the insanity of the move.

"But at least he'd be gone. What if he comes back?" She turned in his arms and held him tightly, pressing her face against his neck.

Jake turned her face back up to his and kissed her softly. He said the words he wished he believed were true, hoping to buy her at least one more night of peace. "It's the least likely scenario. It would be stupid for him to come back. Everyone, even the FBI, will be looking for him now." In his heart he knew his words were just wishful thinking, but he could not bear to worry her. Kissing her again, he whispered at least one truth to her. "I promise I'll keep you safe, Laurie."

She kissed him back, hard. "I'll do everything in my power to keep you safe, Jake. I promise you that."

He looked down at her, warm and beautiful against him, and wondered yet again how he had ever gotten so lucky as to end up with a woman as amazing as Laurie in his arms. He would protect her with his life if he had to. Bringing his mouth down to hers, he kissed her gently, urging her to let him in. Eagerly, she opened her mouth and met his tongue with hers in a deep, soul-shattering kiss. All the anger and fear faded as he lost himself in her, savoring the feel of her soft curves against his now rock-hard body. He poured all the love he felt into his kiss. The world and its ugliness disappeared and there was only Laurie. She was the only thing that mattered, and he needed to watch her come apart in his arms again.

Laurie felt wave after wave of heat wash through her as Jake lovingly kissed every inch of her body, stopping to pay special attention to her straining breasts and then working his way down her stomach. He gently kissed the skin above the simple cotton panties she wore and then slowly pulled them down her legs. He caressed her thighs with his large, calloused hands, his lips following each touch until he had her open before him. The look of desire on his face made her lift her hips toward him with a low moan. She felt dizzy and weak as he lowered his mouth between her legs and began kissing and gently sucking the center of her passion until she was bucking wildly beneath him.

Jake held her hips down as his tongue took her over the edge. Looking up, he saw her as she thrashed and moaned while he brought her through her pleasure. A fine sheen of sweat covered his body and his erection throbbed almost painfully. Watching Laurie go wild under him was the hottest thing he had ever seen. When he felt her collapse bonelessly into the mattress, he came quickly to his knees and pulled her thighs over them. The look of sensual pleasure on her face almost undid him. She lay sprawled and open before him, soft and disheveled. Feeling his release tightening his lower body, he could not hold off any longer and desperately thrust into her sweet, wet center. Groaning his pleasure, he began thrusting into her, almost mad with his need.

Laurie looked up at Jake and, incredibly, felt passion rise again. Thrust for thrust, she met him until they were both breathless and wild. The second orgasm came upon her suddenly, arching her back like a bow off the bed. Crying out his name, she came as she dug her nails heedlessly into his arms.

Feeling the sharp nails bite his skin as she came around him drove Jake over the edge. Losing control, he came violently, shuddering and groaning her name. After what seemed like an endless release, he fell over her, unable to hold himself up any longer.

The only sound in the room was their harsh breathing. Knowing he must be crushing her, Jake tried to move off her.

"No! Not yet," she begged, clutching her arms around his slick back. "Stay inside me just a little longer. It's such a beautiful feeling." She stroked her hands down his back and kissed his shoulder.

Her words undid him once again. Closing his eyes against the emotion, he stayed where he was, inside his woman. After a moment, using his arms to spare her some of his weight, he lifted his head and faced her. "Laurie..."

"I know, love. I love you too."

The whisper filled his heart with peace. He knew he had to call Sam to give him the update on Morris, but he held on to the joy he felt for just a little longer in the darkness.

Sam hung up after speaking with Jake. It was four thirty in the morning. He was tempted to turn on the light, but he did not want to wake Trish. Sliding his feet into his old loafers, he gently eased out of bed and headed toward the kitchen. He wanted a drink, but he would settle for some warm milk. He had never allowed himself to self-medicate with alcohol and he was not about to start now.

He had a bad feeling in his gut. Logic dictated that they would either find Lacayo tonight or he would be out of the country in a day or two. If the man was smart, he would run like hell. But the man got off on pain and retribution. It was his Achilles heel.

Nothing would ever erase the memory of Jake lying in a pool of blood and piss in that abandoned cabana. A man capable of something like that was not logical. Logic would dictate that you kill your enemy swiftly and efficiently.

A psychopath like Rene Lacayo was not logical. He was just deadly.

As Sam had his warm milk in his kitchen across town, Claire stood in her kitchen petting Moses, taking comfort from his grateful purring. She knew Lacayo had escaped again. She had waited until she felt that Laurie and Jake had been notified and were awake before calling. No need to be the one to wake them with the bad news. Better they hear it from official sources first, even if they did believe in her abilities.

Laurie spoke with her first but did not really know much beyond the fact that Morris was dead and that there was a manhunt going on for Lacayo. Claire knew she needed to speak with Jake but had hesitated to worry Laurie by making her think she was hiding something from her. She was about to say goodnight when Jake had come on the line.

"Claire, if we're lucky, they'll catch him. Even if he leaves the country, I'll always be looking over my shoulder. If it were just me, I could live with that." There was a heavy pause. "I can't put Laurie in harm's way like that. I can't leave her, Claire. Not ever. Even if I wanted to. I need your help. Please."

She knew what it took for any cop to ask for her kind of help, even when they believed her. She had to decide. If she helped him in an official capacity, she knew it would not end with this case, even if he did not know it. Could she even consider such a thing? Was her sanity something she felt strong enough to risk?

"Claire, are you there?" Jake sounded concerned.

"Yes, I'm here." She thought of Laurie, of the man asking for her help. She thought of Sam and Amanda. They were all good people and, whether or not they felt the same, she thought of them as friends now. She could not abandon her friends.

"Claire!" Jake's low voice was now more urgent.

"Yes, Jake, I'll help you. I'll be there once the sun's up." She had hung up the phone and had been holding on to Moses for dear life since then. She tried to see how it would all end, but all she could see was her own fear. Was she afraid for her friends or was she just afraid for herself? Eventually, she was honest enough with herself to acknowledge that it was both.

Rubbing her chin against Moses, she spoke her fear out loud. "Oh, Moses, am I stepping into my own personal hell again?" Moses loving purr was the only response.

The next morning, bright and early, Sam, Claire, and Jake sat around Laurie's kitchen table as she fussed over them. She had busied herself making an enormous breakfast for them all to keep her mind focused on anything but the thought of Lacayo coming back for Jake. She set the steaming mugs of coffee before her friends and sat down. Instinctively, Jake snagged her by the waist and pulled her down for a kiss as he murmured his thanks. Looking down at him tenderly, Laurie wondered how love could feel so wonderful and squeeze your heart so painfully at the same time.

Taking a sip of coffee and gathering his thoughts, Jake looked around the table at the people who sat with him. They were here because they were willing to put themselves in harm's way for Laurie. No, he corrected himself mentally, for them both. He could never repay them for their loyalty, he knew that, but he swore he would do his best to make sure that they were safe. He had never had a family before, but as he gazed at his friend Sam, the very brave Claire Murphy, and finally Laurie, he thought he might now understand what it meant to have one.

Breaking his sentimental train of thought, he started by sharing what Linda de Marco and he had discussed when they had spoken again at six in the morning. At first, she had been a bit elusive about the details involving the DEA's next step. He was, after all, a police officer, not an employee of her agency.

He realized that the only way to get through to her and gain her trust was to tell her the whole truth. There was no jerking Agent de Marco around if you wanted to get anywhere with her. It took a while, longer than pleased him, because she had put him on hold to make some phone calls and to pull records on Claire's work with the Cardozo Police Department. Even after all that, she had continued to hold back and stand her ground. It was not until he told her about Laurie that she changed her attitude toward him.

He told her the whole convoluted story. He confessed that he loved Laurie with all his heart. Embarrassed to be saying it all to a relative stranger, it took him a while to admit that he had finally found love and could not live with the possibility that Laurie could be taken away from him.

Agent de Marco had forced him to sit through minutes of silence. He knew she was still there from the humming of the computer somewhere close to her. After what seemed a lifetime, she told him that he could check his email. He would find not only the classified reports on the entire investigation up to the minute, but that he would also be kept apprised of the ongoing manhunt in an official capacity. He was to await his orders. He had never imagined a hard-ass like de Marco would be a sucker for a love story, but it was his stroke of luck.

"What it comes down to is that most of the agencies involved believe that Lacayo will lay low but will try to make his way out of the country as soon as possible. Neither Sam nor I, or for that matter Agent de Marco, are convinced. The man is a psychopath, and I'm the one who got away." He swung his gaze to Laurie. "I wish you would listen to me and let me get you into protective custody until we can finish this."

Laurie's response was firm and clear. "I will not be kept away from you or from Dorothy's funeral. I will see my friend laid to rest, and I will not have you taken from me."

"Laurie, do you think I want to be away from you? You know I don't! That doesn't change the fact that I'm going crazy worrying that this psycho could grab you to get to me."

The worry in Jake's eyes was enough to make Claire speak up.

"Jake, all I can tell you is what I feel. I believe that Lacayo is coming for you, but I don't see how or when yet. Maybe he doesn't even know that yet. Perhaps there is a way that we can draw him out. I feel he has lost what little control he has left. We might be able to use that to our advantage."

"Let's hear it, Murphy." Sam leaned in eagerly.

Dorothy's funeral preparations went ahead as planned. The obituary was beautifully written by Laurie, and she spared no expense on the arrangements. Her friend had loved excess, and that was how her life would be celebrated. Tears filled Laurie's eyes as she smiled at the thought. She had notified Dorothy's many friends throughout the day. She was amazed at how many organizations Dorothy volunteered with. She cried with many of Dorothy's friends over the phone. So many people loved her. They were all held together by the common bond of that love. Dorothy had been an extraordinary person and an irreplaceable friend.

Three men claimed to be her boyfriend. It took her until the third conversation to realize that they all really were aware of the other two men in her life. None of them cared. They had loved Dorothy whether she loved another or not. One of them had told her that to expect a heart as big as

Dorothy's to make room for only one person was selfish. Selfish indeed. How amazing.

She told Jake the story, and when he started grinning wickedly, she pointed an accusing finger at him. "Don't you dare think that my admiration for Dorothy and her... her friends means that I believe it applies to your heart, Detective!" She grabbed him by the front of his T-shirt and dragged him down for a kiss as he laughed. "Your heart is all mine and only mine. You got that?"

Turning serious, he gathered her up in his arms and whispered, "My heart only just started beating in that hospital room when you came into my life, Laurie. It will beat only for you until the day it stops altogether." It was a promise.

Moved beyond words, Laurie said softly, "I love you, Jake."

"And I love you, angel." Then he shocked her by going down on one knee. With her hands in his larger ones, he looked up into her emerald eyes and said softly, "Laurie James, would you do me the honor of saving my life every day for the next fifty years or so? I can't live, I can't breathe without you, baby. I can't imagine a world in which I would wake without you in my arms ever again. Please, angel, marry me." His silver eyes pierced her soul, reflecting hope and fear and love…such love.

Laurie's heart filled to bursting. Weeping tears of joy, she knelt down before him. "Amor mio." The words of her mother's native language flowed easily from her as she held his face in her hands tenderly. In her heart she thanked God again for the love she had found in the midst of so much loss. "You are my heart. I would die inside if you were to leave me, Jake. Nothing could make me happier than to be your wife!" The joy reflected in his eyes was the most beautiful sight she had ever seen. Filled with more love than she had ever thought possible, she brought his face to hers for a soul-shaking kiss.

Between kisses, Jake promised her that as soon as this was over, they would marry. Showering him with kisses, she just kept saying "yes" over and over again like a giddy schoolgirl.

Holding her face in his hands, he stopped her and stared down at her. "I want a proper wedding, Laurie, with all the bells and whistles. You deserve that. I want your family there. I hope they'll like me, but I'm telling you now that either way they are going to have to get used to me. They are going to have to put up with me for a very, very long time." He said it fiercely, but she could sense the insecurity underneath the intensity.

Laurie knew her family would love him. All they would need to see is the love shining in his eyes as he held her. "They are going to love you, Jake, and you're going to love them. I promise."

He held her tightly and swore that it would all be over soon. "We'll go pick out a ring and you'll not take it off that lovely finger," he grinned. "Those lawyers and judges will know you belong to me from now on."

"Always." They sealed their promises to each other with long kisses that led to gentle lovemaking as the sun set on the horizon.

Chapter Thirteen

Two days later Laurie fussed with the long double strand of pearls she wore over the tailored black sheath that hugged her curves. Jake watched her in the mirror as he shaved. She looked beautiful and elegant in the designer dress that was demure and sexy as hell at the same time. Add in the sexy high-heeled black pumps, he thought to himself, and a man had a hard time keeping his tongue from hanging out of his mouth. He watched her jump as thunder rolled through the sky. Drying off his face, he walked toward her where she paced in front of the bed they had just shared. He grabbed her and held her. "It's going to be okay, Laurie."

"Is it?" She gazed at him desperately. "Promise me, Jake. Promise me that nothing is going to happen to you. I couldn't bear it. I couldn't." She cried out as she held her arms out to him.

Claire had seen the vision of Jake being shot at Dorothy's funeral. She had been unable, however, to see how it all ended. "All I can do is tell you what I see. It's not set in stone. As they say in Cardozo, Guerra avisada no mata soldados…a war that is announced kills no soldiers." That was all the hope she had been able to give Laurie.

"I promise you that nothing and no one is going to keep me from you, Laurie." Jake tried to ease her fears. "We're ready for him. I need to know that you're okay, that you can handle this. Please, angel." What he did not say was that he did not know how he was going to keep it together. Just the thought of losing her put his emotions into a tailspin. He was barely hanging on to his sanity as it was, but he knew that they had to see the plan through or they would never have a moment of peace. They would be living constantly looking over their shoulders. That was something he just was not willing to do.

Taking a deep breath, Laurie tried to pull herself together. "I can't believe it is raining. Dorothy would have hated that. She loved sunshine above all else. It was why she moved to Miami, you know."

Knowing that the change of subject was a way to distract herself from her worries, Jake followed her lead. "Well, Miami is famous for its afternoon showers. You always say she had a flair for the dramatic. Nothing is more dramatic than thunder and rain at a funeral."

"You're right, of course. There is that, isn't there?" She smiled weakly at him, but he knew that the stranglehold she had on those pearls was a sign of her terror.

He wished for the thousandth time that he did not have to put her through this. He acknowledged for the thousandth time that there was no other way. This was the plan Claire believed would work, and he had learned to trust in Claire. He only prayed that there were no mistakes. A mistake could cost him everything.

"Go on now. I'll meet you there soon," he said gently.

Amanda Tavares dressed more conservatively than was her habit. She was, after all, going to a funeral. She looked at herself in the full-length mirror in dissatisfaction. It was a lovely black suit, of course, but so plain and somber. It just was not her style. It certainly was not Dorothy's style either. She had been Dorothy's hair stylist since Laurie had hired her. Against her advice, Dorothy would make Amanda change her hair color so often that even she lost track of the particular mix of dyes sometimes. Regardless of her less than traditional tastes, Amanda had loved Dorothy dearly. The woman had loved her dear cousin like a daughter, after all. Who could help loving someone as generous and vibrant as Dorothy?

Max wandered in looking for his cuff links. She smiled as she watched him rummage through his drawers. He was not exactly the most organized person in the world. She knew where they were, of course, but waited a moment before coming to his aid. She took in his handsome face and sexy, broad shoulders in the pressed dress shirt for a moment.

God, she loved this man!

"They are in my jewelry box, amor."

"Thanks, babe." He came over to the vanity table near her and found them just where she said. He glanced up and saw her worrying her lower lip with her teeth. "What's wrong, sweetheart?"

"Dorothy would just hate this suit, don't you think? She'd want color. She'd want us all to bring color to her farewell party." She glanced at him hesitantly. "I wouldn't want to embarrass Laurie or you, but it just doesn't feel right."

Max smiled warmly at his wife. "I think you're absolutely right. You'd never embarrass me, Amanda. Never. I know Laurie will feel the same way." Looking down at his watch, he continued, "But get a move on, woman, or we'll be late."

"Oh Max, I do love you so!" Amanda hugged her husband and rushed back into her closet.

Claire Murphy wore a navy-blue dress that hugged her torso and then flowed loosely around her calves. She knew that the contrast between the dark navy and the deep red of her hair flattered her skin. She had finally decided to wear her hair loose and allow her curls to lie naturally around her face. She wore the silver jewelry that she had inherited from her grandmother. The pieces were lovely Celtic designs that depicted symbols of loyalty, eternal love, and good fortune.

Each was handmade in honor of the ancestors of the artisans who crafted them.

She had not known Dorothy but felt great respect for the woman after hearing Laurie share so many funny and wonderful stories about her. It was clear that Laurie loved her friend dearly and would grieve her loss for a very long time.

Claire took great care with her makeup, something she usually did without. Today was important, and she needed all the self-confidence she could muster. They all did. She tried not to notice how her hand trembled as she applied the soft gray eye shadow that she knew brought out more of the blue tones in her blue-gray eyes. As the thunder shook the sky angrily, she prayed she had not made a terrible mistake. Taking a deep breath, she tried to steady her hands.

Chief Sam Hollinger went through it again with his men. There would be several of his undercover officers posing as mourners at the service. That team was to be commanded by Detective Ben Ramirez; the man he considered to be his best officer.

Linda de Marco and her DEA agents were to cover the surveillance from the outside perimeter. Her snipers would be in place long before any mourners arrived for the service. Every officer had been thoroughly briefed about each of

Lacayo's known aliases and disguises. They had spent hours studying each photograph and poring through all of the existing written reports.

They had made sure that the obituary and notice for burial service had been printed in every local paper. The local television and radio stations had cooperated with the department and covered not only Dorothy's death but also announced the upcoming services. The television stations had interviewed Laurie about the horrible circumstances surrounding her employee's death. Sam made sure that Jake was visible, standing near her in every shot.

Sam would attend the funeral as a mourner as well. He finished the final briefing and sent his men out to do their duty, to protect Jake North and Laurie James and to catch that filth Lacayo once and for all.

They had all done the best that they could do. They were prepared. Now all they could do is pray that it would all play out the way they planned. Because if it did not, he would have to live with the knowledge that his friend might die because he had failed.

Pulling the tie on his dress blues a little tighter, he stepped out of the conference room and headed out to the officer who waited outside to drive him to the funeral. He fervently hoped it would be the only funeral he would be attending in a long time.

Rene Lacayo seethed as he watched the midday news. His rage was such that he had to bite down on his fingers to stop himself from hurling anything he could get his hands on at the screen. The sight of Jake North, alive and well, with that bitch lawyer was like acid burning him from the inside out.

He was in a hotel room in Miami Beach but far from the South Beach crowds. The place was a dump, but the fool at the registration desk accepted cash instead of a credit card for an extra twenty bucks and a blow job. Dump or not, he could not afford to bring any undue attention to himself.

When the DEA agents had arrived at Morris's house, they had been properly fooled by the blood he had trailed across the street earlier that night. It would take them a day or two to confirm that it was good old Myrna's blood and not his or Morris's that he had dripped along on the bottom of his shoes. He had often gambled and won that people would believe what their eyes told them even if it did not make sense. Many a magician made a good living that way. The broken pane in the kitchen side window and tracks of blood convinced the agents that he had gotten away on foot.

Soon the cops would question many things that did not add up, but in the short time it took the agents to run off in search of him while backup arrived, he had been able to get the protective clothing he wore off and slip out of his little hideaway in Morris's house. He had taken a risk stealing a neighbor's car and driving out of the neighborhood, but the gamble had paid off. He was gone before the cops had time to set up their barricades.

He knew that they would be watching every airport, train station, and major roadway, but he had many safe houses between New York and Miami. He also had his choice of chop shops, many owned by him, to get rid of the car and pick up a new one. In his current disguise, it was next to impossible that he be recognized. He had made it down to Miami in less than a day and a half.

And now he would finish it. Jake North would pay for betraying him. More importantly, he would pay for underestimating Rene Lacayo. It made him furious that he would not be able to kill North the way he truly wished to. But the many mistakes of the last few weeks had taught him a valuable lesson. His need for revenge was greater than his lust for blood. Besides, killing the woman who belonged to North before his very eyes would make up for each and every cut he would be denied.

He began pulling clothes out of his suitcase. He had to dress for a funeral, and he wanted to look just so.

Chapter Fourteen

Mourners milled about the tent covering the area where the coffin was to be interred. Close to the outer edge of the structure, Jake and Sam stood alert, scanning the faces beneath the umbrellas of the hundreds of people there to pay homage to the deceased. There were all sorts of people attending the service, from the conservative to the flamboyant. Jake knew that among them were dozens of Sam's officers and that somewhere unseen, Linda de Marco and her agents scanned the crowd through the scopes of their rifles, hoping to catch sight of Lacayo. He should feel confident, but instead his gut kicked like a bronco.

Lacayo was no fool. He was not just going to walk in here in plain view. Claire had been unable to see much. He had sat with her for a while as she tried to see more but to no avail. She apologized over and over until he had stopped her by giving her a big bear hug. He was almost as shocked as she was when he did it. "Listen, Claire, you've done more than anyone could ask. If you can't see more, there must be a reason why. Now please, go on. Be careful, ok?"

With tears in her sad eyes, she had whispered something in a language he did not understand. He knew a prayer when he heard one, regardless of the language. He would take all the help he could get on this rainy afternoon. The umbrellas hindered de Marco's people. He knew that without having to be told.

"This weather is a real bitch." Sam scowled at the sky and the water running from the edges of the large tent.

"Yeah, let's just stall the pastor a bit, Sam. We need to buy some time." The weight of Jake's gun beneath his sports coat was his only comfort.

Lacayo milled in the center of the crowd under a large black umbrella. He stifled a giggle as he thought of how stupid that dog North and the big cop next to him were. He was here, right under their noses, and they had no clue. He twirled the umbrella a bit, watching the raindrops fly from the edges, and then made an effort to contain himself. He caressed the gun and its long silencer with the hand he had tucked inside the pocket of the raincoat he wore. It was a shame he would have to burn a hole through it soon. It was such a lovely shade of blue.

Fondling the gun once more, he thought sarcastically that all girls appreciated a long gun, and he was no different. He raked his long acrylic nails along the side of it the way he had for the pimply hotel clerk before he had serviced him. Even the clerk had no clue his pleasure had come from a man instead of a woman.

In his early years on the streets of Managua, he had often had no choice but to sell himself to men. He had learned to dress the part from the best ladies of the night. He was small and thin and easily passed as a young girl. Since most men paid for oral sex, the majority never knew that they had been with a man. The fools had paid him happily and driven home feeling like "real" men. Those who did find out often enjoyed having sex with him anyway. An occasional few beat him in their rage and then raped him. Those were his favorites, of course. He always thanked them before they died.

It was one of these killings that had given him his leg up into the world of organized crime. That dead john had been a member of a gang that ran drugs and a relatively well-organized burglary ring. Some jealous whore sold Lacayo out to the gang's leader. It was not long before he was warned that the gang was out combing the streets looking for him to kill him for the death of their blood brother. Having nowhere else to go, he decided not to run. Instead, he went to his pimp, asking for protection. With no guarantees, a meeting was set. He painted himself as having no choice but to defend himself against attack. He offered to work for the gang running drugs on the street. After several terrifying moments during which he was sure they would kill him, the gang's leader decided in his favor. The man he had killed was one of the few in the organization who could pose a threat to the leader's position, and he was secretly relieved to have him out of the picture.

It was not long before he moved up in the organization. Not only was he successful in expanding the drug business for the gang, but he also proved himself a talented killer. His lust for blood and sadistic cruelty soon made him feared by the entire gang as well as its enemies. In less than two years, he had killed the gang leader who had spared his life, making it appear to be a rival gang's attack. Soon afterward, it was he who ran the entire operation. The rest was history.

Humming to himself as he recalled the past, he took a seat at the end of one of the rows of folding chairs set out for the mourners. It was closest to the restrooms on the side of the mausoleum just a few feet away from the burial site. The restroom was out of order, of course. He had put up the sign himself. Inside was the body of one of the cemetery's gardeners, naked and shoved into a stall. His overalls were safely in Lacayo's roomy handbag along with a pair of lightweight sneakers.

By the time the panic of the crowd subsided and North and his bitch were dead, he would be long gone.

Amanda held Laurie's hand in hers as Dorothy's closest friends filed past to pay their respects. Each had a kind word for the woman they considered their friend's family. They hugged her, cried with her, and told her stories of how Dorothy had raved about her constantly. Amanda could see that although there was great grief over the loss of her friend, the love these people expressed for Dorothy consoled Laurie tremendously.

Her dearest friends chose to honor Dorothy by wearing bright colors to the funeral, much to Amanda's relief. She had finally chosen a vibrant purple dress and matched it with high-heeled red patent leather pumps. She smiled to herself as she looked over the crowd. She was subdued compared to some of the other mourners.

Amanda looked back at Laurie to see how she was holding up. She looked every inch the beautiful, classy woman that she was. Gracious to everyone who came to pay their respects, regardless of their appearance, she was every inch the lady Dorothy had so loved and admired. She looked composed but exuded warmth as she took each hand and accepted each embrace. Amanda felt great pride in her cousin and was grateful that she could be here to support her. She knew that Dorothy was looking down upon them, happy that Laurie and she were receiving her friends as she would have wished.

It had been especially moving to see the three men in Dorothy's life console each other. While she did not understand that type of openness in a relationship, she could see how much the men had truly loved Dorothy. At their request, Laurie had introduced them to each other as soon as each had arrived. At first the gentlemen had greeted each other with great formality and restraint, but as they began to talk about Dorothy, they had each broken down into tears, and now they sat together as if they were old friends.

She looked over to where Max stood with the rest of the family. Her parents, Laurie's parents, and Laurie's brothers all wore somber colors, but each wore a bright flower on their clothing in honor of the deceased. She squeezed Laurie's hand as she looked upon her loved ones. She was so blessed. Silently, she said a prayer asking God to keep them all safe.

Claire's eyes scanned the crowd worriedly. She concentrated so intently on picking up any kind of image of the man they were after that she almost came out of her skin when she felt a big, warm hand at the small of her back.

"Easy there, Red." The hand came attached to the arm of the ridiculously attractive Detective Ramirez. As she tried to regain her composure, she looked him up and down, very much as he had done to her at their first meeting. He certainly did clean up well, she mused. Handsome as the devil in a well-tailored gray suit, he looked like a model for some fancy ad. He smiled down at her, flashing brilliant white teeth that reminded her again of a shark. She got the impression that he found her to be an interesting snack.

"Detective Ramirez," she nodded coolly. She tried to step away from his hand, but he only stepped closer, keeping his hand where it was. She suddenly saw an image of herself being crushed against his chest as they devoured each other in a steamy kiss. For a moment she was not sure if the desire was hers or his. She blushed furiously and felt heat inundate her entire body. Damn, this gift was a curse sometimes!

Trying unsuccessfully to snatch his hand from her waist herself, she snapped, "Do you mind? I don't let strange men manhandle me!"

Ben enjoyed how her eyes sparked and her little chin jutted out in anger. He had been watching her for a while now. She looked lovely in the flowing navy dress. The silver jewelry she wore seemed to shine with a soft glow around her face and wrists. She looked even sexier today than she had outside the Ambrose. She also had a great pair of legs. She had looked delicious in the jeans she had on the last time, but she made him want to sit up and beg in that dress. It was the sight of those legs that had made him stop watching from behind the tent and go get her. He knew he should be ashamed of himself for being so brazen with her. His mother had certainly raised him better, but something about her brought out the devil in him.

"Now, don't get your back up, Red. I'm not a stranger. I'm on your team." He smiled charmingly at her. "I have a feeling we got off to a bad start the other day, and I just wanted to say I was sorry."

"My name is Claire, not Red!" She hated that she sounded childish as she said it, but it was a nickname that brought back memories of being teased as a child. Besides, she still could not get the image of that passionate kiss out of her mind, and that was a distraction she could not afford.

Her words did nothing to dim his smile. "Ok, Claire. Nice to meet you. I'm Ben." He brought his hand back to offer it for a handshake and managed to caress her back and side as he did. Claire struggled not to lose her cool.

"Detective Ramirez, we are here to catch a murderer, not indulge in your sexual fantasies! You are distracting me and I don't appreciate it." Claire glared at him and ignored his hand.

"That's right. The Chief told me about you." He reached out and captured her hand in his. As he held it firmly, despite her tugging to get it back, his smile faded and eyes as black as night seemed to freeze her into place. He looked into her stormy gray eyes and whispered, "You're right. This isn't the time or the place for fantasies. But just so you know, that was nothing compared to what I'd like to do to you, Red. Let's get back to work now, but I give you my word, once this is over, you and I are going to have a long conversation about fantasies." He squeezed her hand gently. "For now, get out of my head until I invite you in." He turned suddenly and walked away, leaving her staring at his back as he melted into the crowd as quickly as he had appeared.

Claire stood open-mouthed for a moment and then snapped back to reality when she heard the pastor's voice asking everyone to take their seats. Who the hell did that man think he was? As she tried to make her way to her seat, muttering to herself about arrogant, rude sharks, she bumped into several people along the way. Everyone seemed to be moving at once to be seated.

Suddenly, she recoiled, almost in pain, from contact with one of the people moving alongside her. The image of a gun and long red nails came as vividly to her as if she were actually seeing it. Desperately, she turned, searching the crowd for Jake or Sam but could not find them anywhere.

Ramirez! She had to get to him to warn the team! Fighting the flow of people moving along the makeshift aisles of wooden folding chairs, she searched frantically for Ben. Finally, she saw him from the corner of her eye, speaking with a short, heavyset man dressed in a baby blue suit, asking him loudly if the seat next to him was available. She wanted to shout in her terror but knew she could do nothing to warn Lacayo.

Finally pushing her way out of the crowd, she maneuvered toward him as quickly as possible without calling attention to herself. "Ramirez," she said urgently. When he did not turn, she spoke more loudly. "Ben, please!"

Hearing her, Ben turned toward her with a smile that was replaced instantly with concern when he saw the look on her face. He excused himself quickly and grabbed her arm. "What happened? Are you alright?"

"I'm fine. He's here! He's here, Ben!" she whispered frantically. She leaned into him to hold herself steady.

"Are you sure?" He held her arms in his hands and pulled her close. Lowering his voice, he asked, "Where?"

"He's dressed as a woman, Ben. I saw the gun, the long red nails…" Claire was breathless with panic. "We have to tell Jake and Sam!"

Suddenly she looked up and he saw her eyes glaze in fear. "Oh my God," she cried. "It's too late. There they come."

Ben looked up to see Jake holding the arm of a good-looking brunette in a black dress and pearls. She wore a wide-brimmed black hat that blocked her face from him. Chief Hollinger was entering with them. Unable to make eye contact, he put his arm protectively around Claire. Reaching up with his other hand, he activated the small radio located in the pin on the lapel of his suit. Talking down into it, he said urgently, "He's disguised as a woman. Repeat. He's disguised as a woman. He's got a gun. Repeat. The subject is disguised as a woman and armed and dangerous."

Ben almost dragged Claire along trying to get her to safety. He saw the moment Hollinger's and Jake's heads snapped up, searching the crowd and looking for the suspect. As soon as he had Claire off to the side and away from the people seated waiting for the service to begin, he turned her toward him and shook her gently. He needed her to focus, and she looked dazed and confused in her terror.

"Listen, Red, I need your help. There are too many women here. I need you to focus. Can you see anything else?"

His deep, calm voice brought her out of her anxious fog. For a moment, she had let the panic she used to feel daily get the best of her. She needed to concentrate on the moment she had brushed against the man with the gun if she wanted to save Jake and Laurie. The image of the gun had scared her so much that she had not concentrated on anything else. Looking up at Ben, she nodded. "I need you to let me go. I can't risk picking anything up from you and making a mistake. We have no time."

Ben released her immediately and nodded. "Do your thing, Red."

Claire closed her eyes and took herself back to the moment of contact with Lacayo. She pictured the hand holding the gun. "His gun has a silencer. Long red nails. A black umbrella…"

Next to her, Ben repeated every word she said softly into the transmitter.

"Blue! He's dressed in a blue coat. I see long brown hair."

Claire opened her eyes suddenly and grabbed Ben's hand. "Too late!" she cried in anguish. "Oh my God, we're too late!"

Lacayo watched North and his woman walk up the center aisle to the seating reserved for family and close friends of the deceased. He knew he had to make his move before they were seated and before the rest of the crowd finally took their places, or he would lose the chance to stand without being noticed.

Standing up, he lifted the gun still inside the pocket of the raincoat and aimed for North. He would have just enough time for a second shot. He would try for the woman but would settle for the big, burly cop on the other side of North if she moved out of range. He could always take care of her later. Distracting the people around him by shaking the water from his umbrella, they never noticed his arm lifting.

Blood-red lips curved into a smile as he squeezed the trigger.

He got the first shot off and saw North go down. The big cop scrambled forward as North fell, and he was able to squeeze off the second shot straight into the chest of the woman next to them. He gave himself a second to enjoy watching her crumple backward, knocking over chairs on her way down. Perfect! He turned and moved quickly across the grass as the mourners who had been seated near him began murmuring and craning their necks to see what the commotion was about. In seconds he heard someone yelling, "Officer down!" As people began to understand that someone had been shot, they began running out of the tent in a panic, many screaming hysterically. Walking quickly away from the crowd, he headed toward the mausoleum.

Ben threw Claire down onto the ground beneath him and drew his gun. He looked up, scanning the horizon. Claire was struggling to get up, crying and yelling that she had to get to Jake. "Stop it, Red!" he yelled, putting his face close to hers. "Stop it right now. Getting yourself shot isn't going to help anyone." He stared into her eyes, willing her to understand. "Stay down! You hear me?" Getting no response, he pushed her down with the weight of his entire body. She struggled but eventually seemed to realize that though she was strong for her size, he was much bigger and much stronger.

Letting his words sink in, Claire finally nodded her agreement, though he was no longer looking at her to know it. Closing her eyes, she laid her head back on the wet grass of the cemetery. Thunder sounded yet again and rain fell upon them. Thousands of images swirled through her mind like objects picked up by a tornado. The only thing keeping her from falling apart and being taken away on the wild wind in her mind was the very large, very solid weight of Ben Ramirez sprawled across her.

She knew the only way to keep her mind intact was to focus on him. She pictured him in her mind and allowed herself to feel his hard length all along her body. She began to pick up on his feelings and thoughts. Fear for her safety was the first thing that came through. He would protect her, no matter what. Then she could feel his fury at the shooter. Suddenly she heard him barking into his radio transmitter. "There! There near the mausoleum! There's a woman in a blue coat running toward the side of the building!"

Claire prayed they would get Lacayo. She knew that if he escaped this time, he would elude justice permanently.

The pain was excruciating. The bullet had caught him almost square in the center of his still-bruised chest. Jake stared up at the ceiling of the tent, trying to breathe and barely succeeding. He could hear Sam yelling his name. He could also hear the undercover agent posing as Laurie next to him on the ground, trying to breathe through her own pain. The idea that it could have been Laurie lying hurt on the damp grass was enough to snap him out of it.

Though the body armor had done its job, it still hurt like a bitch to get shot. He ripped open his shirt to take a look at the slug lodged in the Kevlar. Wincing at what could have happened without the protective gear, he looked around to get a bearing on the current situation.

He could hear Detective Ramirez yelling over the radio. Struggling to sit up, he tried to make out what the detective was saying.

Seeing Jake attempting to stand, Sam grabbed his arms and hauled him up. Seeing stars, Jake grated out, "Shit, Sam, are you trying to finish me off?"

Relieved to hear his friend well enough to complain, Sam scanned Jake from head to toe in search of blood. "Jesus, Jake! Are you alright?"

"I'm fine. Hurts like a bitch though." Looking down, he asked, "How's she?"

Breathing roughly, the woman nodded at them that she was okay.

"Where the hell is Lacayo? Did they get him?" Jake looked around desperately. "Sam, he can't get away!"

Yelling over the noise, Sam brought his radio up out of his pocket and started barking orders. Undercover agents yelled at the mourners to get down on the ground and stay there.

Suddenly a shot rang out. Focusing on the area where the sound came from, Jake's eyes scanned the distance. Through the rain, he saw a woman go down. "There, Sam, there!" He took off running.

A few blocks away, at the Wilson Funeral Home, Laurie felt the room spin for a moment. Jake was in danger. Turning to Amanda, she whispered, "I have to go. Something is wrong. I have to get to Jake."

Grabbing her cousin's hand tightly, she begged, "Have the pastor wait, please, Amanda. I have to go."

"I'll go with you!" Amanda replied.

"No, Amanda, please. Hold the fort down here. Dorothy deserves her funeral to be uninterrupted. Please." Green eyes pleaded.

"Ok, Laurie, but please be careful!" Amanda's worried gaze followed her cousin as she rushed out into the rain.

Jake pointed his gun as he stood over Rene Lacayo. Through the long hair of the wig, he could see that he was bleeding from his right shoulder onto the wet ground of the cemetery. Looking down on the man he hated, he could hardly believe it was Lacayo. The rain made the makeup on his crazed face run, giving him the look of a mad clown.

"You! It can't be! I killed you!" Lacayo screamed in a high, shrill voice as he stared up at Jake.

"Sorry to disappoint you, you bastard! We knew you'd fall for this very public funeral. I'll let you in on a little secret, you shit. One that only you, me, and the dozen or so law enforcement officers that brought you down know. The coffin is empty." Jake took real satisfaction at the rage on Lacayo's face. His finger itched on the trigger. Every instinct he had made him want to finish this evil bastard off and end this once and for all. "You just can't seem to do anything right, can you, little man?" he spat out viciously.

"You bastard!" Lacayo screamed. "Why won't you die? You have to die!" From the pocket of the coat wrapped around him, Lacayo began to pull out his gun. He would rather North kill him than have to live with the fact that the cop had beaten him.

Just as he began to raise the gun, before Jake had even squeezed off his shot, another shot fired, slamming through Lacayo's head. Jake turned away from the gruesome sight. As he turned, he saw Sam running toward him, still holding up his gun, ready to take another shot if needed. Only a professional marksman could have made that shot on the run. Sam had been the best shooter in their unit when they had served together.

Behind Sam, he saw another figure running toward him. It was Laurie, her beautiful dress soaking wet and her feet bare. What on earth was she doing here? She raced for him with the speed of a gazelle. He could hear her yelling his name as she ran. Relief washed through him, leaving him weak. It was over. She was safe. He wanted to run toward her but could not seem to move. All he could do was watch her and wait with open arms.

She slammed into him, jumping into his arms and wrapping herself around him tightly. "Jake, are you ok? Please tell me that you're ok!" She had seen him standing with his gun pointed at the figure on the ground. Sobbing, she kissed his face as he held her. "I love you! I love you, Jake. Please be ok."

"I'm fine, angel. I'm ok. What are you doing here? Didn't I tell you to wait for me at Dorothy's service?" He began to get mad as he thought of what might have happened if Lacayo had not been taken down. The thought of her being in danger was enough to bring his heart to his throat.

Beyond any notion of decorum, Laurie lifted her legs and wrapped them around Jake's waist. She did not care how high her damned skirt rode up. He was alive! Her man was alive and well and mad as hell. Laughter welled up suddenly. She let herself laugh out loud and feel the release of the fear she had been clutching onto all day. The monster was dead and they were alive!

Jake stared up at her, all his anger fading in the face of her joy. He did not think he had heard her laugh before. It was the most beautiful sound he had ever heard. Pulling her face up for a kiss, he awkwardly said a silent prayer of thanks as his knees buckled and he dropped them both down onto the wet grass.

Two hours later they stood quietly holding hands as they listened to Dorothy's pastor speak glowingly of the woman whom they had all come to honor. Jake looked at the photograph Laurie had arranged to have enlarged and framed for display at the service. It was placed close to the closed casket with a colorful spray of wildflowers beneath it. Laurie had picked a candid shot of her friend, rosy lips smiling widely as she stood in a saucy pose with a hand on her broad, curvy hip. In the shot, she sported bright red hair and was dressed in a hot pink dress. He had heard about the lady's style and now knew that no one had exaggerated.

She looked every bit the firecracker Laurie had described. He believed he would have liked Dorothy if he had had the opportunity to meet her. He was sorry he had never had the chance.

Looking over at Laurie, he took in her lovely profile. He could see her lower lip trembling and the tears that threatened to fall from her eyes. She held herself together, though, as she listened intently to the words the pastor offered as consolation. Once more, he felt pride in her strength. Squeezing her hand gently, he let his mind wander back upon the events of the day.

Once the mayhem had ended at what he had come to think of as the "sting" burial service and Lacayo's body had been taken away, along with the body of the groundskeeper they found in the restroom, he and Laurie had headed to her house to bathe and change. Laurie called Amanda and asked her to hold off the real service until she and Jake arrived.

They showered together quickly and though they could not seem to stop touching each other, they knew that the lovemaking would have to wait. Dorothy's service had been held up long enough.

Laurie had been horrified by the new bruise starting to discolor his chest from the impact of the bullet against the body armor. She had kissed it gently as the water ran over them both, promising to take special care of him later.

Reluctantly, they finished bathing and dressed quickly. Laurie replaced the soaked black sheath with a soft pink wool suit. Jake watched her loop the same elegant pearls over her neck and was glad to see she no longer fussed with them. He breathed a sigh of satisfied relief that her fears were now gone.

He had dressed in the dark blue suit he had had delivered to her home earlier that morning. While she stood before him helping him with his tie, he allowed himself to imagine her doing the very same thing every day for the rest of their lives. It was a peaceful happiness that settled in his heart at that moment, one that he had never felt before.

He was brought back to the present when Laurie leaned her head against his shoulder. Wrapping his arms around her, he did what he could to comfort her.

Once the services were over, Laurie was quickly surrounded by family and friends. Jake tried to pry himself loose and step into the background, but she was having none of it. Dragging him against her side, she introduced him to her family.

"Mom, Dad, everyone," she beamed in pride and joy, "this is Jake, the love of my life."

Epilogue

Four weeks later...

Claire stood quietly amid the music and lights beneath the beautiful tent set up in the gardens of Laurie's parents' home. She held her drink and watched the happy couple dance beneath the tiny, twinkling lights that illuminated the inside of the tent and the surrounding gardens. The beautiful décor made her feel as though she were inside an enchanted dream. Jake and Laurie seemed oblivious to everything and everyone around them as they twirled to the soft love song celebrating their commitment to each other. She felt her heart tighten with happiness at the miracle love had wrought in both her friends, but most especially in Jake. Claire had seen inside his soul just a few short weeks ago and had been saddened by the loneliness and pain that had lived within him for so long. Laurie's love had changed all of that. It transformed pain and sorrow into love and hope. It had also created life. They did not know it yet, of course, but Laurie was expecting. She hoped they would forgive her as she allowed herself a small peek at the child as they danced.

Tears filled her eyes and her breath caught as her mind's eye saw the tiny speck and met the soul of the babe. It radiated happiness and love as brightly as the sun's rays.

Thankfully, she could see that the beautiful baby girl would be healthy. Coming back to herself, she swiped her hands over her face to wipe away the tears.

"I'm a sucker for a happy ending myself." A large, very male hand offered a snowy white handkerchief. Annoyance rose within her and, to her chagrin, so did the heat in her body. Frowning, she looked up at Detective Ben Ramirez. Her smart retort died in her throat as she saw that tears shone in his eyes as well.

"You really are crying!" The shock in her voice made him frown. Studying him in a new light, she mused that he looked like a dark, dangerous pirate in a fancy tuxedo as he scowled. It was the watery eyes that ruined the overall menacing image. She smiled at the thought.

"Red, if crying is what it takes to be graced by your beautiful smile, I'll cry for you every day." The smile was back, as was the hungry look he seemed to carry each time they met. He always made her feel as though he might lean over and take a bite out of her, she thought in irritation. Heat pooled low in her body against her will. As she stared at him, the smile faded from her face. She looked into his midnight eyes, seeing a deep and dangerous passion within, and suddenly knew that this man could rip her heart to shreds if she allowed it. He made her feel things she had not permitted herself to feel in a very long time. Fear made her tremble as she stepped back to distance herself from him.

Ben watched the emotions cross her lovely face as she pulled away from him. An unexplainable anger gripped him suddenly at her withdrawal. She would not walk away from him ever again; he thought with a possessiveness that was entirely new to him. He had never been jealous or possessive of a woman in his life. He was a free man and had always been more than happy to remain so, until the day he sized up this little redhead standing in the street with her nose turned up at him. This woman made him want to claim her, body and soul. Just looking at her in that sexy green gown that made her curls shine like fire made him want to place his mark on her so that no one else dared to come near her. He remembered her vulnerability during the terrible moments when they did not know if Lacayo would kill Jake and his team. If he had not held her down, she would have thrown herself into harm's way to protect her friends. The memory made his stomach twist with fear again.

An unmistakable fury laced his tone as he reached out and grabbed her arms, dragging her roughly back against him.

"Don't you dare pull away from this!" he growled.

Shock widened her beautiful eyes as Claire found herself pressed against him from chest to thigh. The heat shooting through her was like lightning searing her flesh. Gasping, she pleaded, "Please don't. I can't. I don't play these games."

He could feel her reaction to his embrace. The heat from her body burned him like a brand through the thin material of the dress she wore. She trembled and he realized it was both desire and fear. Softening his hold, he bent his head and kissed her cheek gently before dragging his mouth to her ear, holding her head in place with his hand at her slender neck.

"Shhh, baby," he whispered against her soft skin. "It's no game. I won't hurt you, Claire. I swear."

He sealed his promise with soft kisses to her ear and neck. God, she smelled incredible. Like spun sugar with a hint of vanilla, he thought as he breathed her in.

Claire braced herself for the pain as he held her. She had been through this before. A few men had held her, forgetting that she could see into their thoughts and their very souls, and hurt had always followed. Usually, it only left her vaguely disappointed, but she knew this time it would be devastating. She could not deny the intense attraction she felt for Ben. This embrace was going to cost her dearly, she thought, as she allowed him in.

Closing her eyes, she saw a blur of images, some violent, as she melted into his arms. Her legs seemed to lose the strength to hold her upright. She saw him chasing a man through a dark hallway, shouting for him to stop. The man turned and aimed a gun but fell in shock as Ben's bullet tore through his heart. Great sorrow and regret washed through her. She saw him hugging an older woman with the same beautiful black eyes as his and felt a surge of profound love.

Softening, she was unprepared when the final image tore through her.

She was on the ground, bleeding, as he held her, sobbing her name and begging her not to die. Despair and a deep, undying love washed through her. As darkness overtook her, her last astonished thought was that there was no deceit in him. There was no deceit. But there was a relentless need for justice that could lead him down a dark road of revenge... revenge for the death of the woman he loved.

"Shit! Claire, wake up, sugar! Wake up!"

His voice seemed to come from a million miles away, but it was drawing closer. There were other voices too. She realized she was lying on a couch. She could make out Amanda's worried voice and Sam's irritated bark.

"Murphy, so help me God, if you don't cut this fainting nonsense out, I'm going to lock your ass up for your own good!"

Slowly she regained consciousness. Her eyes fluttered open and she found herself staring into a pair of very worried midnight-black eyes.

"You're going to love me, you know."

The words slipped out the way things always did after a vision. Once the words were out, she squeezed her eyes tightly shut and wished she had died instead of merely fainting. How could she blurt out something like that? Stupid, stupid woman.

The other voices suddenly fell silent. She heard a door open and close, and then nothing but complete silence. She knew Ben was still there because she could feel him hovering above her. She did not dare open her eyes.

"Well, sugar," his voice washed over her like smooth, dark whiskey, "that may be true. But first things first. Open those beautiful eyes and look at me."

Mortified, she found she could not. She could feel the heat of embarrassment burning across her face and neck. She knew she was beet red, another unfortunate downside of being a fair-skinned redhead. Like a stubborn child, she squeezed her eyes shut even tighter and shook her head.

Laughter rolled from his chest and shook the strong arms that surrounded her. She felt his forehead rest gently against hers.

"Sugar, open your eyes. It's just you and me."

One gray-blue eye opened, then the other. They were nose to nose.

"I'm sorry," she whispered. "I can't control what I say when I'm coming out of it. It doesn't mean anything. I'm sorry." She fidgeted in his embrace, trying to get away.

"Why are you always moving in the wrong direction, Claire?" he asked dryly.

Tightening his hold, he lifted her chin with his hand and forced her to look at him.

"I'm going to kiss you now. A proper kiss. You aren't going anywhere except toward me. Understand?"

Speechless and with her heart racing again, she nodded.

"Good girl. Once I've kissed you properly, we are going to get up, go dance, and toast our friends. Understood?"

She nodded again.

"Then, Red, you and I are going to make arrangements for our first date. One that you will not break. If I'm going to love you, I think we should get to know each other better. I also require some time to make sure that you're going to love me back. Understood?"

Claire could not understand why her brain would not make her head stop nodding.

"Good girl. Now one more thing. You will absolutely not faint in my arms again. Understood?"

Stormy gray-blue eyes met steady midnight eyes, and a slow nod made him smile as he leaned down to claim his kiss.

The smile faded the moment his lips met Claire's. It felt like sinking into warm honey.

He felt her tremble and it made him want to soothe her. With a soft groan, he let his mouth explore the shape of her lips until he could no longer resist the need to taste her more deeply. His tongue demanded entry and she opened to him with a soft sigh.

Somewhere in the back of his mind, a warning bell rang, trying to remind him that though they were in the study of Laurie's parents' home, they were still technically in a public place. The warning was quickly drowned out by the soft sounds escaping Claire as she wrapped her arms around his neck and pulled him down into a fierce kiss that burned through his soul.

Straining against each other, mouths tangled in a battle for dominance, they lost themselves in a sea of sensation. Ben pulled the delicate straps of the emerald green bridesmaid's dress down her arms, desperate to see and feel more of her. Creamy, rose-tipped breasts lay exposed to his hungry eyes. "Beautiful," he breathed before lowering his head to feast on her. Just a taste, he told himself, just a little more before he stopped. He wouldn't take her here, this way. He wanted to be naked with her, buried inside her, the first time she came apart for him. He wasn't going to take her like a randy teenager on a couch, he told himself, even as he couldn't seem to stop tasting her, reveling in her hot little moans.

Claire could not get close enough to Ben. It felt as though a dam had burst inside her and every emotion she had suppressed for years rushed forward in a flood. All she could feel was Ben. His rock-hard body pressing into hers, his tongue demanding her surrender, and his heart pounding against her breast.

For the first time in her life, she felt no fear. No hesitation. Only passion.

It was like being set free after a lifetime of solitary confinement.

Later, Ben would be embarrassed to admit that the only thing that stopped him from stripping them both down and taking her with no finesse at all was the urgent knocking on the door.

Breathing hard, he dragged himself up and her with him. Sitting up with her still in his arms, he took in the most beautiful sight he'd ever seen. Claire was flushed with passion, her red hair a wild cascade around her beautiful face, her lips red and full from his kisses, her nipples stiff and rosy, begging for his mouth to take them again. But it was her eyes that he'd never forget. Wild and hot, they seemed to see into his very soul and demand him to give her fulfillment. She looked like a long-ago queen commanding what was hers. Dragging her to him for a quick, hard kiss, he released her roughly and stood, trying to get some distance between them before he lost all reason.

"Claire, sugar…there's someone at the door." He saw her confusion and smiled painfully. "Come on baby, straighten your dress." His eyes darkened as he stared at her and promised, "We'll finish this, I promise you."

Shaking her head, Claire tried to regain some semblance of control. What the hell had just happened? She'd never felt anything akin to the passion that Ben made her feel. She could feel the blood pounding through her body as if she were a thoroughbred racing across the wide-open fields.

◐◯◑

"Come on, you two!" Sam's voice thundered through the door. "This is not the time or place. Open up. It's important!"

Flushed and trembling, Claire straightened her dress as best she could.

Sam strode in like an impatient giant, stopping abruptly when he saw the sparks between his detective and the small woman trying to sit primly on the couch.

"She's not one to play with, Ben," he said quietly.

"As I explained earlier, this is no game to me... sir," Ben replied, the last word edged with sarcasm.

"Oh stop it, both of you," Claire snapped. "For heaven's sake, I'm a grown woman."

Sam sighed heavily.

"I need both of you on a case. The daughter of the State's Attorney General is missing. We believe it may be the Machetes."

"Are you crazy?" Ben exploded. "She's not a cop. She could get hurt!"

Claire closed her eyes briefly.

She had known this moment would come.

Opening them again, she looked at Sam and Ben. Two men are now woven into the fabric of her life. One trusted friend. The other man she knew would one day be her lover.

"We need to save her," she said softly.

And so it began.

www.ingramcontent.com/pod-product-compliance
Lightning Source LLC
LaVergne TN
LVHW020659110826
845149LV00012B/2045